CW01211274

Copyright © 2018 Stephen J. Hird
All rights reserved
ISBN-13: 978-1986642118
ISBN-10: 1986642119

CONTEMPLATION ZONE

STEPHEN J. HIRD

Contemplation Zone

Jason Mighty wormed his way through the throng of disgruntled commuters onto the platform. Most of them were leaving in disgust having conceded defeat. The usual build-up of would-be suicides, grouped with their backs to the wall, was a sure sign that no trains had passed through the station for quite some time.

With a rail network such as this; hijacked by new companies every month – each of them seizing and claiming territory, lines and zones – the service was at an all-time low. Since hacking had been fully legalised, its use as an acceptable, competitive business tool meant that warring rail companies could tamper with the information of their enemies to such an extent that trains were cancelled, times altered, and misinformation spread across the city like an autumn infection.

This state of affairs had led to the Contemplation Zone: a reserved area marked off at the back of the platform where those desperate to kill themselves could stand and wait, on the off-chance that a train might finally arrive. If it did, those showing no signs of the intended restorative, palliative effects of their time in the Contemplation Zone were led forward by the Suicide Monitor, whose whistle was a lower pitch than the regular Station Guard's whistle, and blown as the train approached, thereby signalling to the unfortunate few that it was time to step forward and into position. It also served as a shrill indication to the commuters that the approaching train could be cancelled immediately upon entering the station due to the allotted jumpers' final act.

Jason placed his camera bag on the platform between his feet and turned up the collar of his coat. He had to be at the bereaved family's house at 11.30 am in time to prepare his equipment. He was hoping to get some good shots of dread and anticipation in close-up before the hearse arrived. His business had become competitive in the last year or two. Despite being the first funeral photographer, as far as he knew, his well-earned reputation for providing the "grief shots" that people craved in the traditional film format seemed less of a guarantee of work than it once had.

Everything was copied, imitated, revamped, regurgitated and popularised to within an inch of its life, forcing people to abandon the quest for originality in any art form; at least originality that they were willing to share. If anyone happened, by some miracle, to create something original – a song, an idea – they would keep it secret, revelling in the fact that they alone were in possession of something that would not be destroyed by insidious repetition.

Jason's photographs of mourners' tears shed amongst flowers and black ties; their red-eyed despair in their moments of loss, had found a niche market early on after social media networks had banned all photographs of pets, food about to be eaten, drunken nights out and anything which represented fun. He was fully aware that what he did was a trend and therefore ephemeral. He was determined to photograph as many mourners as he could before the fickle hand of whatever force controlled online fads snatched his career away from him. Maybe he was the last person to have done something original openly, the inevitable result being that inferior imitators were cropping up with frightening regularity, each one topping him up with cynicism for the ridiculous, vapid circumstances in which he lived.

A train was now approaching. Jason turned towards the Contemplation Zone, hoping that none of the suicides was ready to take the leap onto the cold tracks. He needed this funeral. He needed to work. He looked at the platform display. It read, NEXT TRAIN TO ARRIVE IN THREE WEEKS. He turned to look at the oncoming train, smiling at the old man standing next to him, with the intention of sharing a moment of mutual disbelief which, really, wasn't disbelief at all, but rather the eye-rolling look of frustration and acceptance which had become all too common on the faces of those who still bothered to attempt rail travel. He's obviously not a regular, thought Jason, as he observed the old man's frown, which was given in response to the young photographer's fruitless attempt at solidarity.

The Suicide Monitor's hand disappeared into his whistle pocket, but instead of retrieving its piercing content, the hand stayed put until its owner was sure of the optimum moment in which to unleash its cold, harsh signal. Were he to have stood in readiness with the whistle poised at his parted lips, panic might easily have ensued.

The company/government department which had won the contract, thereby putting them in charge of platform control, had at least had the foresight to train their Suicide Monitors in what they considered to be the finer details of Insecurity Security. 'THEY'RE ALREADY PANICKING,' the trainee monitors had been instructed forcefully on the first day of their training. 'LET'S NOT ADD TO THAT WITH

INJUDICIOUS WHISTLE-BLOWING!'

The various cowboy train companies which now wrangled over the network control had invested a modicum of time and funds in the retraining of their drivers. Pertinent changes had been made to speed regulations, permitting drivers to enter the stations at a greater speed, therefore minimising the risk of any jumper's endeavour resulting in mere injuries only; their chances of survival sensitively lessened by the network's accommodating "Altruistic Acceleration", or so it was described in their training literature.

There was movement in the Contemplation Zone as the train drew nearer. Other commuters never really liked to appear to show too much interest in which last-minute difficult decisions were being made behind them in the designated area. However, surreptitious glances were cast during the often lengthy waiting time, with some people picking out a favourite, a most-likely-to-jump candidate for whom they would root, as subtly as possible and in complete silence so as not to demonstrate anything that could be construed as influence, let alone interest. To most commuters, the Contemplation Zone had become an accepted feature of the train station and, in some ways, as mundane and practical as a ticket machine, as inescapable as advertising. Occasionally, someone might even wonder whether the train companies were considering how to counter the loss in potential customers brought about by the number of successful jumpers. They might then think that the infrequency of the trains could be their method of countering this loss. But really, most of the people travelling by rail, or at least attempting to, had given up pondering these seemingly unfathomable aspects of what now constituted modern-day transport.

Suddenly, an impeccably trained hand went into a very specific pocket, drawing forth the tool of the trade slowly and most professionally. There was shuffling in the Contemplation Zone; feet on the verge of panic. The whistle was raised, along with twenty or so pairs of desperate eyes casting their final glances at the oncoming metal death machine. With an expectant hand, Jason took his Yashica Electro from his camera bag as people started to move slowly towards the platform edge. He turned in one fluid movement and pointed the rangefinder towards the unfortunate souls. The shoe tips of those nudging themselves forward encroached on the yellow line, threatening the vacation of their zone. He opened the shutter and, in one sixtieth of a second, captured the front line; faces riddled with bewilderment, grimacing, flinching, cringing squirms cast forward despite their origins being deep within their perpetrators. Whistle poised, the Suicide Monitor raised his arm. More of the yellow line was covered by apprehensive toes. Jason's shutter opened again. The train's engine was more audible, its clickety-clack crescendo propelling its metallic odour down the track towards those hoping to embark; towards those hoping to disembark forever.

'THE TRAIN NOW ARRIVING ON PLATFORM ONE WILL...' said the recorded announcer, cut off with no destination. It doesn't matter, thought Jason. It's here. We might not know where it's going, but it's here. The platform was swept by a metallic breeze. There was movement to his right. People had started pushing forward with sheer determination. He heard the Suicide Monitor's whistle blow. The pushing increased as the train entered the station. Jason was pushed back and he tripped over his camera bag. As the first carriage whooshed past him, he felt a sharp pain in his back and shoulders as he fell backwards onto somebody. He was momentarily relieved to find that his camera was clutched safely to his stomach and he congratulated himself on his tight grip. The Suicide Monitor's whistle blew again. Or was it the Station Guard's whistle? He couldn't tell in the confusion. There was a mad scramble during which Jason heard shouting. He didn't realise immediately that it was directed at him. The whistle blew and blew; its shrillness increasing as it approached him and the source of the shouting.

'What the hell was that?' a male voice shouted from amongst the mass of people. The train drew to a stop. The whistle blew again. Jason managed to find his feet. He turned, camera in hand, to see an elderly man which he recognised as one of the Contemplation Zone front line whom he had just photographed.

'Is there a problem?' Jason asked him.

'You blocked me!' he responded.

'What do you mean I blocked you?' Jason asked.

'Blocked! You know what blocked means, don't you?' the man said.

'Look, I'm sorry. I was pushed, it wasn't my fault!' Jason said. The man was silent for a second. Jason offered him a hand and he got to his feet just as the Suicide Monitor arrived.

'Did this man obstruct you?' the Suicide Monitor asked the man.

'Now just a minute,' Jason said. 'I was pushed by these people here.' He motioned towards those commuters close by, whom he assumed were deserving of his accusation. The train doors opened and the accused began pushing their way into the carriage.

'I see,' said the Suicide Monitor. His tone sounded overly

officious for a man with a whistle. 'You do know that obstructing the path of anyone exiting the Contemplation Zone carries a hefty fine?' he said with a hint of derision. He couldn't pretend that he didn't enjoy informing people of railway regulations.

'Well, we wouldn't want any survivors, would we?' Jason said.

'Don't take that tone with me, lad! I'm just doing my job.'

'...and what a noble profession it is!' Jason said.

'Are you hurt, Sir?' the Suicide Monitor asked the obstructed man.

'Is he hurt!?' Jason said. 'He was about to jump in front of a train!'

'Yes, but you stopped him, didn't you, young man?' the Suicide Monitor said. 'I now have to ascertain as to whether there has been any injury added to that insult.'

'...and what if I'm injured?' Jason asked.

'Are you injured?' the Suicide Monitor said.

'Well, no...' Jason responded.

'Well let's just focus on the matter at hand, then. Shall we?' Jason looked at the obstructed man and rolled his eyes with incredulity at the whistle-blowing jobsworth who seemed to be revelling in the activity.

'Look,' Jason said, 'is this going to take long? I have a funeral to get to.' As he finished his question, the train doors started to beep in preparation for closing. 'Oh, that's just great!' he said. The platform had emptied quickly. Nobody had jumped. As he looked around, he noticed that the Contemplation Zone was almost empty, too. The doors closed and the train moved slowly out of the station.

'I am sorry to hear that, Sir,' said the Suicide Monitor.

'Oh, it's "Sir" now, is it?' Jason said angrily.

'If you'll just bear with me, you'll be able to catch the next train.'

'Yeah, right, the next train!'

The Suicide Monitor turned his attention to the obstructed man, who had been waiting silently during the pointless conversation. What an observer might assume to be a sense of failure at having been thwarted by the young photographer, had kept his mouth shut throughout the confrontation. He looked slightly uncomfortable with the situation and appeared more than a little guilty at drawing attention to what he knew to have been merely an accident.

'Well, Sir, do you wish to file a formal complaint against this gentleman?'

'You've got to be kidding!' Jason said.

'Please,' said the Suicide Monitor, 'I think this gentleman deserves a chance to speak, don't you?'

Jason raised his hands in an accepting gesture.

'Now, Sir,' the Suicide Monitor continued, turning once again to the obstructed man. 'You would be quite within your rights, under subsection 3D of the Insecurity Security Act, to file obstruction charges against this gentleman.'

Jason sighed deeply.

'Do you wish to do so?'

'No,' the obstructed man said in a weak voice. 'It wasn't his fault. I see that now.'

His face displayed embarrassment, as if he felt ridiculous at having failed to make his jump, as if trying to blame that failure on somebody else was just one more self-recrimination to add to the list which had forced him to attempt the jump in the first place.

'Perhaps you're not fully aware of the extent of your rights in such a situation,' said the Suicide Monitor.

'Oh, that's nice...' said Jason before the obstructed man could answer. 'Do you really think now is the time to patronise him?' he asked, with an accompanying gesture of frustration.

'Please, Sir,' the Suicide Monitor said with an admonishing tone. 'I am quite capable of dealing with this. My extensive professional training has more than equipped me with the faculties necessary to judge this predicament fairly and sensitively.'

'What a relief!' Jason said. He turned to the obstructed man. 'You're in good hands, don't worry.' He picked up his camera bag.

'Excuse me, Sir, but I can't let you leave until you have provided me with your details,' said the Suicide Monitor as he waved an official yellow coloured form in front of the young photographer. 'What's your name?'

'Jason Mighty,' he replied. He doubted he would make the funeral in time to finish all his preparation. He would have to take a taxi there and just do everything hand-held when he arrived.

'Mighty?' asked the Suicide Monitor with a raised eyebrow.

'Yes, Mighty,' Jason said assuredly.

'I see. And is that your real name?'

'Does it really matter?'

'Well, it certainly does under subsection...'

'Your whole life is a subsection!' Jason's grip on his temper was loosening. He snatched the yellow form.

'I fail to see how any of this gives you cause to be rude, Sir,' said the Suicide Monitor, making good use of the calm tone he had been instructed to adopt in his extensive training scenarios. 'If you would allow me...' he said as he took the form back from the photographer's hand. 'A few brief moments in my office will soon resolve this matter in what I am sure will be a satisfactory manner for all concerned.' Jason sighed as he looked at the obstructed man, whose presence he had almost forgotten.

The three men left the platform in the direction of the Suicide Monitor's office. As they walked, the obstructed man continued to make ineffective attempts to halt any record of the proceedings. With Jason's help, the two of them finally managed to convince the Suicide Monitor that there really was nothing to pursue. However, Jason was not let off the hook completely and his details were taken politely and filed conscientiously, once the form had been rubber-stamped NEGLIGABLE in big red letters. Underneath, a second rubberstamping read AMICABLE BACKDOWN.

Outside the train station, Jason folded up the yellow obstruction form in disgust. He had been informed by the Suicide Monitor that he should report to the office of Platform Irregularities where his form would be stamped a third time. Resisting the urge to vent for fear of never making the funeral on time, he had simply taken the pointless document and left.

Stuffing the form carelessly into his camera bag, he suddenly became aware that the obstructed man, who had left at the same time, was now standing just a few feet away. Under the surprisingly laissez-faire terms of the yellow obstruction form completion process, the obstructed party was under no obligation to provide personal information and could choose to remain anonymous, in what Jason assumed was a show of support for those desperate enough to dash from the Contemplation Zone. Inside the box marked OBSTRUCTED, appropriately, Jason's new acquaintance had simply written MAN. Outside, he looked lost; an aimless expression projecting from between his sunken shoulders made him seem just pathetic enough for Jason to speak to him.

'Where are you going?' he asked. He felt sorry for him. He thought about the fact that this man had been on the verge of jumping but, instead of meeting his end, he had ended up in the office of some pumped-up, thoroughly trained individual with a title and a whistle. The poor man must be feeling totally disorientated.

'Well, to be honest, I have no idea,' he replied. He looked at Jason with imploring eyes.

'Do you want to come to a funeral?' Jason found himself asking the question before he had had chance to consider the sensibility of inviting a suicidal man to a funeral.

'Ok,' he answered.

'I could use some help, really. I'm going to be late.'

Jason hailed a taxi and they set off towards the house of the grieving family.

Insecurity Security

Antony Manbag was, arguably, the perfect perfectionist. Anyone who got to know him would see, in time, that he was in possession of an intrinsic ability which would surprisingly, and quite endearingly for those involved, negate just enough of his fussiness so that he would appear charmingly, yet temporarily, laid-back. He was able to conjure up this capacity at what he believed to be the optimum moments, when it became clear that letting go would serve his objectives better in the long-run than his usual reluctance to relinquish any detail of what he was engaged in performing perfectly.

This facet of his character would eventually grow in proportion; forcing him, after being made truly aware of the sterile nature of his efficiency, to loosen his once rigid grip and allow himself to rebel against the rules and regulations he had always held sacrosanct.

There were, of course, certain machinations which would lead up to this loosening. Such a man could never reject his obsessions out of hand. They were his life. He had never needed to justify his behaviour in the face of others' ineffectiveness. To him, it wasn't obsession, but merely his organisational prowess, kindled by an uncanny ability to foresee potential problems where others could not. He certainly would never have admitted to making such a conceited explanation to himself, although, his own opinion might easily inflate his sense of superiority.

His position as Project Manager of the Insecurity Security Act had provided him with more professional fulfilment than any previous undertaking in his long career. Even those who worked for him would admit that in spite of his meticulous, demanding nature, he was a good boss. He wasn't without the ability to laugh at himself and he certainly wasn't without a sense of humour when it came to making jokes at others' expense. He never took himself seriously; the work, however, was very serious, the work was everything.

To Manbag, Project Management made more sense, and held far greater importance than it once had, due to the dwindling number of completely controllable circumstances remaining in the chaotic field of public transport. He tongued the dregs; firm in his conviction that professional organisation could never be completely wiped out. He could easily convince himself that he was part of an elite force when given praise for his performance. "There are very few of us left", would be his typical humblebrag. He was doing vital work.

He was occasionally employed as an Expert Tie Analyst by a handful of companies who would rely on his extensive knowledge of gentleman's apparel and how an unsuspecting male interviewee's choice of neckwear revealed his personality. To Manbag, it had become an exact science. His exceptional taste afforded him a superior understanding of how spots or stripes; be they vertical, diagonal or otherwise, when combined with colour combinations, divulged valuable information about the job candidate. For this insight, the companies paid him ridiculous amounts of money. It was an enjoyable sideline which kept him in pocket money.

On his desk lay two freshly printed documents, aligned in parallel symmetry by his fussy fingers, ready for his perusal. The production of paper was kept to a minimum. This did not display a dearth of documents which might imply a lack of serious work. It displayed a singular focus on only those most important documents which merited desk space.

Document one was his revised introduction to the Suicide Monitor training literature. He was proud of his alterations. His need to tweak the twaddle which functioned as motivation for these new employees was evidence of his conscientiousness.

DEPARTMENT OF INSECURITY SECURITY ACT

Introduction to Suicide Monitor Training:

Congratulations on gaining acceptance into what has become a vital and exciting arena of transport control. The position of Suicide Monitor is one which we are proud to extol, and one which carries a great honour which you should feel fortunate and thankful to have bestowed upon you.

Please remember, at this preliminary stage, you are nothing more than a Monitor in the making, a vessel yet to be filled with the requisite whistle-blowing proficiency that is establishing our Monitors as consummate professionals.

Welcome to the first day of your step toward vocational enlightenment. Don't blow it!

"Which" is in there too many times, he thought. 'Don't blow it!' he said, chuckling at his own turn of phrase. He had never been convinced by his assistant's advice. The odd splash of humour never hurt anyone, Manbag thought. His assistant wasn't against humour per se, just Manbag's attempts at it.

The document was still not quite perfect. It probably never would be, not to Manbag's eyes, anyway. He took a yellow highlighter pen from his inside jacket pocket. He always carried one with him. He was, after all, paid to highlight mistakes, and couldn't be caught without instrument one. He sometimes liked to imagine colouring somebody's face with it in order to show his disdain for what they had just said to him. Carefully, he applied three yellow horizontal lines; one for each use of the repetitive pronoun which would force yet another re-write. He considered, for only a brief second, leaving the highlighter out on his desk. He placed it down between the two documents but was immediately unhappy with the new symmetry it created, so he deposited it back inside his pocket. He smiled as the space was returned to its previous state, free from the yellow intruder.

The second document was a confidential memo which he had released from its hiding place within his desk. It had been seen by only the most apposite collection of eyes on a need-to-know basis. It had been typed several times and each previous version had been shredded by Manbag personally, the shreds disposed of in a secret location known only to him. Its contents had already been implemented. It was customary for him to re-read active literature regularly. He touched the top left-hand corner of the document but did not lift it. He read it once more.

MEMO
ALTRUISTIC ACCELERATION
SPEED DIRECTIVE

With the newly established Contemplation Zone now up and running, the Department of The Insecurity Security Act, to be referred to henceforth as D.I.S.A., is implementing changes to speed regulations specific to all trains approaching a station.

An agreement between D.I.S.A. and executives representing local hospitals has been finalised wherein all train drivers will accelerate to an as yet to be determined velocity. In accordance with the findings of studies undertaken by independently contracted experts, the aforementioned executives, in an effort to streamline the casualty admissions process, have asked that all trains entering stations be driven at an increased velocity in order to avoid those exiting the Contemplation Zone being unsuccessful in their final aim. The objective of this agreement is to guarantee a lower number of "unsuccessful unfortunates" being admitted to local casualties, thereby putting unnecessary strain on precious medical resources. Instead, it is our primary intention to ensure a higher number of "successful unfortunates" are ultimately dealt with by the wonderful team working in our Contemplation Zone Disposal department.

For one calendar month after the final implementation of this directive, once the appropriate velocity has been determined and all train drivers have been re-trained accordingly, these changes will be subject to alterations at the behest of D.I.S.A. management.

It certainly flowed nicely, thought Manbag. Its quality produced a flicker of pride inside him. There was a knock at his office door.

'Come in,' he said. A Manbag minion entered. 'What is it?'

'Well, Mr. Manbag, I thought you would like to know that a yellow obstruction form has just been issued,' said the minion.

'Well, thank you, but I'm sure your office is quite capable of dealing with that without my input.'

'Usually, yes, with no problem whatsoever.' The young minion smiled smugly before continuing. 'But this particular one has been issued to one Jason Mighty, Sir.'

'Mighty?' Manbag said incredulously.

'Yes, sir, Mighty is his name.'

'I see, and...?' Manbag said.

'Mr. Mighty has been under observation for some time due to his tendency to take photographs on his local train station platform.'

'Not of the Contemplation Zone?' Manbag said.

'Well, Sir, not always, but today he did.'

'Is that right?' Manbag said.

'Yes, Sir, and he was involved in a rather unfortunate obstruction incident which resulted in him being quite rude to one of the monitors.'

Manbag chuckled. 'I wouldn't worry about that. They're more than capable of dealing with a little rudeness. They are superbly trained, after all.'

'But of course, Sir,' said the minion.

'Leave it with me,' Manbag said.

'Very good, Sir,' the minion replied.

Frown, please...

The funeral photographer and his new assistant arrived at the grieving family's house in reasonable time. Jason pulled two black ties from his camera bag as they neared the house. They had spent most of the taxi journey in silence as he had been checking his camera equipment and cleaning his lenses. The obstructed man, understandably, had not been so chatty.

'Put this on,' he said as he handed the tie to the obstructed man. 'Just stay with me and try to blend into the background, ok?'

'No problem,' said the obstructed man.

The taxi driver, having seen the hearse outside the house, drew to a respectable stop some distance away. Jason paid him and they got out. The two men stood on the pavement, tying their ties. Jason looked at the obstructed man. His tie was perfectly tied, which led Jason to readjust his own. He raised his Yashica quickly and snapped a sullen portrait of his new assistant.

'You're late!' Both men turned to see a harassed looking undertaker walking towards them. 'You've already missed countless opportunities!'

'I'm sorry,' Jason said. 'It wasn't my fault.'

'No, of course it wasn't,' said the undertaker. 'It's never anybody's fault, is it?'

The obstructed man looked at him. 'Excuse me,' he said. 'My young friend here was delayed by matters beyond his control, but he is here now, so why don't you let him do his job, lest the missed opportunities become even more countless.'

The undertaker gave the obstructed man a withering frown but did not comment.

'Well, let's go, then,' said Jason, smiling at the obstructed man. He almost managed a smile in return, but not quite.

Jason could feel the heavy sense of grief as they approached the house. On other occasions, he had noticed the lachrymose atmosphere build up inside the houses of the grieving. But now, as he was arriving late, they were walking directly into it. He thought about the obstructed man as he lifted his Yashica to capture a middle-aged woman in a sombre hat as she stood on the doorstep, holding a cling film-covered cut-glass bowl filled with trifle. The front door of the house opened to reveal a teenage girl whose expression was not one of grief but rather of annoyance at having to answer the door.

'Hello, Mrs. Bracewell,' she said as the woman thrust the bowl of trifle at her.

'Be careful with that, love. It's my best crystal,' said the woman as she pushed her way inside, leaving the teenager alone on the doorstep.

'Yes, I'm doing ok, thanks for asking,' she said to herself.

Jason captured her frustration as he and the obstructed man approached. The undertaker pushed past them and into the house.

'Is that really necessary?' asked the girl.

'What?' said Jason.

'Photographing me holding a trifle on the day of my

grandfather's funeral,' she said.

Before Jason could answer, the obstructed man stepped in once more.

'I'm very sorry, my dear. I truly believe it shouldn't be necessary at all. However, my young friend here has a job to do, a job which he does with the greatest respect for his subjects.'

Jason looked at him, surprised by his defence for the second time in only a matter of minutes.

'Martha!' said a voice from inside. 'Don't keep these gentlemen waiting outside in the cold.'

'Yes, Father!' she replied.

Martha's father, the son of the deceased, introduced his family as Jason and the obstructed man entered the living room. The atmosphere was indeed heavy with grief, as Jason had expected. They were each handed a small glass of sherry. It was Jason's custom to have one drink with the grieving family, if offered, as a sign of respect to the dearly departed, before beginning his work. The obstructed man turned to Martha, who was still holding the trifle, and raised his sherry glass.

'To your grandfather,' he said with a subtle smile which she returned in appreciation of the gesture. Both he and Jason sipped their sherry as Martha's father began gathering the rest of the family.

'Nicely done,' Jason whispered to the obstructed man, who gave the same smile in return to the compliment.

'I thought we could begin with one of us all together. Immediate family, that is,' said Martha's father. 'Of course, you're the expert, so I'll leave it up to you.'

'As you wish,' said Jason. 'I'm happy to oblige. I will take several shots throughout, of course, but any ideas you have, then please tell me.'

In front of the fireplace was the coffin in which grandfather could be seen at rest. The only three people in the room who seemed to pay it any attention at all were Martha, Jason and the obstructed man, who gave grandfather a woebegone look. The rest of the family were busily trying to organise themselves around the coffin. This seemed to involve a lot of repositioning which produced sighs from Martha. Her mother looked at her sternly.

'What about this?' Martha's father asked Jason. 'It's just that we wanted one of us all that we could hang on the wall.'

Martha sighed again. The young photographer took the final sip of his sherry. His empty glass was taken from him by Mrs. Bracewell. He handed his camera bag to the obstructed man. Producing a light meter, from his pocket, Jason set about checking the set up. He anticipated the dreary light surrounding the fireplace would be suitable for such a family photo.

'I think it's fine,' Jason finally answered.

'Ok, then,' said Martha's father.

'The Hasselblad, please,' Jason said to the obstructed man.

During the course of the next twenty minutes, Jason took several medium format shots of the family surrounding grandfather's coffin. Before the first one or two, he said, 'Ok, and frown, please...' Quite soon after, the family members, with the exception of Martha, needed no such direction from their photographer as their natural mourning demeanour readied them perfectly before every shutter release. Martha hated every sixtieth of a second. She was glad when the family was finally released and she was able to slope off into a corner and sneak a sherry or two.

Despite being eighteen years old, her mother would not approve of her sampling the sherry. Her grandfather would have given her some. He always thought his daughter-in-law was too uptight and would gladly have given his granddaughter sherry if only to rock the boat. The only other person in the family like Martha was now gone, in fact he was lying in a box in front of the fireplace. She despised this whole situation. The family wasn't that religious and, in her mind, she was convinced that the only reason they were having a wake such as this was for the sake of the photographs. Her grandfather would have hated it, and she hated her father for not taking that into account when planning this tasteless display. Such was the main fuel which fired her sighs; sighs which her parents assumed were merely teenage emissions of hormonal feelings they had long since forgotten and with which their patience was waning.

Jason had exchanged his Hasselblad for his Yashica and was now mingling with mourners, taking discreet shots of melancholia. This left the obstructed man free. He came and sat down next to Martha in her well-chosen quiet corner. She gave him a thin smile.

'You don't have to force anything for me, love,' he said. Her smile widened slightly. 'I agree with you.'

'Agree with what?' she asked him.

'You hate this situation, you think the need for these photographs is macabre and callous.'

'Yes, I do,' she said. 'Why can't we display happiness anymore?'

'Because of the austere time in which we live,' replied the obstructed man.

'But shouldn't that be the best time to display happiness?' Martha said.

'You and I may think so, perhaps even thousands of others, too. But unfortunately our opinions carry little weight when it comes to how we live. Choices are made for us. Decisions are made on our behalf.'

'But how is that fair?' Martha asked.

'It isn't,' replied the obstructed man.

'Martha, dear,' said her mother as she approached them.

'Yes, Mother,' said the teenager.

'I hope you're not distracting this gentleman with your wild ideas. He is here to do a job, after all.'

Martha's mother stood in front of them with a glass of sherry in one hand, the other hand on her hip.

'Not at all,' said the obstructed man. 'Although, I should be happy to be distracted by such a pleasant and intelligent young woman. You must be very proud of her.'

'Erm...yes,' said Martha's mother, sounding surprised by what she had heard. 'She certainly is spirited, shall we say.'

'Thank you, Mother,' said Martha with a sarcastic smile.

'Well, I must get back to it,' said the obstructed man, taking his leave. As he walked away, he heard Martha and her mother discussing something that almost led to raised voices. However, the mother's sense of her surroundings forced her to silence her daughter before too many heads were turned.

Before long, they set off to the funeral where the obstructed man continued to assist Jason. The photographer was happy with his new assistant, who seemed to blend in better than he himself ever had on any previous occasions. The obstructed man found the whole experience uplifting in the sense that the opinions of the teenager had provided some glimmer of hope, some anticipation of a younger generation who might buck the system rather than simply following their parents into a life of well-planned wakes in order to create photo opportunities. Why should displaying grief be necessary? Why must that be the logical response to not being able to display happiness? His new friend had built up a business based on that idea alone. He wondered how many photos Jason had taken of the Contemplation Zone; how many unfortunate souls, photographed seconds before their desperation had taken its final shot, slapping them in the face and then pushing them in the back towards the platform edge.

As the day wore on, Jason thought more about the obstructed man and wondered how many times he had found himself in the Contemplation Zone.

Stamp Collection

The sign on the door read, ANTONY MANBAG: PROJECT MANAGER. Jason turned to the faceless minion who had accompanied him.

'There must be some mistake,' the young photographer said. 'I'm sure it doesn't take a project manager to stamp a yellow obstruction form.'

'There's no mistake, Sir,' replied the minion. He knocked and a voice from inside invited them in. The minion opened the door and ushered Jason inside. He was immediately welcomed by another minion.

'Mr. Mighty, my name is Workman,' he said, offering a clammy hand which Jason shook reluctantly. 'And this,' he continued, gesturing towards a man seated behind a very tidy desk, 'is Mr. Manbag, our Project Manager.' An obsequious smile underlined the proud tone he adopted when saying his boss's name.

'Mr. Mighty,' said Manbag as he stood and offered a hand across the desk. 'What a noble name you have.' Jason leaned across the desk to take Manbag's hand. Less clammy than Workman's, he thought. 'Well, and yours, too, if somewhat metrosexual,' Jason said.

Workman winced at Jason's comment. Manbag laughed, perhaps louder than was necessary.

'An excellent start,' he said, curtailing his faux amusement. He gestured towards a chair and Jason sat down. 'You're probably wondering why you've been brought here, to my office, as opposed to simply having your yellow obstruction form stamped by one of our clerks.'

'It had crossed my mind, yes,' Jason replied. 'One thing...' he continued. Manbag gave him an unctuous smile. 'Everyone keeps referring to it as yellow, it's obviously yellow,' he said, holding up the form in question. 'So why not just refer to it as an obstruction form? Don't tell me...there is more than one type of obstruction, right?'

'There most certainly is,' said Manbag, 'each type having its own corresponding colour.'

'I see,' said Jason. 'And what classes my particular offence as yellow? What is yellow?'

He heard an intake of breath as Workman reacted to the questions.

'Well, Jason,' Manbag began, 'I may call you Jason, or do you prefer Mr. Mighty?' He grinned.

'Please,' Jason said, permitting the drop in formality.

'I'm sure you are not really interested in the various types of colour-coded obstruction and their protocol,' Manbag said.

'Actually, I am,' Jason said.

Workman interjected. 'Mr. Manbag is a very busy man. Unfortunately, we have to limit ourselves to the matter at hand.' Jason looked at Manbag's virtually clear desk.

'Well, he certainly does look busy,' he said, smiling insincerely at Workman. Manbag raised a hand to halt Workman's response.

'Take his form, stamp it, and wait for my call, please,' Manbag said to Workman, who immediately stood and did as instructed.

'What an obedient staff you have working for you,' Jason said, once they were alone. Manbag sighed professionally. Jason spied the faint hint of jowls appearing on Manbag's face.

'I can see you're not happy about being here, so why don't I cut straight to the chase,' Manbag said.

'Cut away.'

'Well, first of all, let me say that nothing I'm going to say should alarm you in any way; there really is no cause for concern,' Manbag said, adding a diplomatic smile.

'Isn't that usually how people sitting behind tidy desks preface alarming information that should cause concern?' Jason replied, mimicking Manbag's smile.

'You might be right,' Manbag said. He cleared his throat and straightened the papers on his desk unnecessarily. 'It seems your photographic activities have drawn attention.'

Jason displayed as little surprise as possible at what Manbag had just said.

'It seems that our Contemplation Zone has become something of an attraction to a young photographer, such as your good self,' Manbag said.

'Really, how could it not?' Jason asked. 'It's a government approved area, rapidly becoming commonplace in all train stations, installed for the sole purpose of suicide control.'

Manbag smiled. 'Well that really is the key word, isn't it?' he said.

'I used several key words,' Jason said.

Manbag's smile changed slightly. 'You certainly did, but I'm sure you realise that I meant CONTROL. That is what I'm talking about.'

'I imagine you talk about little else in this office,' Jason said.

'You might be right,' Manbag replied. He would not let the young man's aggression register in his replies. He couldn't lose control when talking about control; that would be very unprofessional.

'So I assume I'm here because my photographic activities are in some way illegal. Am I in contravention of some colour-coded subsection?'

'Forgive me, Jason, but you seem to have a very negative attitude. What exactly is bothering you?'

'What's bothering me? Well, because of your Contemplation Zone regulations, I was penalised for obstructing a suicide, I missed the train, and then I arrived late to a funeral, which is not professional.'

'You're quite right, that certainly is not professional for a funeral photographer. However, you must understand that these rules are in place for very serious reasons; without them we would have chaos.'

'You don't think that people being encouraged to jump in front of trains is already chaos?' Jason said.

Manbag continued to smile. He admired the young man's fervour.

'Because of my regulations, it is, at the very least, organised chaos,' Manbag said.

'Ah, so as long as it's organised, it doesn't matter that it's tragic?' Jason said, his temper rising. Manbag wanted to say no, but he felt steering Jason away from this point would be more judicious.

'I believe your obstruction incident was NEGLIGABLE and resulted in AMICABLE BACKDOWN; there were no hard feelings?'

Manbag said.

'No,' Jason said, calming down a little, 'in fact, after we left the station, I took him with me to work.'

'You took a suicidal man to a funeral?' Manbag asked.

'Yes.'

'I see. A very bold move,' Manbag said.

'Not really. To be honest, he seemed to enjoy it, in his own way, I guess.'

'Interesting...'

'How did you know I was a funeral photographer, anyway? Jason asked.

'You wrote it on your yellow obstruction form,' Manbag replied. Of course, he had already been informed of Jason's profession as a result of his team's surveillance, but there was no need to share that fact.

'Look, why am I here? Why does a project manager need to deal with this?' Jason asked.

'Well, let's get back to the matter of control, shall we?' Manbag said. 'I'm sure you can appreciate that control is paramount. It pains me to say it, but this office is not infallible. Inevitably, there are occasional glitches. Within my purview exists the responsibility to seek potential damaging influences, either information or other material, and eliminate that potential, by whatever means necessary, to ensure the on-going success of the project.'

'You really do take this very seriously, don't you?' Jason said.

'I most certainly do,' Manbag replied.

'But what does all this have to do with me?' Jason asked.

'Your photographs,' Manbag said, 'I need to be sure that not one single image could cast a negative light on our operation. If you have captured anything at all that might be unfavourable, I need to know.'

'And if I have?'

'If you have, which I seriously doubt, in light of the professionalism of my team, but, if you have, then we would have to reach an agreement regarding control of the images in question.'

'This certainly is CONTROL!' Jason said. His flippancy was starting to grate in Manbag's ears. 'You're in luck,' Jason added, reaching in his bag and producing a file. 'I just happen to have some of the photographs in question right here.' He held the file out reluctantly, not quite putting it in Manbag's hand.

'It's paramount, as I said,' Manbag said, reaching further across his desk to take the file from the photographer's stubborn hand.

He opened it and was confronted by images for which he had in no way prepared himself. Jason was quick to notice the Project Manager's physical reaction. Running, jumping, dashing, pushing, and of course, contemplation: each of these activities had been captured, within their horrid context, on faces so desperate – faces attached to numerous bodies – just how many people were contemplating? Manbag was momentarily enthralled with what he had laid before him. The shift in his demeanour – the sudden departure from his collected ultra-professionalism was brief – but not so brief that it escaped Jason's observant eye. The photos he had shared with him were only of people in the Contemplation Zone, or people attempting a dash. There was nothing so graphic, other than the blatant intention on a slew of wretched faces.

He paused. He picked up the phone and after a couple of

seconds said, 'Ok.'

'Is that it?' Jason asked.

'Almost,' said Manbag, 'but I'll need to hang onto these, for the time being, and I would like to see your archives, anything relating to the train stations. I assume you have archives?'

'I do indeed have archives, all organised. It's paramount in my business,' Jason replied.

'Mr. Mighty,' Manbag began, 'this whole process will be far simpler for both of us if we undertake it in a civil manner. Can we at least agree on that?'

'We can,' Jason said.

There was a knock at the door and Workman reappeared.

'Your copy,' he said as he handed the yellow obstruction form to Jason. Across the form was a third stamp which read, CONTROLLED.

The Flushed

At the end of each working day, Antony Manbag left his office replete with a sense of achievement; taking comfort in the knowledge that any issues which remained pending would be tackled again tomorrow with the benefit of a fresh suit and a rested mind.

It being a Wednesday, he felt particularly confident in his predictions for Thursday's professional grapplings. His Wednesday evenings were spent in the company of the E.F.A., or Enema Fanatics Anonymous. The group's name, which its members had often pondered changing, implied, through the inclusion of the word "Anonymous", that there was some obligation for them to participate, that they were addicts who used first names only. This wasn't entirely untrue.

Amongst the various factions in the group were the Gersons, who sat around eating fruit during every session; the Holistics, who participated fully with both body and mind; the Carcinophobes, who would try anything to delay the inevitable; and the Klismaphiliacs; those who were sexually aroused by the introduction of liquids into the rectum and colon via the anus.

Manbag fitted comfortably into the Holistics. He tried his best not to enter into any unpleasantness when one of his number occasionally tried to steal fruit when the Gersons weren't looking. Nor did he intervene, unless absolutely necessary, when the Carcinophobes criticised the Klismaphiliacs for enjoying something that was intended to prevent a horrible, withering death.

Despite the internal wrangling which only sometimes occurred, Manbag did enjoy being part of a group. His particular taste was for coffee enemas, which he regularly administered in the privacy of his own home. There was no administering within the group sessions, although he had been witness to the odd couple of Klismaphiliacs sneaking off during a boring testimony in the past.

Almost as enjoyable, for Manbag, was when new members came to their first meeting. He was able to use his powers of perception, often deploying his tie-analysis prowess, and predict with frequent accuracy which particular penchant the new member had. His reward after each successful prediction was coffee before bedtime.

During the meeting, which progressed in what had become the typical fashion of the Klismaphiliacs addressing everyone with insidious recruiting tones, Manbag found himself distracted by the idea of Jason Mighty's photographs. It was rare for him to be burdened by thoughts of work, so assured was he of the efficiency of his office. But, sitting there, amongst the intoxicating aroma of fresh fruit, his mind wandered away from the guest speaker's talk on nozzle hygiene. Could we be open to scrutiny if any of these photos became public? He considered the extent of his endeavours during his time as Project Manager of the Insecurity Security Act, and what his office had been able to achieve through its unwavering acumen. He thought about all those faces he had seen. The quality of the images; the composition, the black and white starkness of the subject matter. Men and women, old and young, pushed up against each other, and standing only a few feet away were the regular commuters who seemingly paid no attention.

He left the meeting promptly and drove home feeling somewhat queasy. He phoned Workman and asked him to arrange a meeting with Jason Mighty for the next day.

'No, tell him I will go to his house at his earliest convenience. I have to see everything he has as soon as possible.'

Darkroom

Jason was surprised to receive a call so soon after his visit to Manbag's office. The whole yellow obstruction incident had left him more frustrated with rail travel than he had ever thought possible. There was still the added fact that the obstructed man had accompanied him to the funeral and behaved in quite an un-suicidal manner throughout. Furthermore, he had given Jason his number and said, 'That was erm...well, enjoyable. We should do it again, if you need help, that is...' They had gone their separate ways without any mention of how their paths had crossed. Jason wondered if he would see him the next time he had to use the train. He would prefer to have him as a helper than to see him toeing the line in the Contemplation Zone. The doorbell rang. Here we go, he said to himself.

Antony Manbag's keen eye for detail extracted a reasonable amount of information once he had been ushered into the living room of Jason's house. The room was sparse and practical. He assumed that everything he saw before him had a regular use; nothing extraneous was on display. His first impression was augmented when Jason asked if he would like to see the darkroom.

'You have a darkroom?' Manbag asked.

'Yes, it's where I spend most of my time.'

'How quaint, in this age of technology,' Manbag said with a smile.

'I suppose it is, yes. Now people tend to use apps to make their photos look like they're not digital...where would we be without the concept of retro?' Jason said.

'Well, I don't think all retro is bad, as such,' said Manbag.

'You don't think it's just a euphemism for unoriginal?' Jason asked.

'Perhaps if I were to think about it as cynically as you...' said Manbag.

Jason had led Manbag to the door of the cellar at the back of the house. They stopped and Manbag read out the sign on the door.

'DO NOT ENTER. If this were a horror film, I'd go down there, never suspecting that I was being lured to my grizzly death.'

'That's right,' Jason said, 'unless the poor, unsuspecting fool is me, inviting a maniac into my house.'

'Who knows?' Manbag said with a grin. There was a moment's silence as Jason placed his hand on the door handle. He opened the door. Manbag was disappointed that it didn't squeak. He thought about commenting but then decided that they had shared enough preliminary banter; he was there in a professional capacity, after all.

'Watch your step, here,' Jason said.

Manbag followed the young photographer down into his lair. At the bottom of the steps was another door through which they entered the darkroom. Jason had used the darkroom so much and for so long that he had ceased to think of it with any sense of pride. He did, however, bask in its closed-off wondrousness; its creative functions giving his life a purpose.

Manbag looked around him at the collection of antique cameras.

Hundreds of black and white prints covered the walls; the latest still clipped to lines which hung across the room. The smell of chemicals was strong despite the extractor fan in the corner of the room. It wasn't an unpleasant smell, thought Manbag. He wondered if prolonged exposure to these chemicals could have any adverse effect on their user.

Jason suddenly felt ill at ease having this government body in his darkroom. How much of his private space did he really want to show him? He went to a filing cabinet and retrieved a large file.

'Let's take these back upstairs,' he said. 'The light is better and there's more air. I'm sure you're not used to this type of space.'

'I'm not,' Manbag said, 'but I have to say, I'm very impressed. I can't remember the last time I was in a darkroom.' His tone of voice rarely altered from its amicable register, unless there was true cause for it to do so.

Back upstairs, Jason went to make tea – he felt he should at least show some modicum of hospitality – and left his guest on the sofa, flipping through the previous day's evening newspaper. Manbag looked over the top of the newspaper at the unopened file of photographs which Jason had placed on the coffee table. His desire to inspect its contents was not so strong that he would forget his manners. He was unable to focus on any single item in the newspaper, as the images he had seen the previous day had kept him awake into the small hours, and the anticipation of seeing more provided ample distraction. He felt restless. He didn't know exactly what he was going to see, and he found himself worrying about his own reaction. He was surprised by how difficult it had been to apply his usual sense of detachment to aspects relating to the project. He hadn't considered the possibility of Jason's photographs having any discernible effect on him, but they undoubtedly had, and he felt uncomfortable and somewhat vulnerable. Casting the newspaper aside, he stood and began inspecting the bookshelves. They were filled with books which he realised he should probably have read. He wondered why Mighty had seemed so keen to get him out of the darkroom.

'Here we go,' said Jason as he appeared with a tray bearing a teapot, two big cups, milk and sugar. 'I hope you like Ceylon; it's my favourite, at the moment, anyway...'

'Lovely,' said Manbag. He turned away from the bookshelves. 'You must spend a lot of time reading.'

'Yes, but never enough,' replied Jason. 'My work takes up a surprising amount of time.'

'Why is it surprising?' Manbag asked.

'Well, I suppose the idea of a funeral photographer being very busy is somewhat depressing, wouldn't you say?' Jason asked in a tone which made Manbag feel he was being tested.

'Of course,' he replied, 'although, it's good for you.'

'And for you, too, I would imagine,' Jason said.

Manbag recognised that tone from when they had met in his office. 'Why would it be good for me?' he asked calmly.

'Well, I'm not implying that the funerals which provide me with work are exclusively the fruits of your Contemplation Zone. That would be ridiculous. However, you can't deny that your work is basically managing death.' Jason began pouring the tea slowly, forcing Manbag to wait to give his answer.

'I'm sorry you see it that way, Jason,' he said, taking the cup Jason had placed before him whilst considering the possibility that he could be right. 'Perhaps you will never be able to see it as we do.'

'Which is?' Jason asked.

'That we are minimising the distribution of suicides by providing an outlet, thereby concentrating the unfortunate incidents within a manageable space.' Manbag took a sip of his tea. 'Delicious,' he said.

'Oh, so you can at least see that these are "unfortunate incidents"?'

'Of course I can, but one has to be realistic about how much control is necessary in these situations.'

'I don't even know what that means!' Jason said.

'It means that, in these times of austerity...'

'Oh, please,' Jason said, interrupting Manbag. 'If I hear one more government suit begin an "explanation" with "in these times of austerity" ... it's just another way of saying everything's shit so you have to adapt to any macabre reform we choose to push through.'

'I think you'll find, down the line, that it's not as simple as that,' Manbag said, sipping his tea.

'...down the line?'

'Yes, down the line, people will eventually see that the Contemplation Zone works on many levels. It's only because the project is in its infancy that people still have to get used to its radical approach. Give it time; you'll see,' Manbag said. 'I can see why you like Ceylon so much.' Jason said nothing in reply. He simply leaned forward and flipped open the file of Contemplation Zone photographs. He saw an immediate reaction in Manbag as his eyes fell on the first shot. It had been taken two days earlier, just before the obstruction incident, when Jason had turned towards the group of suicides and captured a melee swathed in despair. Among them was the obstructed man, before he had earned his name; when he was just a man caught up in what almost became the final moments of his life. A frown wrinkled Manbag's forehead as he put his tea down on the table. He said nothing as he lifted the photograph. He had never really thought about the desperation of those poor unfortunate souls who populated his Contemplation Zone. He had never been present in any of the stations where his wonderful facilities had been introduced and, consequently, had never witnessed the Zone in operation. It had been easy to focus on the project on paper and in principle and leave the practical side to his capable assistants. He put the photograph down on the table and picked up a few more. Spreading them out on the table, he surveyed their tragic implication. He sniffed loudly as his eyes followed the line of images. Jason watched with fascination, hoping that his photographs might inspire some shame or perhaps even regret at having been part of the Zone's implementation.

Manbag touched his bottom lip with the first two fingers of his left hand as his eyes continued. A shot of the sign, CONTEMPLATION ZONE, seemed to lend a horrifying title to the table's montage – a close-up of a skinny young woman with a speckled, drawn face of addiction; a middle-aged man in a tie which escaped Manbag's analytical eye as its focus was elsewhere; face after face of black and white gloom-laden wrinkles; furrowed brow after furrowed brow of doleful forlornness; each aspect filled his eyes.

Jason continued his observation as Manbag continued his. The young photographer was surprised that the Project Manager had not made one single comment since his perusal began. He had no desire whatsoever to be complimented on the quality of his work. What he did want, however, was some sign from Manbag that he acknowledged the gravity of what he was observing

Manbag was experiencing an internal struggle. He had felt himself filling with a profound discomfort as he realised that, in that moment, his professional duties seemed beyond his capabilities. He had come to investigate the possibility of wrongdoing and here was ultimately damning evidence laid out in front of him; evidence which made him feel, for the first time since the project's inception, that there were real people involved; they weren't just numbers on a page of projections, they weren't just figures in hospital documents. He could not let Mighty know that his thoughts were about anything other than the continued success of the project. He could not let Mighty know that the potential wrongdoing of which he had come in search was not potential at all, but very real and splashed all over every single evocative, awful image.

He gathered the photographs together.

'There are more,' Jason said as Manbag placed them back in the file.

'I think I've seen enough, thank you,' he replied as he closed the file and picked up his tea. He had to try to direct the focus elsewhere before leaving. He couldn't leave Jason's house without injecting a more positive note into his visit. 'So, Jason,' he began. Jason cringed at Manbag's repeated use of his name when speaking to him. 'What else occupies your time, besides photography?'

'Why?' Jason asked.

'I just find myself interested in what else such a creative young man might turn his hand to, that's all.' Manbag replied.

'Well, since traditional photography tends to be so expensive these days, I have been supplementing my income by writing. Kind of a sideline, you might say.'

'Is that right? How interesting. What do you write?'

'Erotic fiction.' Jason looked at Manbag, waiting for his reaction of surprise.

'Erotic fiction, really? I must read something of yours, what do you say?' Manbag said.

'You don't have to,' Jason said.

'Nonsense,' Manbag replied. 'I'd like to.'

'Well, if you really want to, you can find my work under the name of Cristina Hart.'

'Ah, a female pseudonym, wise choice,' Manbag said with a smirk.

'Look for Roger 'N Granny online.'

'Roger 'N Granny,' Manbag said. 'It sounds very specific.'

'You could say that, yes,' Jason replied. 'But why are you asking me all this? I can't believe you're really interested, especially after what you've just seen.'

'Speaking of what I've just seen…I need to take the photos with me, I'm afraid.'

'But…'

'Don't worry, you will get them back, undamaged and just as they are now,' Manbag said. He finished the last of his tea. 'You should try tea from Rwanda. It's not unlike this, you'd like it, I'm sure.' He stood up and held out his hand for the photographs. 'You have my word,' he said in response to Jason's reluctant expression. The young photographer handed him the file. 'I'll be in touch. Thank you.'

As soon as Manbag had gone, Jason returned to the depths of the darkroom. Opening the bottom drawer of the filing cabinet, he retrieved a much thicker file than the one Manbag had taken with him. He sat down on a tatty old leather armchair in a corner of the room. He opened the file and studied the first photograph, angling it so as to avoid glare from the lamp above him. He had come to realise, during his repeated attempts to catch a train, that once the Suicide Monitor's whistle had sounded, there was far less chance of being noticed with a camera in his hand. Once people started running and pushing, once the fear became more palpable, nobody was going to be paying attention to him. Consequently, he had managed to capture the horrific images he was now examining; the images he hadn't shared with anyone else, although he had added a few to Manbag's file; images taken by shooting away from the Contemplation Zone towards the tracks, which captured the appearance of sinister station staff dressed in what seemed to be plastic protective clothing, entirely covered from the head down to black wellington boots. What Jason didn't know was that these people were Manbag's Contemplation Zone Disposal Team assuming their positions, as per their rigorous training; training that might easily be open to scrutiny were the existence of such photographs to become known.

Again, shooting away from the Zone, Jason had captured the blur of the train – post-whistle – with the slower unfortunates frozen in time, mid unsuccessful dash, destined to remain as non-jumpers. More and more images; Suicide Monitors at the crucial point of inflated cheeks; regular commuters caught in backwards turns in the morbid intention of witnessing something they didn't really want to see; a lone jumper in mid-air, with only the tip of one shoe pointing back to the platform, the result of a perfectly-timed dash which came to fruition, thanks to an old Nikon at 1/8000th of a second. In the next image, the point of impact that all those dashing were hoping to achieve; the final release as metal meets skin and bone.

      The collection continued until the bottom of the file, but Jason had had enough. It had only been recently that he had experienced the uncomfortable sensation of not wanting to look at his own photographs. He did, however, feel proud at having been responsible for the contents of the file, if only because he hoped that they might prove important at some time in the future.

The Manbag Abode

Locking the door behind him, Antony Manbag placed the folder of photographs on the floor as he bent down to unlace his shoes beneath the hallway mirror. Awaiting his tired feet were his slippers; left aligned and adjacent to the place where he discarded his shoes. He looked at the folder as he flexed his toes. He grabbed it; his knees cracking as he straightened up and set off into the kitchen.

He dropped the folder on the kitchen table, its weight producing an ominous thud which seemed to encapsulate its profound cargo. A smoothie; that's what he wanted. The buzz of the fridge interrupted the silence of the kitchen as he opened the door in search of ingredients. Gathering what he needed, he turned and placed everything on the table next to the folder. He didn't really want to examine any more of Jason's photographs, but he had to. He thought about the images he had already seen as he dropped the fruit methodically into the blender. He pressed the button and the silence was interrupted once more. The whirring, whizzing metallic noise usually started off his breakfast routine, during which he would watch the television news. He flipped open the folder as he waited and spread the photographs across the kitchen table. As he looked at the contorted faces, the blender noise made him think of trains. Its volume seemed to increase in his ears as he stared at grotesque moment after grotesque moment of pain, despair, anticipation. His eyes flicked from one face to another until he had to switch off the blender. The room was returned to its previous state. His imagination was released from the blender's locomotive force. He filled a big glass to the brim with the viscous, fruity beverage and sat down at the table.

Could he have been wrong? Was Jason's aggression justified? He took a sip from the glass; the pureness of its restorative contents making very little intervention on the ghastliness welling up inside his stomach. I am a Project Manager, he thought. The completion of the project is everything. I am not supposed to care. I am unaffected by collateral damage.

He continued his perusal, finding new images from beneath the ones he had already seen, each of them opening his eyes further. I am a Project Manager. The completion of the project is everything. I am not supposed to care. I am unaffected by collateral damage.

Another sip from the glass turned into a gulp as he felt his body begging him for a cleansing. The system is supposed to work perfectly. We have streamlined all operations. Another gulp. Another image. Have we totally overlooked the glaringly obvious? Such a high number of suicides, potential suicides, would-be suicides, but why? Are we content to let it continue, our only focus being how we tidy it up? Another gulp gave way to a retch, bringing with it a small bit of blueberry.

The faces of the photographed; those referred to in the literature, his literature, as "unsuccessful unfortunates" whom they were hoping to convert to "successful unfortunates", were staring back at him. He was disgusted with himself. He was disgusted by the fact that he felt disgusted with himself and that his professional endeavours had provoked such events to become commonplace. His Contemplation Zone, his baby, which had been, by any measure in the minds of his collaborators, a success; a true labour-saving, cost-effective phenomenon which had driven him to career heights beyond his imagination, was now making him retch, turning him away towards a new understanding of all the dreadful elements of the Insecurity Security Act and the schemes that had been put into action in its name. He turned quickly, ran to the kitchen sink and vomited the smoothie; banana and blueberry spattering the stainless steel with a sweet acidic splat.

What can I do? He thought about this as he spat the final fruity dregs into the sink. I can't continue. It can't continue. But I can't resign. It is my project. I am the project. I am unaffected by collateral damage. I can't stop it. I am collateral damage...

He continued to swing back and forth between what he considered to be one impossibility after another. Nobody would believe my resignation. I have been too committed. Nobody would accept my abandoning the project. I have been too efficient. He sent a hurriedly thumbed text to Workman telling him that he would be in the office the following morning for their meeting but then he would have to leave, taking care not to sound anything other than thoroughly professional; something about further investigation being necessary. That ought to do it. He had to think. Turning away from the sink, almost hoping that the photographs wouldn't be spread across the kitchen table, he retook his seat. There they were. What am I going to do?

He had never been a bad person. Confronted with the photographic evidence of his office's handiwork, he felt an undeniable surge, a sensation akin to nothing he remembered from previous experience. Any compassion, any emotional attachment in his colleagues, upon which he had been required to frown for the sake of the continued smooth running of every project he had ever worked on; all consideration for anything other than the greater good, or at least his version of it, all of it now had been laid bare by the power of Mighty's photographs, Mighty's evidence of Manbag's project and its gruesome achievements. The smoothie had purged his stomach, but he needed more. He needed to be cleansed inside. Time for a coffee.

The Contemplation Zone was a damage control method, part of the concatenation brought about by industrial espionage within a privatised rail network. Hacked systems, train delays, train cancellations; various machinations had made Manbag's project necessary. Is that really as elegant a defence as I can muster? Excusing ourselves as being a mere cog; as accurate as that might be, will do nothing to persuade the cynics that the Zone is not despicable.

The organic fine blend coffee was ready. He switched off the heat in order to let it cool to the optimum tepidness. During the summer months, Manbag's neighbours frequently smelt the fine aroma wafting through the open windows and often commented on its quality as well as on how late it seemed to be drinking it. Of course, he only bought fair trade coffee, as better conditions for farmers somehow seemed even more important, in his mind, when said farmers were producing something which was ultimately going to be swishing around his colon. Strangely, he had never drunk it. He had no idea how it tasted. He kept a different brand of fine organic coffee solely for drinking. His need to separate the two might seem at odds with the holistic methodology espoused by his more fervent E.F.A. colleagues, but he had never really felt the need to share details of his personal coffee preparation habits.

He went to the bathroom to retrieve his anal accoutrements. He often thought about the fact that he kept the coffee in the kitchen yet his sundry items were stashed in the bathroom in a fine, wooden case which he had bought at a convention some years before, when his self-cleansing had first become a regular part of his regime. He opened the case and set about assembling his apparatus. The coffee was just about the right temperature. After lowering his trousers, he applied coconut oil to a fresh nozzle. The coffee was in place, the clip on his tubing was closed. Everything was ready for insertion. He lay down on his side. With one foot extended, he pushed the bathroom door closed.

 He emerged from the bathroom, having lain down for an hour, during which time he had pondered his situation, considering each circumstance while undergoing his coffee-induced cleansing. He still didn't know what he was going to do about Jason's photographs. He had no idea how his position had changed. However, he did feel some benefit.

 In his bedroom, he began changing into his pyjamas. He smiled to himself as he started to think that his vomiting and coffee before bedtime had gone some way towards ridding him of his initial disgust. He felt a sort of loosening, as if his eyes had been opened to his own up-tightness. He opened the drawer in which his boxer shorts lay perfectly folded and aligned according to colour. He laughed out loud as he began grabbing them in handfuls and throwing them up in the air over each shoulder.

 Something; he didn't know what, but something had to change. He thought about Jason. He would go and see him tomorrow. He suddenly remembered what the young photographer had told him about his erotic writing. Roger 'N Granny; that was it, he thought. In search of distraction, he rushed to his computer and quickly found and downloaded the book. He collected the rest of the smoothie from the kitchen; now believing he had the stomach for it. On top of the bed, he placed a pile of toilet paper squares, folded with the experience of one who cares about effective absorption. He may have been loosening up but he wasn't an animal. He kicked off his slippers without bothering to put them together in the usual spot next to the bed. He laughed once more at the pairs of boxer shorts strewn across his bedroom before climbing onto the bed.

'Roger 'N Granny,' he read aloud as he found the first page. 'Roger was sitting in the corner of the Denmark Café, on his third coffee.' Manbag could still smell his own coffee. He smiled as he continued reading, curious to know if Jason Mighty's story would reveal anything interesting at all about his character.

Further Loosening...

The following morning, Workman knocked on Antony Manbag's office door at 8.57, three minutes earlier than the scheduled meeting. These three minutes were the result of rigorous time management. Manbag, at the first of their meetings, had asked Workman if he could arrive at 8.57 so they might feel free to settle down, exchange pleasantries, and then attack the day's agenda head-on, once the clock had reached the hour. In Workman's mind, those three minutes showed him that his boss considered him to be worthy of non-work related exchange, that his valued professional input merited a personal touch - a whole three minutes' worth. To Manbag it was nothing more than basic people management. Make them feel worthy, and they will go above and beyond. Workman's commitment had proved Manbag right on several occasions. A small amount of smugness was apt to power the Project Manager's smiles as he saw the results of such labours.

Workman entered the office without waiting for a reply; a liberty which he believed he was afforded due to those significant three minutes. He found Manbag sitting at his desk, as normal, but looking less than his usual impeccable self.

Workman's scrutinous eye made light work of his boss's appearance: unshaven, no tie, curious; hair not quite perfect, less tweaking between finger and thumb, strange; blank expression, interesting; usual faint aroma of coffee despite absence of coffee in room, check – something normal, phew!

'Are you alright, Sir?' Workman asked. Manbag stared down at the typical military tidiness of his desk. Workman sat down opposite.

'Something's...' Manbag said, waving his arms over the desk.

'Something's?' Workman said. 'Is everything ok?'

'Workman!' Manbag said, making eye contact with his assistant, as if only just aware of his presence. 'It's erm...well, let's begin, shall we?'

Workman tried to control his sense of puzzlement.

'Well, Sir, we have one or two rather pressing matters relating to disposal,' he said.

'Disposal, ah yes, very interesting...' Manbag replied. His eyes were back on his desk. 'Do go on...'

As Workman continued to explain, Manbag began shifting the pile of papers in front of him to different locations on his desk. Left or right, corner or more central, nothing seemed to provide enough satisfaction to relieve his tired face of the frown of disappointment which occupied it. Despite his movements proving somewhat distracting, Workman continued.

'We have received unconfirmed reports of Disposal Team members removing jewellery and other valuables from the "successful unfortunates" during the course of their disposal duties.'

Having decided to separate the pile of papers into two and place them adjacent in the centre of the desk, Manbag was now unhappy with the location of his pen holder. He began trying out different possibilities based on the symmetry of the two piles of paper.

'So, Sir, I'm sure I don't have to explain the gravity of such information becoming public,' Workman said.

Manbag sat back in his chair, trying a different perspective, moving his head from left to right. The pen holder just wasn't right. He sat forward again. Workman sat quietly, watching his boss make increasingly frustrated adjustments to his desk. *Does he even realise I've stopped talking?* In one rapid sweeping movement, Manbag knocked over the pen holder, scattering pens and pencils across the desk. Workman jumped. *That was deliberate,* he thought.

'Sir...,' he said, leaning forward to begin restoring Manbag's desk to its usual clinical state.

'This is just not working for me!' Manbag said loudly. 'Let's sit over there, come on!' He gestured to the sofa, which had never been sat on, at least as far as Workman knew. Manbag stood up, totally disregarding the stationery nightmare he had caused, walked across the room and flopped down onto the sofa. It was such a nonchalant gesture that Workman had trouble believing that it was his boss who had just made it. He then saw Manbag readjust his position, the nonchalant slouching obviously not providing the perfection he was seeking, and his faith that it was indeed his boss was restored.

As Workman approached the sofa, Manbag leaned forward nervously and took a magazine from the tidy array on the coffee table. He flipped through a few pages, looking at nothing, as his confused assistant stood before him. Workman sat down in the armchair opposite the sofa. He looked back at the desk, at the assortment of writing implements left scattered there. He checked his watch again. They were now three and a half minutes into their meeting with absolutely no progress made; highly irregular.

Manbag closed the magazine and threw it back on the table, out of place on top of the others, the space from where he had taken it remaining unoccupied. Sitting back, he lifted his right leg and rested his ankle on his left thigh. He was in danger of looking relaxed. Workman looked at the discarded magazine in wonder, then at his boss's casual pose.

'So, you were saying...' Manbag said. Workman displayed a glimmer of relief at the intimation of work.

'Yes,' Workman began, 'these reports need to be confirmed before any action can be taken.'

'Of course, yes,' Manbag replied. 'I assume you are already on top of it?'

'Absolutely, Sir, I am just keeping you abreast.'

'Well, abreast I am kept,' Manbag said with a grin. His ankle was uncomfortable. He changed legs. He suddenly noticed that he was wearing odd socks. He let out an uncomfortably loud snigger. Workman jumped.

'Well, I think we're done here, don't you?' Manbag said, acting quickly. Workman responded with a nonplussed expression.

'I must go,' Manbag said, standing up from the sofa. He watched as his odd socks were obscured by the bottom of his trouser legs. 'As I said, I will be out for the rest of the day. I trust there is nothing that needs my immediate attention?'

'Not presently, Sir, no,' Workman said, bemused by Manbag's behaviour.

'Well, then...'

The Gathering

Since his unfortunate obstruction incident, Jason had found himself thinking about the obstructed man, especially since his visit from Manbag and the showing of the Contemplation Zone photographs. As he was finishing off the funeral prints, he suddenly thought, without knowing exactly why, that the obstructed man should be there. He had been present at the funeral, as a willing assistant, and it seemed only right that he should be present to see the finished product.

As Jason dialled the number that the obstructed man had given him, he hoped that he would be there to answer the phone, that there wouldn't be some terrible reason why he was no longer available for anything. He was relieved to hear the obstructed man's solemn voice after five rings. His tone changed after hearing Jason's invitation. He would be right round. Jason hung up feeling positive, as if he had done his good turn for the day.

A few minutes later, he was surprised to hear the doorbell ring. He wondered how close the obstructed man lived as he opened the front door. Standing on the doorstep with a sullen expression was Martha, the young woman from the funeral.

'Hi Jason, remember me?' she asked

'Of course I do. It's Martha, right?' Jason replied. She was very pretty, he thought. He didn't remember thinking that at the funeral. He managed, briefly, to convince himself that this had been down to his sense of decency. He smiled at her.

'My father said I should call you Mr. Mighty, but that seems ridiculous,' she said with a grin.

'Does it now?' Jason said. 'Why's that?' She gave him an incredulous look but didn't reply. 'I guess you'd better come in,' he said after it became clear that a response to his question would not be forthcoming.

'I know I'm early,' she said as they entered the living room, 'but I was hoping you wouldn't mind showing me your darkroom. It is here, isn't it?'

'Yes, it is here,' Jason said. He was pleasantly surprised by her interest, but tried not to show it too much. 'I have everything set up in the cellar.'

'Ok,' she said passively. 'Oh, here,' she added, pulling an envelope out of her jacket pocket and handing it to him. 'My father said you wanted to be paid in cash. I'd count it, if I were you.'

'I'm sure it's fine,' Jason said. He put the envelope down on the coffee table. 'Let's go downstairs, then, shall we?'

She followed him down the cellar steps in silence. Inside the darkroom, she looked around in much the same way as Antony Manbag had the previous day.

'You have a lot of cool cameras,' she said.

'Do you like old cameras?' he asked.

'I do,' she said. 'My grandfather gave me his old Zeiss Contaflex not long before he died.'

'Oh, that's a really nice camera. Have you used it yet?'

'No, but I'd like to. I like the idea of using something that was his.'

Jason smiled at the sentiment just subtly enough so as not to be patronising.

'Don't you take pictures on your phone?' he asked.

'Why, because I'm eighteen years old and that's all we do?' She smiled at him with one raised eyebrow; thereby tempering his reaction to what he had assumed was aggression. He didn't bother trying to explain himself.

'Your photos are here, just drying,' he said. She walked over to the line he indicated, where the prints hung. The doorbell rang at the optimum moment as he had just been considering leaving her alone with what he assumed would be emotional images for her to look at.

'I'll be right back,' he said.

She was mesmerised by the first photograph she saw which showed her grandfather lying in his coffin beneath the mantelpiece. The first few seconds of surprise gave way to a different feeling - one almost of disbelief. She knew it was him, but being displayed here, in black and white, made him seem like somebody else. It could have been an old press photograph of some dead prime minister lying in state. She liked it, though. He looked peaceful. He looked free from his suffering, and from the nagging of her mother. Moving down the line, the next few images were ones of the family standing around the coffin. How ridiculous, she thought. Look at their stupid sad faces.

On the table next to the old leather chair, she found three enlargements of family shots. These must be the ones my father asked for, she thought. Why would anyone want that hanging over their fireplace?

The door opened. She turned to see the obstructed man followed by Jason. She smiled when she saw who it was who had rung the bell.

'Martha, how nice to see you again,' the obstructed man said. He walked over to her and grabbed her hand in his. She appeared to be very comfortable around him.

'And you,' she said, retrieving her hand after a polite amount of time.

'You're here to see the photos too, I presume?' the obstructed man said.

'Well, actually, just to collect them. I was more interested in seeing the darkroom.'

'I see. Jason invited me to see them, as I was acting assistant on that day. I hope that's ok with you.'

'Of course,' she said. 'To be honest, I find them quite disgusting, but...'

Jason was taken aback by her remark. The obstructed man understood perfectly.

'Don't get me wrong,' she said, looking at Jason's unsettled face. 'I think they're amazing. It's just the whole concept I find disgusting.'

'But this is my work!' Jason said.

'...and this is my opinion!' Martha replied.

'So you like my work, but you don't like that it's necessary?' Jason asked.

'It's NOT necessary,' she said, 'and I hate the fact that it even exists!'

'I know exactly what you mean,' said the obstructed man as he stood inspecting the hanging prints as they dried.

'Oh you do, do you?' Jason said.

'Of course I do. It's rather simple, really. Like a lot of people, Martha believes that the wanton display of grief which has become so commonplace, is a symptom of austerity; we're no longer permitted to display facile images of fun on social networks and somehow, this restriction has led to an appalling trend which she refuses to accept.'

'...an appalling trend?' Jason said.

'Quite frankly, yes,' the obstructed man said. 'Let's be honest about it. The social network restriction on fun wasn't entirely a bad thing. We were becoming a race of desperate over-sharers, convinced that our lives were fascinating. I hesitate to use the 'S' word, but really, how many photos does anyone really need of themselves?'

'Exactly!' said Martha.

'But don't you think these photos are the opposite of all that?' Jason asked them.

'In what way?' Martha asked.

'Well, they're not facile, they have emotional depth. It's not just another picture of your dog...' Jason said.

'Jason,' the obstructed man began as he inspected the images, 'these photographs are wonderfully profound.' He smiled at the young photographer, who allowed himself a little up-turning at the corners of his mouth as a result of the compliment. 'But don't you see? It's the displaying of them, as people would do with any other family photographs, that is vacuous. People are so intent on proving that they have substance that they are willing to exhibit what should be their most private moments of grief. It's desperate over-sharing to the nth degree.'

'I have to admit,' Jason began, 'I agree with everything you've just said, but this is my work, these photographs are good, and I'm proud of them.'

'We can't disagree with that,' Martha said. 'But you have to see that hanging them on your wall, posting them online; being careful to make a point of mentioning that they are "real" photographs made in a darkroom, is just wrong.' She looked at the obstructed man as he nodded in agreement. The doorbell rang again.

Jason opened the door and was surprised to see a very different looking Antony Manbag standing before him, clutching the folder of Jason's photographs. Instead of an impeccable suit and tie; chosen judiciously for its accompanying impact, Manbag was sporting a more casual yet still co-ordinated look. He hadn't shaved and the reddish-grey stubble on his chin made him feel on the edge. His overall air was of a man with a preoccupation. He looks really clean, Jason thought. He detected the faint aroma of coffee.

'Mr. Mighty,' said the visitor.

'Mr. Manbag,' said the host.

Standing down the hall behind Jason, Martha and the obstructed man both waited nosily, wondering who the latest arrival was. As soon as they heard Jason invite the visitor in, they dashed into the living room and sat down.

'This is Mr. Antony Manbag, Project Manager,' Jason said, presenting his visitor to Martha and the obstructed man.

'Hello,' they said in unison.

Manbag advanced on them both, shaking their hands and smiling.

'Good morning,' he said. 'I hope I'm not interrupting anything.'

'Antony Manbag?' said the obstructed man, struck by a sudden realisation.

'That's right!' Manbag replied.

'Project Manager?' the obstructed man asked.

'Yes,' replied Manbag.

'Insecurity Security; you're the one who controls the Contemplation Zone, aren't you?' the obstructed man said.

Manbag blushed slightly. 'Well, I'm flattered that you've heard of me,' he said uncomfortably. Martha studied him closely. Jason watched the obstructed man apprehensively.

'There's nothing flattering about it,' the obstructed man said seriously.

'Oh, I see,' replied Manbag, anticipating more discomfort. 'Why is that?'

'Why would I flatter you? Perhaps you make a perfect soufflé...' the obstructed man said. Manbag raised his eyebrows smugly in recognition of what he knew to be true. 'Maybe,' continued the obstructed man, 'you are nice to your mother, maybe you give money to charity, who knows? You might even help your elderly neighbour inside with her shopping bags. It doesn't really matter how many qualities you have that might very well inspire compliments and flattery from your obsequious subordinates. The simple fact is, that anything positive that your life contains will be forever overshadowed by the grotesque work that you do.' The obstructed man took a much-needed breath.

'Well,' Manbag said after a few seconds of silence during which Martha had struggled to stifle a laugh. 'It's not often one receives such a warm welcome.' Nobody said anything. Jason looked at Martha; they both then looked at the obstructed man.

'Perhaps I should sit down,' Manbag said.

'Please...' Jason replied, gesturing to a chair opposite Martha and the obstructed man. Manbag sat down, putting the folder of photographs on the table. Jason sat down on the sofa between Martha and the obstructed man.

'Well...' Manbag said, addressing the three of them. 'Let me begin by saying that you may well be right.' His listeners showed subtle signs of surprise as they waited for him to continue. 'I've always prided myself on my professionalism; my desire to do the best possible job in fulfilling the objectives of the project has been paramount.'

'Wow,' said Martha, 'you people really do speak like that.' Jason raised his hand to imply that she should let him finish.

'But, I have to say,' Manbag continued, 'I came here today to say that yesterday, after looking at your photos, Jason, I had what I can only describe as an awakening which, I should say, has left me in an impossible position.' He suddenly thought about his squeaky-clean innards and how they didn't seem to be making this any easier.

'What position is that?' asked the obstructed man.

'One in which I am suddenly unable to function as I have, one in which I have no idea what to do,' Manbag said.

'Is that right?' Jason said.

'It most certainly is. I am the Project Manager of The Insecurity Security Act,' Manbag said. His demeanour had changed since he had sat down. 'I am in charge of the continued smooth running of all Contemplation Zones. Their number is due to increase slowly over the next six months. Huge amounts of money have been invested in this project.'

'We know all this already,' the obstructed man said.

'That may be so, but my point is...' Manbag paused. 'What I'm trying to say is that I don't see how I can continue. I don't see how I was able to get this far without considering the gravity of the situation, without seeing the Contemplation Zone for what it truly is.'

'...and what is that?' the obstructed man asked.

'I'm sure you don't need me to tell you, you seem quite capable of forming an opinion,' Manbag said.

'I would like to hear it from you,' said the obstructed man.

'I think it's abhorrent!' Manbag said. 'I feel ashamed to have been so obsessed with completing the brief, that I was blind to what it really represented.' He paused, as if surprised with himself for actually saying it out loud. 'But you must understand,' he said to the three of them with an earnest look on his face. 'I don't know what I can do. For the first time in my professional life, I find myself totally at a loss. After what I have just said, I have to say also, that I don't see how I can leave the project either.'

'It's almost as if you are expecting us to tell you what to do,' said the obstructed man.

'What I don't understand,' said Martha, 'is how the Contemplation Zone even works anyway. I mean, how can people just use the train platform, knowing that that's what's happening? How can they just stand there, waiting, with those poor people there behind them?'

Manbag looked at her.

'Well, after extensive research, we came to the conclusion that the majority of people, when confronted with something which should horrify them, are content to look the other way and focus on their own immediate situation. They might feel guilty for having done nothing, for not even acknowledging the supposedly horrifying circumstances, but really, they can assuage that guilt by quite easily convincing themselves that somebody, somewhere, will do something, so they don't have to.' He paused, scratching the top of his head with the fingertips of one hand. 'Think of it in much the same way as people ignoring the homeless when they ask for money. How many people have you seen who don't even answer when asked, almost as if the situation is embarrassing?'

'Ok, said Martha, 'that does happen, of course, but it's hardly the same as standing by whilst people jump to their deaths.'

'No, that's considerably worse, without a doubt, but isn't that what makes it easier to ignore?' Manbag asked.

'...and isn't that what allowed you to manage the whole thing?' asked Jason. Manbag gave him a resigned look. Jason continued. 'Isn't that what allows people to ignore the fact that an enormous number of people seem to be committing suicide? Instead of asking why, instead of going to the root of the problem, they simply make it easier for them to do so in an organised, tidy way. How can something like the Contemplation Zone even become a viable project? How can it possibly be justifiable for a society to offer this as an option for suicide control?'

'As one of my superiors said when the project was first proposed,' Manbag said. "We don't have to solve the problem, as long as we can clean it up!"'

'That was really their attitude?' asked the obstructed man.

'Perhaps not everyone shared that opinion, but it was definitely agreed upon by some, yes,' Manbag said. It seemed as though discussing these points outside of his usual sterile environment allowed him to see them more clearly, which in turn made him feel ashamed. It was all suddenly more real; having only brainstormed around conference tables and perused details on the drawing board meant that, in Manbag's imagination, the project had retained an element of the hypothetical. But perhaps, somewhere beneath the veneer of conscientiousness, there had always lurked an iota of unease, a doubt which had kept him off-site, away from construction; delegating to those he was now starting to believe were more blessed with the efficient emotional detachment which his superiors had seen in him.

'You mentioned that research had been done,' Martha said.

'Yes,' replied Manbag.

'What kind of research?' she asked him.

'Really, if I told you about that, you would just hate me even more,' he said.

'Assuming that were possible,' Martha replied sharply. Manbag didn't respond. He just looked at her in acceptance of her criticism; his thick skin deflected it more readily than his three detractors might have preferred. But then, one could never become the Project Manager of Insecurity Security with no backbone.

'So,' she continued, 'your organisation conducted research into the likelihood of people ignoring horrifying situations?'

'More into the likelihood of them accepting them as normal,' Manbag said. The obstructed man raised his eyebrows as he looked at Manbag. 'And the findings were such that the Contemplation Zone was given the go-ahead?' he asked.

'Basically, yes,' said Manbag.

'Well, isn't that depressing!' said the obstructed man.

'It certainly is,' said Manbag. 'But it's nothing new, now, is it? How many despicable acts of the last century were ignored, mainly by people who did actually have more power than the common man to act, to protest, at the very least to speak out?'

They sat in silence for a moment. Manbag was thinking about what the obstructed man had said, about expecting them to tell him what to do. He didn't really expect anything. He did wish they had some answers for him, but he certainly wasn't about to ask them for anything.

Breaking the silence, Martha said, 'So why are you here?' Manbag wasn't surprised by the question, but he hadn't expected it to come from the young woman. She was shaping up to be the toughest of the three, he thought.

'I'd be lying if I said it was only to return Mr. Mighty's photographs,' Manbag answered.

'So then...?' the obstructed man said.

'I guess I had to come here, and in my own bumbling way, try to express what a profound effect they've had on me,' said Manbag.

'So Dr. Frankenstein comes to apologise for his monster's bad behaviour?' the obstructed man said.

'Something like that,' Manbag said with a nervous smile. 'Although, to whom, for what?'

'You feel like you should apologise, but you don't know why,' the obstructed man said. 'That is something else you will have to determine for yourself.'

Manbag looked at the three of them. He was making a concerted effort to appear as though their criticism was not finally finding its way beneath his skin. He began to wonder if relaxing this effort might render him pitiable at all; perhaps just the smallest amount may prove enough for them to extend their compassion in his direction. He felt slightly pathetic, sitting there under scrutiny; with virtually nothing to offer in his defence, unable to be sure that they believed anything he had said about agreeing with their opinions. Why would they? It seemed as though he had walked into a house and found the three people who were most unforgiving of his situation. What is my situation? I'm the big bad wolf, in odd socks. He scratched the hair on his chinny chin chin and sighed; maybe I'm not. They were still looking at him, waiting for him to continue.

'What do you want from us?' the obstructed man asked.

'It doesn't really seem like I'm able to ask you for anything,' said Manbag. 'Even if I were, I wouldn't know what it would be. I understand that you must be very sceptical about all this, my turning up on the doorstep with what appears to be no firm intention, yet somehow claiming to find the project, which I have worked so hard to develop, abhorrent. I would struggle to believe that a man from my professional background could suddenly deviate from the cause, yet here I am, going through some sort of crisis, sitting before you in desperate need of help but fully aware that you consider me totally undeserving.'

'What do you want to do?' Jason asked him. Manbag's eyes widened.

'I want to destroy the whole thing!' Manbag said, raising his voice in the excitement of finally getting that sentence out of himself. 'I don't know how, I haven't got a fucking clue what I'm doing, but ever since I saw those photos...' he pointed to the folder, 'I... I just... I'm losing my mind, or something...'

'Steady on,' said the obstructed man, 'or you'll end up toeing the yellow line in your own zone!' The apparent sensitivity of his comment was belied by the slightest hint of suggestion in his tone. Only Martha picked up on this, which she conveyed in a sideways glance at him. It wasn't enough to turn his head and she remained in his peripheral vision, his eyes forward and fixed on Manbag.

'You say you want to destroy the whole thing, yet earlier you said that you didn't see how you could leave,' the obstructed man said.

'I know,' Manbag replied. 'I have no idea what to do, as I've tried to explain. I just know that something has to change. I can't pretend I haven't seen those photos, I can't just carry on and try to forget them.'

'But if you resign, because you've somehow developed a conscience just from seeing some photographs, the project will continue without you. The number of Zones will increase due to the efforts of some other corporate robot,' said Martha. 'No offence,' she added, bitingly.

'You really are a very sharp young woman, aren't you?' Manbag said, tiring of her attitude.

'What do you expect?' she replied. 'I'm sorry, but I just find it hard to believe that a person like you can just suddenly turn on his professional creation, his pride and joy...'

'Have you seen these photos?' Manbag asked, interrupting her. She picked up the folder, opened it and began inspecting its contents. Manbag rubbed his eyes. Jason watched him, wondering what he was going to do next. Martha started passing photos to Jason who in turn passed them to the obstructed man.

'Jason, please forgive me,' Manbag began, after composing himself. 'It certainly wasn't my intention to come here and create tension in your house.'

'No, I wouldn't have thought so. It's ok,' Jason replied. He felt about as sceptical of Manbag's about-turn as Martha and the obstructed man obviously did. Yet, there was something in the Project Manager's demeanour which inspired pathos. The photographer just couldn't be sure whether it was genuine, or simply the well-versed mind of a master manipulator plying them out of some greater, more sinister self-interest.

Manbag watched carefully as the obstructed man and Martha perused the photographs in horrified silence. He made eye contact with Jason, who remained quietly still between them. The obstructed man looked up from the table at Manbag, casting an accusatory glare, the weight of which filled its recipient to the brim with opprobrium.

'Jason, these are incredible!' Martha said, without taking her eyes off the overwhelming images.

'What you have here, young man,' said the obstructed man, without taking his eyes off the overwhelmed Project Manager, 'is the perfect protest.' All eyes were suddenly on him. 'Yes,' he said, in answer to their unasked questions, 'the perfect protest, just look at them. We could go to the relevant government offices and file carefully-worded complaints and we'd be fobbed off with bureaucratic delay tactics; years of ignoral.'

'But...' Martha began, 'if we used these photos...'

'Covertly,' Manbag said. They looked at him. 'We use them

covertly; we plan a strategy, our intention being to shame the system...'

'He's already making it his project!' The obstructed man said. Manbag allowed himself a slight smile.

'I need to think about this,' he said.

'What you need,' the obstructed man said, 'is a field trip!'

'...where to?' Manbag asked.

'...to the Contemplation Zone!'

Zoned Out

Jason Mighty and the obstructed man returned to the scene. The location of their first meeting; the meeting which was yet to be properly discussed by the two, was quieter than it had been when Jason had become the proud owner of a yellow obstruction form. The two men knew almost nothing about each other, yet they were there with a shared purpose. Closely behind them strode the feisty teenager who had only called to collect her grandfather's funeral photographs. Behind her shambled the newly awakened Project Manager; his current surroundings made him feel like washing his hands. He thought about coffee. He thought about this being his first ever visit to a Contemplation Zone.

In the station entrance, Manbag suddenly felt vulnerable, as if his appearance there might attract the wrong sort of attention.

'Should I buy a newspaper?' he said as they walked past the ticket office.

'You didn't come here to read,' said the obstructed man.

'No, I meant to appear less obvious. I don't want to...' Manbag said.

His three companions giggled.

'You're already wearing that ginger wig, nobody'll recognise you,' said Martha. Jason and the obstructed man giggled louder.

'There really is no start to your talent, is there?' Manbag replied. She joined the other two in their giggling instead of replying to the Project Manager's umbrage.

A cold wind whistled through the station, making an unwelcome impression on the bladders of those for whom waiting included the need for relief. As the arrival information was likely to be hacked at any moment, nobody could trust anything on the display. Therefore, a mad dash to the toilet was just too risky. The facilities went almost unused from one day to the next, the consequence being that they were in surprisingly clean and fragrant condition; resulting in the station's cleaning staff taking advantage of this lack of activity by allowing themselves a modicum of false pride at their spotless condition, not to mention the surplus toilet rolls, which frequently became the convenient spoils of unused conveniences.

The downward escalator was out of order. A large hole, in which a group of overalled men stood talking, was barriered off, forcing commuters to use the stairs to gain access to the platform.

The three men and the teenager walked slowly through the doors and out onto the platform. To their left, along the station wall, was the Contemplation Zone. Manbag's eyes widened. He felt the chill of the afternoon air accentuate his discomfort. Perhaps, if the Zone had been empty, he might have found it less of a daunting experience. However, the presence of a few unfortunates gave him goose pimples. His sphincter tightened more than any self-respecting member of the E.F.A. would care to imagine.

Jason looked at the obstructed man. The two of them turned to look at the exact spot where they had collided. Martha looked up at the display. It said, NEXT TRAIN TO ARRIVE HAS A BLOCKED TOILET. There were sighs from those who hadn't risked the station toilet dash.

Manbag was ushered into the zone by his companions. He lowered his head and began rubbing at his forehead; shading his face in unnecessary anonymity.

'No-one's going to recognise you!' said the obstructed man. 'Are they?'

'You did,' said Manbag.

'Your name,' said the obstructed man, 'not your face!'

'Be that as it may...' Manbag said.

'What?' Jason asked. 'You're the Insecurity Security Project Manager. Surely it wouldn't be so unusual for you to be here.'

'You're hiding your face out of embarrassment!' said the obstructed man. After everything you've said today, you're ashamed to be here.'

Manbag's expression was confirmation.

They moved backwards and into the Contemplation Zone. Manbag found himself amongst the users of his efficient facility. He avoided eye contact with them by casting a glance forward at the yellow line. If he didn't look at them directly, he could try to convince himself that they were ordinary commuters. He wouldn't have to witness their contorted expressions of fatal intent. But, he wasn't there to ignore the situation. His eyes soon diverted from the yellow line, forcing engagement with his immediate surroundings. He pulled up the hood of his coat, its material doing little to isolate him.

Martha had moved back out of the Contemplation Zone and was

standing a few feet away, looking at the regular commuters. She turned to a smartly-dressed man standing next to her. He was oblivious to her, until she spoke to him.

'How can you just stand here?' she said. The man didn't answer. 'Excuse me,' she continued. The man looked at her. 'I said how can you just stand here?'

'I'm waiting for the train, why?' he said.

'...and you can do that, no problem?' Martha said. 'This doesn't bother you?' She gestured towards the Contemplation Zone.

'I'm just waiting for the train, nothing more,' he said.

'You can see those people, I presume?' she said to him, still gesturing.

'What do you want?' he asked. He peered at the teenager.

'I want you to...' She felt a hand on her shoulder. It was the obstructed man.

'There you are,' he said, cutting her off. 'We're over here.' He took her arm and led her away from the smartly-dressed man, who resumed his incurious wait.

'What are you doing?' she said to the obstructed man.

'We don't want to attract attention,' he replied.

'I can't believe my asking him such an obvious question would cause any fuss. They all seem so oblivious to everything!'

'Remember what Manbag said,' the obstructed man said. 'They choose to ignore it. They're not oblivious at all.'

'He's right,' said Jason, as they arrived back in the Zone. 'How do you think I met Manbag in the first place?' The three of them looked at the hooded Project Manager. He was static, facing forward; the tip of his nose protruding moistly into the cold air.

'I don't know,' Martha said in exasperation. 'Maybe you took his passport photo or something...'

Jason gave her a derisive smile which she reciprocated. He continued.

'There are cameras everywhere. I was caught on CCTV the last time I was here, while I was taking photographs. When I went to get my form stamped...well, it's a long story. Let's just say Manbag already knew who I was. Everything is monitored. So just blend in, ok?'

'He's absolutely right,' Manbag said, breaking his silence but still facing forward. 'Everything is monitored. You cause a disturbance now and you could end up in my office tomorrow.'

'Assuming it still is your office,' Martha said.

Manbag didn't answer. Across the tracks, he noticed the Disposal Team appear on the opposite platform. A train must be due, he thought; they do look professional.

They stood for a few moments in silence. The wind blew. A muffled announcement from inside the station provided no distraction from the disquieting anticipation.

The information on the display disappeared. It was replaced momentarily with, THE APPROACHING TRAIN COULD WELL BE YOUR LAST.

At the other end of the platform, a door marked PRIVATE opened and the same Suicide Monitor who had penalised Jason for obstruction, wandered slowly from inside. As he inhaled the cold air, he straightened his regulation hat from the jaunty angle to which he usually pushed it whilst reading the newspaper on the toilet. Manbag spied this activity, unable to fully alleviate himself of the feeling that he should be monitoring the Monitor. But then, he wasn't there in an official capacity. Based on the Monitor's rearranging of his hat and trousers, plus the final inward tuck of his shirt, Manbag knew, without a doubt, what he had been doing. He thought about the Monitor's whistle, and whether he had washed his hands.

'Look who it is,' said the obstructed man quietly. Jason turned.

'Oh, great!' he replied. 'It'll seem strange to him if he sees us together.'

'Why is that?' the obstructed man asked. 'Is it so unlikely that we could have become friends?'

'No,' Jason replied. 'But it is unlikely that we would be standing in the Contemplation Zone together, later the same week!'

'Well, that's true,' the obstructed man said.

Like Manbag, both Jason and the obstructed man pulled up the hoods of their coats.

'I thought we were trying not to stick out!?' said Martha as she looked at the three of them; the only people in the Zone with their heads covered. They didn't answer her. She pulled a green, woollen hat from her bag and put it on. Jason smiled at her for following suit in her own way.

'It's cold, ok!' she said to him.

From somewhere in the distance came the faint clickety-clack. The approaching train would soon be upon them. Manbag could hear it. He couldn't remember the last time he'd stood waiting for one. He was sure this would be the last. Carefully, he looked around at those who were counting on it being their last, too.

The long-anticipated locomotive was drawing nearer. Martha, Jason, Manbag and the obstructed man inched forward, the four of them looking down at their eight feet as the tips of their shoes toed the yellow line. None of them had the faintest idea what was going to happen. Clickety-clack...

Movement in the Zone... Shuffling of feet... The Suicide Monitor adjacent... Clickety-clack... Manbag turned in the train's direction; anxiety curled his toes... Clickety-clack... Movement behind as if Manbag's toes had started a chain-reaction which rippled to the Zone's edge... CLICKETY-CLACK... Closer and closer... The well-trained hand delved into the whistle pocket... Altruistic Acceleration... He could see it... CLICKETY-CLACK... Disposal Team... CLICKETY-CLACK... At the ready... It was coming... A hand... CLICKETY-CLACK... CLICKETY-CLACK... CLICKETY-CLACK... CLICKETY-CLACK... Pushed between... CLICKETY-CLACK... CLICKETY-CLACK... Manbag and the obstructed man... CLICKETY-CLACK... The whistle... CLICKETY-CLACK... There was a runner... Manbag stumbled... CLICKETY-CLACK... CLICKETY-CLACK... 'STOP!' he shouted... And then the JUMP...

The jumper, a young woman, had perfectly timed the whole manoeuvre. It was almost admirable. She made her final contact. It was over... Deceleration... Cli-cke-ty-clack...

The train stopped and its doors opened. Manbag was rooted to the spot. It had worked perfectly. He was horrified. The regular passengers embarked. How was it possible? He couldn't fathom it. In front of the train, down on the tracks, Disposal Team Technicians went about their business, cleaning the point of impact with their specially designed equipment. Through the train's windscreen, they saw the driver emerge from his isolation booth and resume his position at the controls. This facility was the last modification Manbag had introduced. The driver was to reach the desired speed, in accordance with the Altruistic Acceleration Directive, and then switch to auto at the precise moment indicated by the train's computer. This left time for the driver to enter a wardrobe-sized, sound-proof compartment to the rear of the carriage where he was able to isolate himself; free from the dangers and the sights and sounds of impending impact.

He switched back to manual from auto and gave a thumbs-up to the Disposal Team. They turned to their colleagues who were busily removing all trace of the "successful unfortunate" from the track. There was one shoe missing.

On the platform, Manbag maintained his position. Martha, Jason and the obstructed man were amongst those who hadn't run. Finally breaking from his rigidity, Manbag walked slowly towards the platform edge. As the train doors beeped and then shut, he bent down and picked up the young woman's shoe, the only trace of her final moment of success which remained, thanks to the efficiency of his project.

Aftermath

The platform had emptied quickly. The Contemplation Zone had cleared; its users dispersing, some to return another day. Its four observers had gone their separate ways, each with their own tenuous grasp of the next logical course of action.

Antony Manbag had returned home and locked himself in for the weekend. He had forty-eight hours in which he had to force himself towards some type of conclusion.

He tried to convince himself that he was in full possession of the facts. He had witnessed the potency of the Contemplation Zone first hand. He had observed the efficiency of the Disposal Team. He had stood by whilst commuters, plagued by indifference, had jostled for access to the train which had just taken the life offered to it, the life of the "successful unfortunate", whose stray shoe now rested forlornly in the centre of his kitchen table. Saturday morning smoothie in hand, he sat there, looking at the abandoned brown item. He wasn't sure what had prompted him to retrieve it from the platform edge and take it home with him. It seemed so desperately sad to him; half a pair, reduced, bereft; entirely more significant now than any one shoe should ever be. He was surprised that it looked new and wondered if it had only been worn that one time. Why would she jump in new shoes? He couldn't comprehend it.

He took a gulp of his celery and spinach smoothie and sat quietly for an hour until he finally broke free from the shoe's allure. If he was going to get through the weekend, he would need to talk; he would need some sort of indulgence. He suddenly became aware of the fact that there seemed to be only three people in the entire world with whom he could even begin to consider spending time.

Jason came right away after receiving Manbag's call. Despite being a regular train user, yesterday's incident had been the worst such experience for the young photographer; so close, so appalling, so perfect.

Manbag's thinly disguised call for company served Mighty's need for answers. As he rang the doorbell, he found himself hoping that the Project Manager would know what to do.

The door opened and Manbag appeared. Any strangeness that Jason might have felt at being comforted by this new association vanished as he spied his host's outfit. Manbag was wearing a white woollen cardigan, on the front of which, two red wolves faced each other, their mouths snarling either side of a zip, which nuzzled at maximum height beneath the Project Manager's fuzzy chin. Around the cardigan's hem and cuffs ran red paw prints.

With one hand on the door and the other in his cardigan pocket, Manbag smiled at his guest. The smile was partly emitted in warm welcome, but it was topped off with a decent amount of enjoyment at said guest's reaction to his sartorial uniqueness.

They shook hands, which seemed appropriate somehow. Jason smiled. 'Please, come in,' Manbag said. Jason put down his camera bag in the hallway next to a jumble of shoes which, until only a couple of days earlier, had been aligned neatly in pairs. At one time, Manbag might have worried that such disorderliness would've created the wrong impression of his abode, but now, as things were, he wallowed in his newfound ability to discard things rather than putting them away.

'Thanks for coming,' Manbag said as they entered the living room. Jason looked around the room as he took off his coat. Even after the Project Manager had daringly let things slide, the place was still tidy compared to the photographer's ramshackle residence. Manbag's unplumped cushions and the smoothie glass, stained with arched remnants up to its rim; discarded, coasterless and threatening to leave a ring on the coffee table – none of it registered with Jason, nothing looked out of place. However, Manbag picked up the glass as Jason continued to survey the room.

'Can I offer you anything?' Manbag asked, waving the smoothie glass suggestively.

'Whatever you're having,' Jason replied.

Manbag disappeared into the kitchen, leaving his guest alone. Jason studied the music collection, which was carefully alphabetised and spread extensively across several shelves. There were many albums which he thought he probably should have heard. In a corner of the room, he spied a small glass display case. Inside, lying atop a red velvet cushion was something Jason had never seen before, indeed, something he didn't even recognise at first glance. It appeared to be an antique implement of some sort, perhaps medical; a right angle shaped metal object that looked like copper with a carved wooden handle.

'I see you're admiring my antique enema syringe,' Manbag said proudly from across the room. Jason turned with a start to see his host holding two small glasses of the leftover breakfast smoothie.

'Your what?' Jason replied.

'It's a pewter enema syringe from around 1840; wonderful isn't it?' Manbag said.

'Erm…yes, I…so, is this part of a collection?' Jason said.

'I wish it were. This is my only antique, I'm afraid, unless you count the odd Christmas jumper I have stashed away.'

Jason glanced at the wolf cardigan again and cleared his throat.

'And what is this?' he asked, feigning enthusiasm for the glass of green liquid he was handed in an attempt to steer the focus away from Manbag's antique.

'It's celery and spinach; my current choice for Saturday mornings - very fortifying after a five-day slog.'

Jason took a sip warily. Manbag smiled at the young photographer's face.

'That's actually nice,' Jason said.

'You sound surprised,' Manbag replied.

'I guess I am,' Jason said, taking another sip.

Manbag gestured towards a chair and they both sat down. There was a brief silence, as if mentioning the events of the previous day needed to be prolonged, despite it being the reason for Manbag's invitation.

'Can I ask how you feel about yesterday's field trip?' Manbag began. 'I imagine you've thought about little else.'

'To be honest, I don't really know what to think. How are we supposed to feel after seeing something like that?' Jason said.

'I wish I knew,' Manbag replied.

'I still can't believe people will just stand by, as if it's nothing more than a normal feature of any station,' Jason said.

'Therein lies the problem,' Manbag replied. 'It is becoming a normal feature of any station.'

'Along with the indifference of regular commuters,' Jason said.

'That was what our studies suggested,' said Manbag. 'We were convinced it wouldn't take long for people to accept it.'

'And how do you feel, more importantly?' Jason asked. 'Now you've seen it function, and let's be honest, it really does function well, how do you feel?'

'Part of me wishes I could just accept the compliment; that it was nothing more than the success we planned on. But that would mean wilfully rejecting the revulsion it inspires; it would imply that I saw no need for redemption.' Manbag sighed and sipped his drink.

'And do you?' Jason asked him.

'Do I what?'

'Do you see the need for redemption?'

'I think I at least have to try,' said Manbag with a frown. 'Although at this precise moment, I have no idea how to go about it.' He paused and put down his glass. 'What I do know for sure is that I need your help and I'm pretty sure that after yesterday, you feel you ought to do something, too.'

'I don't know what I can do,' Jason said. Manbag's demeanour changed and he leaned forward in Jason's direction.

'Why did you take all those photographs?' he asked.

'I'm a photographer. I'm living in a time where grotesquely photogenic events occur every day, and yet no-one seems to be documenting them.'

'But did you have any intention of doing anything with them?' Manbag asked him. 'Or were you just documenting the societal quirks of our day, to be gawped at in years to come by disbelieving future generations of exhibition goers?'

'Yes, I was doing that. But, the more graphic they became, the more I started to think that some sort of protest should be made; an exposé, perhaps.'

'Yes, but an exposé of something in which everyone is already participating. How do you expose us to ourselves?' Manbag said.

'Well, that would be a problem…' Jason said.

'No!' Manbag said, interrupting. 'I'm asking you, how? I want to know…because that's what we're going to do.' He stood up and clapped his hands together. 'What are you doing this evening?'

'Nothing, why?' Jason said.

'Let's call our two co-conspirators. You're all having dinner here. We need to talk.'

'You may think, just because you're 18 years old, that you can waste your life laying in bed…' said Martha's mother through the bedroom door.

Martha sighed. 'I'm not laying, Mother, I'm lying,' she shouted back from beneath her duvet.'

'What was that?' her mother answered.

'It's Saturday morning!' Martha shouted.

'Not for much longer…!' said her mother.

The bedroom door opened and Martha appeared. Barefoot and scowling beneath a mop of tousled hair, she pushed past her mother and into the bathroom. Sitting down to pee, she was only alone for a second before her mother was outside, now with a different door through which to annoy her daughter.

'Your father and I would like to see the funeral photographs before our guests arrive. Did you remember to collect them?'

Martha threw her head back in frustration.

'Well, did you?' her mother asked again.

'Yes, Mother, I got them. But maybe you could let me pee first.'

'People will start arriving at 2.30, so please hurry up!'

'What people?'

'…for the presentation of the photographs. Honestly, I think you don't listen to a word I say.'

'I try really hard not to,' Martha said to herself.

'Pardon, dear?'

'I said ok, I'll bring them down.'

She listened to her mother's footsteps as she went downstairs and finally left her in peace. She pulled off a length of toilet paper and clutched it, her hands resting on her thighs. A presentation of the photographs! She couldn't stand another day with the house full of her parents' friends. The very idea of their facile comments in false admiration of the true depiction of family grief filled her with dread. Her stomach rumbled in support of the sickening notion.

Back in her room, as she put on a hoody and tried to tame her hair, her phone buzzed on the bedside table. The message was from Jason Mighty: Dinner at Manbag's this evening at 7.30. I think you should come. I'll text the address later.

The obstructed man was in his back garden, lovingly tending to his gerberas. The conservatory door opened and his wife appeared. 'There's a Jason Mighty on the phone for you,' she said. He turned to look at her. She looked small from the other end of the garden as she stood, holding her reading glasses. The phone had interrupted her crossword. He rubbed his hands together, shaking the soil from them, and stood up with as quiet a groan as he could, lest she should hear evidence of the physical strain his favourite activity now took at his age. 'Coming…' he said. She went back inside. By the time he reached the phone, she had resumed her puzzle.

Unlike his young friends, the obstructed man had been able to compartmentalise the events of the previous day. His experience of the Contemplation Zone was more extensive. It wasn't the first successful jump he had seen. It hadn't proved as encompassing for him as it had for Jason, as it had for both Manbag and Martha.

Breaking Bread

Punctual to the second, the obstructed man arrived at the Manbag abode. Bearing no trace of his beloved garden, his spotless hands held onto homemade tea bread which his wife had insisted he take. The door opened and Jason stood before him. They exchanged a look of unspoken solidarity; their previous meeting's shared experience, combined with their first obstructive encounter, having instilled something concrete which was, as yet, undefined, yet tangible, nevertheless.

'Manbag's in the kitchen,' Jason said, 'so I've been put in charge of greetings.' They shook hands.

'I hope you're ready for such a responsibility,' the obstructed man said with a smile.

'I've been fully instructed, don't worry,' Jason said. 'Come in.'

'Thank you,' said the obstructed man as he entered the hallway. A wonderful smell emanated from inside, where he assumed the Project Manager was hard at work. 'How does he seem, after yesterday?' he asked.

'Difficult to say, really,' Jason replied, 'although he's definitely not lacking enthusiasm. He just doesn't know for what, yet.'

'I imagine that's why we're here, isn't it?' the obstructed man said. Jason answered with a shrug as he ushered him through to the living room.

Manbag appeared from the kitchen in a waft of fragrant steam.

'Ah, welcome to Manbag Towers,' he said, shaking the obstructed man's hand.

'You seem to be in high spirits,' said the new arrival.

'I am, surprisingly... What's this?' he said, gesturing to the obstructed man's cargo.

'Tea bread,' he said. 'My wife made it.' He offered it to Manbag, who took it with a smile and smelt it through the wrapper.

'It smells fantastic!' he said. 'There's nothing like home baking,' he added. 'I'll be back.' He disappeared back into the kitchen, leaving the obstructed man with raised eyebrows which he cast in Jason's direction.

'I see what you mean,' he said.

In much the same way as Jason had, the obstructed man surveyed Manbag's living room for signs of its owner's personality. His eyes finally found the display case and its intrusive content. He approached it and cast a glance through its glass front.

'Have you any idea what that is?' Jason asked him. He leaned in front and opened the case.

'I don't think you should be doing that,' the obstructed man said.

'It's ok, he let me look at it earlier,' Jason replied. He placed the implement in the obstructed man's hands. 'Be careful, though; it's an antique.'

'I can see that!'

'He told me it's from around 1840 or so.'

'But what is it?'

'It's an enema syringe.'

The obstructed man looked up at Jason with a start. 'You might've told me that before handing it to me.' He thrust it back at him.

'It's pewter,' Jason said. 'What's the matter?'

'Do you know how many rectums it's been in?!' the obstructed man said. Jason laughed. 'Put it away before he comes back!' The doorbell rang. 'Concierge, you're needed!' said the obstructed man. He followed Jason into the hallway with his hands held out in front of him.

'Bathroom's through there,' Jason said, intuiting the obstructed man's desire to wash his hands. The doorbell rang again.

On opening the door, Jason was confronted by Martha. She smiled from beneath her green woolly hat.

'Got you working has he?' she said.

'Something like that,' Jason replied.

'Why are we here, exactly?' she asked, as the obstructed man appeared, having washed the unwanted vestiges of who knows how many anonymous arseholes from his hands.

'Hello Martha,' he said.

'Hi,' she replied.

'We're here to have dinner,' Jason said. 'Let's just start there, shall we?'

She pulled off her hat with a sigh. The obstructed man gestured towards the living room and she entered. Manbag appeared as before.

'Ah, good, we're all here. How are you?' he said.

'Fine,' Martha replied. 'I took this from my Dad's collection.' She handed him a bottle of wine which, on inspection, seemed to please him. He thanked her and went back into the kitchen. She spied the music collection and went to inspect it. Jason and the obstructed man sat at the dining table.

Small talk just didn't seem possible, though they did try.

'Here we go,' Manbag said as he carried a tray to the table.

'What's this, then?' the obstructed man asked.

'Mojitos,' Manbag replied.

'I'm surprised,' Martha said as Manbag joined her.

'Why?' he said, handing her a drink. 'Am I too old to like interesting music?'

'You're probably too old for lots of things,' she said. He smiled at her. 'Put something on, if you like.'

She pulled an Ella Fitzgerald record from the shelf.

'This is very nice,' the obstructed man said, slurping his mojito. 'So, what are we having?'

Five minutes later, the table was laden with hummus, tzatsiki, olives, stuffed vine leaves and bread. White wine was opened. The four of them began to eat with no formality; sharing and enjoying, passing the food to one another. Their experience in the Contemplation Zone had succeeded in uniting them and they ate like a family without pretension.

After everything had been tasted; Manbag took a good glug of wine. 'It occurred to me, whilst in the kitchen, that we really know nothing about each other,' he said. 'Well, I know you're a funeral photographer, Jason, but that's it.' He looked at his guests as they chewed. 'Perhaps, as we have the connection we do, we should share something about ourselves. What do you think?' He didn't wait for an answer.

'We know what you do,' Martha said. 'We've seen the fruits of your labours.'

'Indeed you have,' Manbag replied.

'I have a question,' said the obstructed man. He sipped his wine.

'Ok,' Manbag said.

'Why do you have an antique enema syringe in your living room?'

'What?' Martha said.

'He has an enema syringe,' the obstructed man said.

'Ok, as we're sharing,' Manbag began. 'I am a member of E.F.A.'

'What's the E.F.A.?' asked the obstructed man.

'It's an acronym for...'

'Initialism!' Martha interrupted.

'I'm sorry,' Manbag said.

'E.F.A. is an initialism, not an acronym,' she said.

'What's the difference?' the obstructed man asked.

'An acronym forms a word, like NASA, for example, whereas an initialism is also made up of the first letters of each word, but pronounced so, like E.F.A.,' she explained. 'Everybody says acronym when they should say initialism.'

There was a pause. Manbag took a gulp of wine. The obstructed man smiled at the young woman. Manbag continued.

'E.F.A. stands for Enema Fanatics Anonymous.'

His guests were silent. Having encountered dumbfoundedness on several occasions, Manbag had a prepared description of his organisation, to which he had applied his professional skills, in order to pave the way to an understanding of something that he had had to accept was not for everyone.

'It's a group of people who believe in the various benefits of this form of cleansing. It's holistic in nature, for most of us at least, and through presentations from guest speakers and so forth, we embrace the healing power of the enema.'

The obstructed man cleared his throat.

'My preferred method is the coffee enema,' Manbag continued. 'I do hope this isn't inappropriate for the dining table.'

'I did ask!' said the obstructed man.

'You did,' said Jason.

'Isn't it dangerous?' Martha said.

'Only in the sense that inserting anything can be dangerous if not done properly,' Manbag said with an air of expertise.

'Which I assume isn't a problem for you,' Martha said.

Manbag smiled. He was starting to like her.

'Isn't it true that there's absolutely no scientific proof of any beneficial effect from using coffee?' Jason asked.

'The whole idea of "detox" is a marketing scam,' Martha added.

'Are you sure this sharing is a good idea?' said the obstructed man.

Manbag raised his glass. 'To people with opinions!' They raised their glasses. 'I'll get us another bottle, shall I?'

The three guests continued to eat as Manbag disappeared once more. 'So, Martha,' Jason began, 'did your parents like the funeral photographs?'

She emitted a groan. 'I don't know, really.'

'You sound annoyed,' the obstructed man said. She looked at him and sighed.

'They're having some stupid "unveiling" at the house right now.'

'A what?' asked Jason.

'They've invited all their friends round for some kind of catered perusal of your photographs.'

'Sounds terrible,' said the obstructed man.

'It was, trust me,' she said. 'I was glad to be able to slope off without having to suffer anymore well-chosen words of appreciation.'

'Appreciation?' Jason said.

She looked at him. 'Yes, don't worry, even if my parents didn't like them, they will now because all their friends do. They'd never go against the majority; they probably only invited people to see them because they're incapable of forming their own opinions.'

'You really don't like them, do you?' said the obstructed man. She drained her glass in silence just as Manbag arrived back to the table.

'So what are we on now?' he asked.

'Well…' the obstructed man began, more in the spirit of avoiding a return to Manbag's revelation than anything else. He held his glass out for a top-up. He took a generous swig before he continued. 'I am married, I am sixty-three years old, I like gardening and my wife does crosswords all day.' He looked at his fellow diners. '…and occasionally bakes tea bread.' There was a pause.

'What?' the obstructed man said. Martha smiled at him. 'Oh, I see,' he continued. 'You were expecting something a bit more…a bit more…'

'Intimate?' Martha suggested with a look at Manbag.

Jason looked at the obstructed man. The two of them held each other's gaze for a moment.

'I see,' said the obstructed man. 'You're wondering about our first meeting, aren't you? Now being a time for sharing, as it were, would be the time to ask.'

'What's this?' Martha asked. Jason paused, unsure how to proceed. The obstructed man took the lead.

'We met in the Contemplation Zone,' he said.

'He was making a dash!' Jason blurted out. Martha was still. She looked at the obstructed man. Manbag said nothing. Ella Fitzgerald ground to a halt. A beeping sound came from the kitchen. Silence.

'I think something's done,' the obstructed man said.

'It can wait,' Manbag replied.

Jason seemed almost embarrassed by his outburst. He looked down at his plate. The obstructed man sighed.

'The truth is,' he began, 'I wasn't really making a dash.'

They waited for him patiently.

'I deliberately ran into you. I had no intention of jumping.'

'What do you mean?' Jason asked.

'I was there because…well, I just saw you taking photos and I thought it was wrong. I didn't see why those people should be exposed to what I thought was just another ghoul.'

'You think I'm a ghoul?' Jason said.

'I did,' said the obstructed man. 'But now I know better.'

'I'm sorry,' Jason said. 'I hope you realise that I was only taking photographs because it just seemed like everybody else was ignoring them. I have to admit, though, that I became a little overwhelmed by the idea of being able to capture the final moments of a person's decision to take their own life. I certainly didn't take it lightly. I couldn't begin to explain how horrible an experience it was. It still is, even though I try not to look at the photos. It doesn't take much effort to recapture the images when I close my eyes.'

They all drank from their glasses. Manbag topped them up.

'I have a question,' Martha said. The obstructed man looked at her pre-emptively.

'If you weren't there to dash, why were you there?' she asked.

'That's the question, isn't it?' the obstructed man said. Nobody spoke. 'I was there, Martha, because I needed to see it. I needed to be at that point where that was the next step; that was the objective.'

'But why?' she asked. He sighed and looked down at the table.

'Because that's how my daughter died,' he said. Manbag let out a gasp.

'Oh, God!' Martha said. 'I'm sorry!'

'It's ok, love,' said the obstructed man with a wan smile.

'No, it's not!' she said. 'We're here, pushing you, and...' Her eyes glistened.

'I'm sorry, too,' Jason said.

Manbag stood up from the table. His face had reddened. The obstructed man caught hold of his wrist. Manbag froze.

'If it hadn't been in the Contemplation Zone, it would've been somewhere else,' said the obstructed man. Manbag couldn't make a sound. 'Let's just...' He squeezed Manbag's wrist. Martha took a serviette and wiped her eyes as she went to change the music. The obstructed man looked at Manbag. The Project Manager hadn't moved. The obstructed man let go of his wrist. Manbag stood still for a moment, during which they shared a look; an exchange that conveyed within it the older man's acceptance of facts, the stark reality of which meekened Manbag more than he had ever experienced.

'So, what's next?' said the obstructed man, motioning toward the kitchen.

'Moussaka,' Manbag said. He disappeared back into the kitchen.

Jason refrained from asking any questions. He sat across from the obstructed man in silence, somehow sure, despite the briefness of their association, that the elder would open up more at his own speed, and that they should leave him to do so without prompting. Martha returned to the table as the sound of Timber Timbre's Beat The Drum Slowly pierced the silence. The obstructed man looked at the two of them with a rueful smile. Jason's face bore a tinge of surprise at the elder's magnanimous treatment of the Project Manager. Martha's exuded unadulterated empathy. 'Look at you two,' the obstructed man said. 'You weren't to know,' he added, as Martha sniffed up the last of her shame. His smile became less rueful, which in turn tightened his crow's feet. Neither of them answered him. It just wasn't necessary.

In the kitchen, Manbag busied himself with final flourishes which, despite being culinary full stops, not to mention triumphs of presentation, were doing nothing by way of providing the distraction from the scene he had just exited. A suicide with which he now had some personal contact was a huge departure from the tenuous comfortable distance that his power had once afforded him. Not only had he been in the Zone and taken a single brown shoe as a memento, he now had a grieving parent at his dining table; a true victim of the project, not a jumper, but the father of one; left to fathom the unfathomable process of dealing with the loss of a child.

Determined not to allow the music to make the atmosphere any more palpable, Martha stood and walked around the table. She sat next to the obstructed man and planted a kiss on his cheek just as Jason raised his camera and captured the sweetness of the moment of warmth on the recipient's face. 'Perhaps we should offer to help,' said the obstructed man. Jason stood up and went into the kitchen.

Manbag was relieved to see him. He didn't need any help and preferred not to accept it out of politeness.

'He seems fine,' Jason said as he watched Manbag's hands.

'I know,' Manbag said, his hands accelerating. 'If anything, his attitude makes me feel even worse.'

'Why?' Jason asked.

'Because after going through all that, he still has the emotional maturity to sit at the dining table of the man who is responsible, and try to convince him that he isn't!' Manbag froze.

'I don't think...' Jason began.

'What don't you think,' Manbag asked, his face reddening, 'that I'm responsible?'

'I was going to say that I don't think just one person can be held accountable for his daughter's suicide.'

'Then why do I feel like I am?' Manbag asked. His hands resumed their work.

'Because you're just starting to really see the whole concept from a different perspective. You're no longer just the Project Manager of a faceless operation, hiding at a safe distance from the results of your work.'

'Is that so?' Manbag said incredulously.

'Yes. And I'm no longer just a photographer capturing those results yet doing nothing more than sitting on them in fear of the consequences. We're going to act.'

Manbag looked up from his preparation. 'Yes, we are,' he said. They shared a look of determination. The oven beeped. 'Now, let's eat,' he added.

When the two men returned to the dining table, Martha had retaken her seat across from the obstructed man.

'…and by the time they had all arrived, I couldn't wait to get out of there,' she said.

'What's this?' Manbag asked.

'My parents' unveiling of the photographs that Jason took at my grandfather's funeral.'

'Ah, an unveiling.'

'Yes, my mother tries her hardest to turn anything into an event. It's quite sad, really. All she has in her life is her desire for people to find her socially superior, as if her events set some kind of benchmark to which her circle aspires.'

'She has you,' the obstructed man said.

'My mother resents the fact that I don't care about anything she believes in. She says I'm apathetic,' Martha said bitterly.

'In her mind, that's true,' the obstructed man said. 'If you don't care about the things she wants you to care about.'

'She can't see far enough beyond the disappointment she has to even notice the things I am interested in,' Martha said.

Manbag served them each an individual ceramic dish of steaming moussaka. 'Well,' he said, smiling at Martha, 'let's have a drink at their expense, shall we?' He opened the wine she had brought with her. 'This'll complement the food nicely. Let's hope your dad doesn't miss it, eh.'

'I doubt it,' Martha said. 'On the day they have a house full of guests; the perfect time to steal wine.'

They all smiled and started digging into their moussaka.

'So, Jason,' Manbag said after a moment. 'It seems you are the only one who hasn't shared anything with our group.' He had momentarily forgotten a certain erotic story he had begun reading.

'Oh, we're a group now, are we?' Jason replied.

'Well I think so, yes. Don't you?'

Jason avoided the reply by filling his mouth with food. When he had swallowed, finally, he began.

'What can I say? Nothing out of the ordinary, really; I love my mother, I'm careful with my money, and I take my coffee orally.' They all laughed. Manbag took it in good humour. Jason could tell they were expecting something more from him. In light of the obstructed man's woeful story, not to mention Manbag's hobby, it seemed almost mandatory, now, to share one's innermost details.

'Let's try a little experiment, shall we?' Manbag said. 'With your consent, of course…'

'Do I have a choice?' Jason asked.

'You always have a choice,' said Manbag. Not really feeling like he could say no, Jason gave a gesture of consent. Manbag took the lead.

'Stand up and let me inspect you.'

'What?' Jason said.

Martha pushed him up off his seat. Manbag surveyed the young photographer; tall, skinny, thick-haired, with a curving posture which would no doubt develop into a stoop in later years.

'Every female friend you have ever had has told you, maternally, to stand up straight. Your sweet shyness appeals to all women. You like to convince yourself that your boyishness is contrived, but really, you are simply an endearing individual,' said Manbag with a superior air in anticipation of the accuracy of his pronouncements.

'What boyishness?' Jason asked. 'I'm thirty years old!' His three companions looked at him.

'So, is he right?' the obstructed man asked. Jason looked reluctant to confirm anything and simply shrugged in response. His observers took it in the affirmative.

'Of course he's right,' Martha said. 'Do me, now.'

Jason took his seat as she stood in his place. Manbag inspected her.

'Martha,' he began. 'Eighteen years old, intelligent, pretty, sarcastic…'

'Something that isn't obvious, please,' she said with a grin.

'You don't like your parents. You're an only child but you wish you had brothers and sisters, even though you wouldn't wish your parents on them. You're terrified of becoming your mother and you rebel against any hint of it. You judge new people critically. Out of the three of us men here, you will become closest to our distinguished friend,' he gestured toward the obstructed man, 'because he is the oldest and he reminds you of your recently deceased grandfather.'

Martha was silent for a moment. Manbag took a gulp of wine.

'Well?' said the obstructed man. Jason looked up at Martha's face. She mimicked the shrug Jason had given in response to his description. The obstructed man smiled at her.

'So, is this some type of parlour trick, then?' the obstructed man asked Manbag.

'Well, I hope it's a little more than that,' replied their host. 'It's a skill that I have honed in my various professional capacities.'

'Oh, he's talking like a Project Manager again,' Martha said.

'He is, isn't he?' Jason added. Manbag smiled.

'An occasional yet quite profitable sideline of mine is the little-known field of Tie Analysis,' Manbag said proudly.

Martha spluttered a little on her wine. 'Tie Analysis!' she said after a little cough. 'What the hell is that?'

'Well,' Manbag began; glass in hand. 'Really it started off simply with the analysis of job candidates' ties. I was paid by various top level companies to analyse tie choices during interviews as a means of screening.'

'You're kidding,' Martha said.

'It's just one of many methods of profile assessment used, these days,' Manbag replied.

'And for the female candidates not wearing ties?' Martha asked.

'Well, I have only ever been asked to analyse male candidates,' said Manbag.

'Of course,' Martha said with a sneer, 'presumably because they only interview men at these exclusive companies.'

'I couldn't speak as to their gender preferences, I'm afraid. But, the lack would suggest so.' Manbag gave her a sympathetic smile. 'I have to say, though, I'm developing it beyond the tie into a more rounded, fuller sartorial assessment method.'

'Based on what?' Jason asked him.

'No doubt the finer details are not to be shared with the likes of us,' said the obstructed man.

'It can't be that difficult,' Martha said. 'Why don't you stand up,' she said to Manbag, 'and let me have a go?' Manbag smiled at her naïve arrogance. He stood with a welcoming gesture which she took as her cue to proceed. She cast her eyes about his person. He sipped his wine while he waited and wiped his mouth with a serviette. She began.

'Fastidious in everything you do, yet the stubble on your chin would suggest that you are able to let go, once in a while. You are shamelessly metrosexual, which should be applauded in this day and age. You are fully aware of your stubbornness, yet make little excuse for it, as you don't see why you should have to, and, I have to say, the amount of irony in that cardigan might just make it the coolest thing I've seen for a long time.'

'He looks like Val Doonican,' the obstructed man added with a giggle.

'Who?' Martha asked. The obstructed man was suddenly reminded of her age, despite the skill with which she had just stolen the spotlight. Manbag smiled at her.

'Well?' she said.

'I'm very surprised,' Manbag said.

'Why?' she asked.

'I was expecting something far more insulting,' he replied.

Jason and the obstructed man both made noises of agreement.

'I can't think why,' she said with a smile.

'My Dad actually made this cardigan,' Manbag said.

'It's fantastic,' she said. Manbag's face lit up in what he saw as a bonding moment.

The moussaka had all but vanished. The table was cleared and more wine poured. Manbag had returned to the kitchen, leaving his guests to their own devices once again. Martha continued her investigation of the music collection whilst Jason and the obstructed man remained at the table.

'I have to say,' the obstructed man began, 'I wasn't expecting to enjoy this evening as much as I am.'

'Why's that?' Jason asked. As soon as the words had left his mouth, he thought about the obstructed man's daughter. With the Contemplation Zone being relatively new, he assumed that her suicide had been fairly recent, which then led to the further assumption that the obstructed man must have lost the ability to enjoy anything. Jason gave him a look which conveyed his regret at having asked the ill-considered question. Sparing his young friend any further discomfort, the obstructed man changed the subject.

'What do you suppose will come from this evening?' he asked.

'What do you mean?' asked Martha as she returned to the table.

'What I mean is, as pleasant as all this is, I'm wondering about where we go from here, that's all.'

'I've been wondering about that, too,' Jason said.

'Do you think our Project Manager has come up with anything yet?' Martha said. They looked at her blankly. The kitchen door opened and Manbag reappeared to find his three guests all looking in his direction.

'Have I missed something?' he said.

'We were just talking about what comes next,' said the obstructed man.

'Well, I'm glad you're still hungry, because…'

'No, we want to know what we're going to do after today,' said Martha.

'I see,' Manbag said. He looked at each of them in turn. 'Let me make a suggestion. Let's eat our pudding, and then we can brainstorm.'

Martha raised her eyebrows. 'Has either of you ever brainstormed before?' she asked her two fellow guests with a grin.

'Can't say I have,' replied the obstructed man. 'What's for pudding?' he asked as Manbag turned back to the kitchen door.

'Prepare yourself to flatter me,' Manbag replied as he vanished. The three of them looked puzzled. The oven beeped. A moment later, Manbag returned with a tray. He placed it in the centre of the table and said proudly, 'The perfect soufflé.'

The smell was incredible. They tucked into its chocolaty richness with appreciative noises. None of them really said anything much until each of the four dishes was empty.

'Now,' Manbag said, 'who's for coffee?'

His three guests looked at each other and then burst out laughing.

'…in a cup!' Manbag said.

Waiting For The Other Shoe To Drop

In his bedroom, Manbag opened the door of his safe and retrieved a file box. So assured was he of the power of its contents that he set off back to join his guests with a satisfying sense of purpose and enthusiasm, in no small part fuelled by wine and the novelty of having people at his table.

'What's that?' asked the obstructed man, once he had seen the Project Manager approaching the table.

'This…' Manbag said, raising the file box for effect, 'is what happens next.'

The coffee and homemade tea bread had been dispatched and the group had moved onto sampling Manbag's liquor cabinet. The three guests looked at the file box and then at each other as their host took his seat at the table.

There was an anticipatory pause as the file box lid was removed by its increasingly emotive owner. He reached inside it and, in the fluid, flourishing movement of an expert in corporate presentation, produced his Contemplation Zone souvenir - the brown shoe of the "successful unfortunate" - and placed it in the middle of the dining table, removing his hand from its leather surface slowly in dramatic understatement. He saw from his captive audience's reactions, that it required no details of ownership. This pleased him greatly. As his three guests studied the abandoned item, he sat back and watched in a silence which not only encapsulated the gravity of the shoe itself, but emphasised the palpable, unscripted preamble to his presentation.

He drank slowly from a glass of water until he was sure that the shoe had achieved its full potential. Eventually, all eyes were upon him.

'Friends,' he said, gesturing subtly. 'You see before you something which I believe not one of us here could ever think of as merely a shoe. We have an obligation to think of it as motivation, as reason to act. I sit here; complicit in many things, to which the contents of this box will attest. Yet I sit here; grateful that I have seen what I have seen in the last few days, because, without that truly harrowing, yet beneficial experience, I would not have arrived at this point.'

'And what point is that?' asked the obstructed man. Manbag reached down into the box and produced a file of documents. He handed one to each of them.

'The point where I risk everything in allowing you all to see these,' he replied. 'Take a moment to read what I have given you.'

Martha, Jason and the obstructed man began reading their respective documents. Manbag allowed himself a small glass of whisky in recognition of what he had just done. He sipped it, as he studied the faces of those reading, for signs of what he hoped would prove to be motivation equal to that which he found bubbling away within him. It wasn't long before the signs started to appear.

'What!?' Jason said. '"Train drivers rewarded for successful deployment of the Altruistic Acceleration Principal and monthly total of "successful unfortunates" …'"

'Listen to this,' Martha said. '"Suicide Monitors to be awarded "golden whistle points" for each successful blow, to accumulate monthly and to be converted into pension contributions."'

Both she and Jason continued their fervent inspections.

The obstructed man looked at Manbag and said, '"50% of the money saved by hospitals as a result of the Contemplation Zones' success will be reinvested in the Insecurity Security Act."'

Manbag's face lit up knowingly. He didn't consider for a second that they wouldn't see these documents as evidence of the burden of his position. He didn't expect sympathy, exactly, but perhaps a modicum of understanding, on their part, of the weight he had had to bear. He then wondered, as they continued reading, if he had only come to see his position in this way as a result of the events of the last few days.

The three readers grabbed at the file for more of the documents. In the pit of his stomach, Manbag could feel the swelling shame which seemed to have been festering since his first viewing of Jason's Contemplation Zone photographs. As he listened to snippets of his stash of documents projected across the dining table from three angles, the out of context sound bites became scandalous headlines emitted by disgusted readers. Without the comfort of his office, his crisp suits, and his fawning minions, the printed evidence of his work hurt his ears, made his stomach judder, and his innards feel about as impure as they ever had. And the readers continued.

'"The objective of this agreement is to guarantee a lower number of "unsuccessful unfortunates" being admitted to local casualties, thereby putting unnecessary strain on medical resources."'

"'Identically attractive women employed to walk down platforms as pacifying distraction to early morning male commuters.'"

"'Avoidance Isolation Booths to be standardised for all drivers ASAP.'"

Jason and the obstructed man weren't so full of alcohol that they couldn't comprehend what lay before them, yet they were full enough that their incredulity wouldn't go unexpressed. They looked at Manbag, who raised his whisky glass to his lips and looked down at the table. Martha continued shuffling through the inflammatory pages.

She continued, "'Ours is not to reason why, ours is but to clean and shine.'"

'Martha,' the obstructed man said in an effort to silence her.

'Please,' Manbag said, with a purging flourish of his arms, 'let her continue, by all means.'

She did. "'Suicide Monitors to have absolutely no verbal contact with those occupying the Zone unless a case of post-whistle blow obstruction arises.'"

'Yellow or otherwise,' Jason said, raising a glass in the direction of the obstructed man, in honour of their first meeting.

"'Government mental health cuts will enable D.I.S.A. funding.'"

'Martha, please,' said the obstructed man.

"'Suicide Monitor Five-a-side football tournament…'"

'Enough!' the obstructed man said in a raised voice.

Martha jumped and looked across the table at him. He raised a hand in apology but the firmness of his expression kept her silent. She placed the documents down on the table. Nobody spoke. Manbag topped up their drinks; the sound of the liquid pouring emphasised their sudden break from the revelations. Martha stood and made her way, once again, to the record collection. Keeping his eyes away from the gaze of his guests, Manbag gathered the pages far more nonchalantly than he had ever gathered official documents in his life and, playing to his continuing sense of awe at his recent unclenching, stuffed them back, in no order whatsoever, into the file. In a second, the file was back in the box and its lid had been replaced.

From across the room, with her eyes still scanning the music on offer, Martha broke the silence.

'Is it me,' she began, 'or are we still at a what-do-we-do-now point?'

'Explain yourself,' Jason said.

'Well,' she said, 'we asked what we were going to do, and he showed us all this stuff. All I can think, really, is still, what do we do now?'

'She has a point,' Jason said. 'I mean, what are you suggesting, exactly, some type of Snowdenesque disclosure?'

'That would be somewhat clichéd, don't you think?' Manbag said flippantly.

'Of course,' Martha said, 'you wouldn't want to be unoriginal when it came to doing the right thing, now, would you?'

'Just choose a record, eh!' Manbag said; his patience finally diminishing. She did as he had said without further comment. Richard Hawley's Coles Corner began as she returned to the table.

'Take a drink,' Manbag said to the three of them. They complied.

'Ok,' he said. 'Here's my plan...'

Part Two

Excerpts from the Fall Out

In Print

Front page of **The Anchor**, *1st December 2015.*

INSECURITY SECURITY SECURITY BREACH
Impenetrable office springs a leak

By Madge Nicholson. Photos by Jason Mighty.

Recent revelations regarding the machinations of DISA, The Department of the Insecurity Security Act, have left the once seemingly unblemished government office in an unfamiliar and uncomfortable position, as its highest representatives, not unlike those who make use of its cutting edge facility, the Contemplation Zone, are standing with their backs to the wall. In a statement issued this morning, containing the phrase "we guarantee our full support", DISA tried to make some headway in defusing a situation which extends far beyond a mere security breach and is likely to see them fall under further scrutiny in the coming weeks. When asked to clarify certain comments which have emerged from emails exchanged during the inception of the Contemplation Zone scheme, a DISA representative said that, "comprehensive explanations of the context of such exchanges will be forthcoming in the final report so we therefore ask the public to be patient and allow those in charge of the investigation to go about their work unhindered."

From *The Circumlocution*, 2nd December 2015.

DISA: TIME FOR CONTEMPLATION

Answers due to arrive on schedule

By Edmund Kemplar

With the rail network in a sorrier state than ever before, it would seem that more than a brief moment of contemplation is necessary if DISA, and those recently linked to several inflammatory leaked documents, are to come anywhere near to redeeming themselves. An official independent inquiry, in addition to DISA's own internal security breach investigation, is about to be launched, at the end of which, answers will be demanded, not least of all by a disgusted public.

Centre pages of *The Verbose Evening Post*, 3rd December 2015.

Hospital Executive leaked email: "We're just making their final wish come true." Jeff Peterson ponders the implications

The benevolent, wish-granting executive in question, whose name remains as of yet unprintable due to legal restrictions, was obviously under the impression at the time of writing this comment that the task undertaken by those responsible for the Contemplation Zone was in some way purely compassionate, dare I say, philanthropic. Are we to think of the Contemplation Zone as assisted suicide? Does last year's government U-turn on such euphemisms as "death with dignity" or "aid in dying" perhaps coincide rather too conveniently with DISA's train station installations? By no means can Hospital Executives be thought of as doctors or nurses providing health care, and therefore, their methods of daily operation within their various professional capacities are not subject to any medical oaths or declarations. However, an affiliation with the medical profession, and certainly not a tenuous one at that, should, one would assume, demand that said executives "maintain the utmost respect for human life", as the 1948 Declaration of Geneva dictates.

Should we wonder…?

"Has the local authority or other agency identified any specific locations which provide opportunities for suicide and/or where suicides/attempted suicides have occurred (such as a bridge, cliff or rail crossing)?" Crown copyright 2011 - Department of Health – Prompts for local leaders on suicide prevention

Are we to see the day, not so far in the future, where Contemplation Zones appear on bridges and on rail crossings? Why confine ourselves to train stations when prevention is so blatantly not the motive, here?

When hospital executives join forces with government to implement such brutally efficient means of suicide control - means which in no way include the concept of prevention - somebody has to be brought to task.

Page 3 of *The Explainer*, 4th December 2015.

ALTRUISTIC ACCELERATION: TIME WE PUT OUR COLLECTIVE FOOT DOWN? Stephen Crabtree digs deeper

Inundated as we are these days with intelligence, misinformation, sound bites and factoids, one might expect, *ipso factoid*, that the latest scandalous dirt to hit the headlines may, for most of us, be as easy to ignore as a general election; at the very most providing a mere flash of distraction between hopeful TV singing show contestants, whose passion truly ignites our desire to vote.

If we can project so much indifference in the face of rising suicide rates, if we can stand by idly; not allowing the fate of those who jump to interfere with our commute, their plight not registering on our internal scale, then we have to wonder, right now, how we have any right whatsoever to feel shocked, indignant, appalled.

As a population of ignorers, are we not just as culpable? Do we have the right to become so suddenly interested? Do we even want to be, really?

It has been reported that DISA, after extensive testing under conditions which are yet to be disclosed, found its subjects to be compliant beyond expectation, not to mention passively accepting of suicide control measures which are, only now, as we jump predictably onto the Draconian bandwagon with both feet, becoming controversial. Is this our very own form of Altruistic Acceleration? As we rush to condemn a system which we apparently couldn't have cared less about at the testing stage, shouldn't we stop and wonder if we really do care any more now than we did then?

Front page headline story from *The Tabloid*, 24th December 2015.

CHRISTMAS JUMPER
MUM MOURNS CZ SON AS CHRISTMAS RUINED
By Barry Boggis

Bereaved beauty, Brenda Bradshaw, 40, has space under her Christmas tree. Gary Bradshaw, 23, who was the latest jumper in the grisly Contemplation Zone, has been described by his mother as "a troubled boy". "We all knew something was wrong," she told The Tabloid yesterday, "but we thought we'd get through Christmas with him here to open his presents."

Single and unemployed, she can't afford photographs of her only son's funeral. When asked if she had anything she would like to say to those responsible for this terrible tragedy, she responded with, "They're all bastards! I hope their turkeys are dry, they've ruined Christmas!"

Continued on page 17

Lifestyle feature from *The Sunday Supplement*, 3rd January 2016.

SUICIDE MONITORS NOT WHISTLING WHILE THEY WORK

"I've never done so many sudokus."

CZ Official talks to Florence Bolton

A sudden downturn in the number of Contemplation Zone occupants making full use of the facility has left Suicide Monitors twiddling their thumbs. The controversial Golden Whistle Points scheme, which has become just one of many hot potatoes currently doing the rounds in the wake of what seem to be constant revelations since last month's DISA leak, is now under threat as whistles remain in pockets, unblown. Suicide Monitors are the latest victims in what is being described across the media as a standstill, as fewer unfortunates are making that final jump, and choosing instead to remain with their feet firmly on the ground. The pension augmentation scheme, originally implemented as a training incentive, had flourished since being put into practice, with certain Suicide Monitors riding the gravy train home from work, looking forward to a very comfortable retirement. This has all changed, however, and the Suicide Monitors' Union has attempted to enter the investigation into the identity of those responsible for the leak, with one Union representative directly addressing the anonymous perpetrator in the S.M.U.'s most recent press release. "From a united group of professional whistle blowers to a cowardly whistle-blower whistling in the dark, we will expose you on behalf of those whose pensions you have destroyed."

Across The Airwaves

The 8 o'clock Breakfast Meeting on **Radio Powwow**.
5th January 2016.

RADIO PRESENTER: …and it seems, according to various, shall we say, unsubstantiated sources, that you are alleged to have said that the "CZ is nothing more than assisted suicide."

NONDESCRIPT MINISTER: Well, I'd be curious to know which sources they might be.

RADIO PRESENTER: I'm sure you would, but let's not let that get in the way of your answering the question.

NONDESCRIPT MINISTER: I haven't heard a question, yet.

RADIO PRESENTER: I'm sure some of our listeners might be wondering if you ever hear any questions.

NONDESCRIPT MINISTER: In much the same way as we in the government wonder if you ever hear any of our answers.

RADIO PRESENTER: I haven't heard an answer, yet.

NONDESCRIPT MINISTER: Ask your question, and I shall answer it.

RADIO PRESENTER: Did you refer to the CZ as "nothing more than assisted suicide"?

NONDESCRIPT MINISTER: I was instructed…

RADIO PRESENTER: …a simple yes or no would suffice, Minister.

NONDESCRIPT MINISTER: We're living in times of austerity; a simple yes or no answer is a luxury we simply can't afford.

RADIO PRESENTER: Just one of the many things that the people of this country can't afford, Minister. So in times of austerity, do we actually have more words? As everything else is cut, slashed, decreased and downsized, are your "answers" the only thing that is left growing?

NONDESCRIPT MINISTER: I'm simply saying that there are fewer sound bite answers for your listeners to digest between commercial breaks.

RADIO PRESENTER: Speaking of which, we'll be back to hear the Minister's austere, yet wordy, answer shortly.

Commercial break…

RADIO PRESENTER: So, Minister, I believe you were about to enlighten us… Is the CZ nothing more than assisted suicide?

NONDESCRIPT MINISTER: Well, first of all, I believe we should define the term "assisted suicide" before we set about trying to lump the Contemplation Zone in to any category.

RADIO PRESENTER: …and will our defining it change your answer, should one be forthcoming?

NONDESCRIPT MINISTER: My answer will remain the same.

RADIO PRESENTER: It would seem, then, that a definition really has no bearing, at this point.

NONDESCRIPT MINISTER: …and where would we be if definition had no bearing on political discourse?

RADIO PRESENTER: Perhaps nearer to the end of a satisfactory answer, which would allow me to ask why so many people find themselves in such a situation that the CZ is even necessary?

NONDESCRIPT MINISTER: Is that another question? Perhaps the

people of this country might be better served if they had enough patience to wait for the answer they seem so desperate to hear.

RADIO PRESENTER: I assume, from your attitude, that re-election isn't something that concerns you at this point.

NONDESCRIPT MINISTER: ...sigh...

RADIO PRESENTER: Hold that thought, Minister, while we hear some music from the band everyone is talking about at the moment. This is the new song by Empty Threat, which is available to download from various sources, plus, for all you vinyl lovers who can't believe the cost of records these days, but will buy it anyway, it is available on this very attractive clear vinyl, which I am holding in my hand. Nice, isn't it Minister?

NONDESCRIPT MINISTER: ...silence...

RADIO PRESENTER: There we are folks; yet another unanswered question. Well, here's Empty Threat with *Suicide Backlog*.

Suicide Backlog   Lyrics:

See them fall under further

Those in charge of a mere public

Standing with their backs to the situation work unhindered

Purely compassionate task undertaken

Some way by those in question

Highest position unprintable due to legal wish-granting

A disgusted public redeeming themselves

Seemingly unblemished by a sorrier state

Suicide Backlog   Suicide Backlog   Suicide Backlog

Certainly not a tenuous zone

The benevolent contemplation methods of daily scrutiny

Which have emerged leaked linked to such euphemisms as "death"
Why confine ourselves to human life train?
Name remains inflammatory
Demand more than a brief moment of comprehensive explanation
Implement blatantly control brutally those whose "aid in dying" will be forthcoming
Suicide Backlog   Suicide Backlog   Suicide Backlog

RADIO PRESENTER: Empty Threat, there with **Suicide Backlog**, available now. What do you think of the song, Minister? Quite provocative lyrics, wouldn't you say?

NONDESCRIPT MINISTER: This is certainly a time for populism. I'm sure it'll do very well.

RADIO PRESENTER: Well, you can pass on those encouraging words in person, Minister, as we welcome our next guest, singer of Empty Threat, Johnny Lane. Good morning, Johnny!

JL: Good morning.

RADIO PRESENTER: Wonderful to have you with us. The song is very interesting. It's certainly attracting a lot of attention.

JL: It is, yeah. We're very pleased with it.

RADIO PRESENTER: Tell me, how did you come to write it? Presumably the topic of our discussion this morning was a great influence.

JL: It was indeed, but I have to say that the recent reporting of these events was what really inspired the song, plus the incredible Jason Mighty photographs.

RADIO PRESENTER: So we humble journalists can take some of the credit, then?

JL: Erm, yeah, in a sense. I've always been fascinated by the cut-up method, yer know, Burroughs, Bowie etc., and it seemed to me that the often hysterical reporting of the Contemplation Zone…I've been trying to avoid the word "scandal" because it just seems omnipresent, these days. Anyway, the reporting of the Contemplation Zone opprobrium has been histrionic…

RADIO PRESENTER: It's a very serious subject.

JL: It is indeed, which is all the more reason for the media to limit themselves to reporting the facts in the simplest way possible; honestly, unsensationally.

NONDESCRIPT MINISTER: Is that even a word?

JL: I'm sure your Eton education doesn't require confirmation from the likes of me, Minister.

NONDESCRIPT MINISTER: …harrumph…

RADIO PRESENTER: Tell us more about the lyrics.

JL: Basically, I found myself in possession of various newspaper articles on our theme for the day, so I cut them up and reassembled them in an attempt to find out what the journalists weren't saying.

RADIO PRESENTER: I see. And what we hear in the song is what you think the newspapers should be saying?

JL: What you hear in the song is what I believe is going on, from the subjective point of view of a singer; nothing more nothing less.

RADIO PRESENTER: Interesting. And what would you say to the Minister's view of the song's content being populism?

JL: I would say that empathising with the "mere public" is a concept which might serve politicians well, were they ever to deem it worthy of their time.

NONDESCRIPT MINISTER: It's very easy for your sort to say that, isn't it?

JL: My sort?

NONDESCRIPT MINISTER: ...knowing full well that there will be listeners at home, or on their way to work - from homes to jobs they would struggle to keep without our commitment to improving the opportunities for the man in the street - listening to you, a rock musician, having a Bono moment, out of your studio, tinkering with the real world in which us real people live...

JL: In what sense of the word are you a real person?

RADIO PRESENTER: Gentlemen...

JL: Surely a real person would be someone who finds themselves ignored at every turn; someone who, if they manage to suggest that their mind is plagued by an array of doubts, insecurities and helpless, lethargic self-loathing, is likely to be fobbed off, or even jostled around the system until they inevitably end up with their toes on the yellow line, waiting for a train, their supposed only solution, that might never arrive. Is that you, Minister? Are you a real person?

NONDESCRIPT MINISTER: Populism! Once again, a politician having to converse with a celebrity on political matters in which only one of the two is qualified to have an opinion. It seems there really is no place left these days where one is not forced to look at the bottom of the barrel.

JL: Are you looking up from beneath?

RADIO PRESENTER: Gentlemen, please...a commercial break is upon us. Back to your corners, please...

A quick burst of *Suicide Backlog* leads into the first commercial.

On Air

Excerpt from live television broadcast of ***Question and Answer***. Thursday 7th January 2016.

AUDIENCE MEMBER: …what I think many of the people here are perhaps eager to know; and this is something which goes back to what the Honourable Minister for Avoidance failed to answer earlier, [murmurs from the audience, close-up of said Minister] is how the government can deny the accusations of social cleansing. How can they continue to expect us to believe that any part of the DISA purview was nothing less than despicable?

[Cheers from audience]

DISTINGUISHED HOST: One moment, please, ladies and gentlemen, a most interesting question. Your answer to that, please, Cynical Novelist.

CYNICAL NOVELIST: Well, I'm afraid the simple answer to your question has to be that they are the government; they are in the business of denial. Perhaps, if you will allow, I might ask what the purpose of this debate really is. In the Contemplation Zone's infancy, during the "rigorous testing" conducted by DISA, an insidious notion on whose nature they are yet to enlighten us, it was found that test subjects displayed two key characteristics; apathy and indifference. Let us consider that for a moment. Apathy and indifference, two such impassive human reactions to what we must assume were vivid stimuli.

Let us then consider the fact that, after the Contemplation Zone's grand opening, the general public continued to use the rail service whilst displaying the same vacant acceptance of their changed surroundings…

DISTINGUISHED HOST: Sorry, I'm going to have to press you for an answer…

CYNICAL NOVELIST: I beg your pardon. My answer is that the government can deny anything; quite simply, they can expect us to believe anything. It is absolutely social cleansing, of course it is. However, what truly amazes me is the fact we, as a public, somehow believe we have the right to condemn it after months of ignoring it. [Noise from the audience, raised hands and furrowed brows from the panel members] The one thing that will cure both apathy and indifference is scandal. We have suddenly acquired the right to castigate, the right to be indignant, because health executives have conspired with government to create an unconscionable facility to avoid mental health care, yet until it became a scandal, we had done what we do best, which is to stand around idly, ignoring each other.

[Loud applause from the audience interspersed with booing]

DISTINGUISHED HOST: The Honourable Member for Backwater, your reaction, please.

HON MEMBER FOR BACKWATER (OPPOSITION): I think our eminent friend makes a valid point. This government has brought us scandal after scandal and every day it seems we awaken to news of more corruption. The Prime Minister must surely feel the pressure to act…

CYCNICAL NOVELIST: What does that even mean? "The pressure to act" tells us absolutely nothing.

HON MEMBER FOR BACKWATER (OPPOSITION): I'm pretty

sure you have had the opportunity to express your opinion. Will you afford me the same courtesy?

CYCNICAL NOVELIST [not directly in to microphone but audible] But you're not saying anything.

DISTINGUISHED HOST: Please, if we could move on…

HON MEMBER FOR BACKWATER (OPPOSITION): As I was saying, [Cynical Novelist smiles at the audience] I believe The Prime Minister and the government are under serious pressure to act. They have a huge hole to dig themselves out of.

    [Applause]

CYNICAL NOVELIST: Bravo!

DISTINGUISHED HOST: Quickly now, the Minister for Avoidance, your thoughts, please.

MINISTER FOR AVOIDANCE: I believe my fellow guests have just about covered everything.

DISTINGUISHED HOST: As expected. Time for one more question from the audience. You, Madam, yes, you in the red blouse, please.

RED BLOUSE: Can we expect to be fobbed off with half-truths, once the government enquiries conclude?

CYNICAL NOVELIST: What have you had, so far?

    [Laughter from the audience]

DISTINGUISHED HOST: One for our newspaper representative, I think…

TOKEN HACK JOURNALIST: I would like to assure the audience that all information will be covered as fully as possible, at least by my publication.

CYNICAL NOVELIST: Can we have that in writing?

Online

Headlines, tweets, status updates, blogs etc.

GOLDEN WHISTLE POINTS:

Maybe we should all become Suicide Monitors

#"SUCCESSFUL UNFORTUNATES"

#"We had to call them something!"

"I've answered your question," says Health Minister

#EMPTY THREAT ARE GREAT!

#Top Ten Government Scandals

How many do you remember? Play now.

LIKE and REPOST if you think the Government are a lying sack of shit.

JOIN THE PROTEST AGAINST THE CONTEMPLATION ZONE. BE THERE OR CONTINUE TO IGNORE IT.

We deserve to be represented by decent human beings. Demand an election!

www.onlyonebrownshoe@blogpit.com

Welcome to anyone who has stumbled across this, my blog about what is currently happening in this country. We are bombarded daily, once again, by evidence that those in power have been caught with their trousers down. Newspapers are attempting to take the moral high ground, as they usually do. Journalists are suddenly sounding like they care. People are writing songs, giving interviews, protesting against those they chose to represent them. Even in the grubbiest corners of free speech, there are the tiniest hints of empathy where we might never expect to find it, as could be seen on this month's front page of Union Jack Boy, a far-right magazine, whose focus shifted slightly from its usual thoroughly white bullshit.

It seems as though there really is no other news. Is this the sign of a whole nation deciding to pay attention?

How long will this collective interest last? Will we lose interest some time during the second month, as is usually the case with wars in foreign countries we've never been to? Or after natural disasters, when we've donated sufficiently so as to feel like decent people, only to forget about the plight of those charity cases until lazy journalists reprint their stories at the end of the year? When the next outrage is upon us, will we do it all over again? Of course we will, because we need to feel like we are taking part in something, even if it is from the comfort of our homes, into which we would never consider inviting the homeless, the refugees, the terminally ill, the suicidal, not if we can provide anonymous help from a comfortable distance.

When the Contemplation Zone eventually dies on its arse, which will be the case soon enough, what is going to happen to all those people who have been standing within its cold yellow lines? What are we going to do about all the people who have been denied the help they so clearly need and deserve?

Changing their stories every day, providing little or no explanation which seems remotely plausible, The Spinistry of Health, as I like to call them, should be held accountable and subjected to the most rigorous of punishments. Instead of spending the obviously large amounts of money they have available on mental health care, perhaps to (crazy idea, I know!) HELP people with accurate diagnoses and long term treatment, they have sunk millions into creating DISA, along with hospital executives, in order to cut the problem off, brutally, inhumanely, disgustingly and, to their incredible shame, for a profit.

Sack them, expose them, arrest them; they are white collar cunts who will never give up until somebody stops them!

Video presentation broadcast every hour on train platform monitors. Produced and presented via anonymous hack:

Black screen:

The question, WHY ARE YOU HERE?, *flashes on and off for ten seconds before* Land of Hope and Glory *begins gently. A succession of news footage images, changing slowly and in time to the music, can be seen. Politicians, the Contemplation Zone, Disposal Technicians, Journalists, News Presenters speaking to camera, Empty Threat, the yellow line, The Prime Minister, Headlines, Ministry of Health personnel, Tweets, The Union Jack, Hospitals, etc…*

The images continue as audio excerpts from various reports and interviews, sound bites, phrases, individual words, are heard, in multiple voices which have been edited to form an audio sequence, producing the following message:

'Why are you here? Is this really the only choice available to you? You might be surprised to know that there are still some people who care, still some who want to make sure that you receive the help you deserve. Don't assume, just because your country has let you down, that you are totally alone. Don't think for one second that there is nobody left to listen to you. You have no reason to jump. Don't give them the satisfaction. You can leave here, right now. **You HAVE a future. You have the power to change it.**'

The images change. Family photographs, smiling faces, people hugging, groups of children smile at the camera, the old, the young, the middle-aged; all of them laughing, smiling, kissing, helping each other to exist.

Land of Hope and Glory *reaches its dramatic conclusion as the screen returns to black and the flashing words,* **YOU HAVE A FUTURE**.

Part Three

Getting In Line

The day after the dinner at Manbag's house, the Project Manager had arranged to meet Jason at a local soup kitchen/food bank for the homeless and needy, where, since the death of his daughter, the obstructed man had been working as a volunteer. Every Sunday morning, after trying in vain to convince his wife to accompany him on what he believed to be a cathartic step toward perspective, he set out to feed those less fortunate. He had suggested to Manbag, who had been most impressed by the obstructed man's sense of the spirit of the operation on which they were embarking, that the soup kitchen might provide a neutral location at which they could meet, when need be, to update each other on their individual progress. That first Sunday was marked as day one. From there, amongst the hungry unwashed, the Project Manager met with the Funeral Photographer. Manbag and Mighty sat, one-to-one, at a corner table near the kitchen.

It being day one, Manbag had launched himself fully into clandestine mode. He had arrived at the soup kitchen sporting the ginger stubble, which was now on the verge of wispy. The after-effects of the previous night's overindulgence, plus the calculated neglect of his usual metrosexual ablutions, had rendered him drawn and blotchy about the jowls. Ordinarily, he would have balked at the idea of leaving the house in such a state, but he felt flushed with the excitement of putting his plan into action. He had woken very early, put on the oldest pair of jeans he could find and a frayed jumper. Taking soil from a plant pot in the living room, he had proceeded to daub his clothes with it. Then, having put on an old khaki parka, he'd gone into the garden and rolled around on the ground, after which he'd smoked one cigarette, making sure to allow as much smoke as possible to permeate his clothing. The final result was quite impressive, so he'd thought, although he'd then felt his attempt at authenticity was a little crude, as if all the homeless had to worry about was a bit of dirt and the smell of tobacco. Despite this, he had ventured forth into the first day of his plan, reasonably content that he would both fit in and remain unrecognised.

The obstructed man had barely recognised him. Manbag had arrived with the hood of his parka up. It was only his ginger wispiness that had caught the obstructed man's eye as he was serving stew and dumplings to the first line of people. Manbag had queued up and was standing with a bowl in his outstretched hand at the point of recognition. The obstructed man had to suppress a smile as the Project Manager looked at him seriously. Once in receipt of his steaming stew, he had found his way slowly to the corner table where Jason was already seated.

The room was very practical; Formica tabletops, plastic chairs. Faded posters, designed with the typical neutral, wishy-washy colours of public information literature, admonished from each wall; heroin, cot-death, winter fuel awareness, flu injections, condom promotion - "Don't be silly, cover your willy", "Cover your cough", "Wash your hands".

'Is this seat taken?' Manbag asked in a gruff voice. Jason looked up at him and was momentarily lost for words as he fought to control his face. Manbag gave him the same look he had dispatched in the queue as he had witnessed the obstructed man's reaction. Jason acquiesced. Manbag sat, placing his bowl of stew and dumplings in front of him. Jason had already half-eaten his. 'It's no chocolate soufflé,' he said, 'but it hits the spot.'

Manbag surveyed the room without commenting. In spite of the facility having washrooms with bathing amenities, not every diner made use of them. As a result, Manbag decided to breathe through his mouth, as the miasma overwhelmed his delicate nostrils.

'This is the perfect place,' Jason said. 'Nobody will pay us any attention here, if that's what you're worried about.'

'I'm not worried,' Manbag replied. 'I'm just being cautious.'

'So it would seem,' Jason replied, as he scanned his companion's garb. The young photographer had also made some effort to dress down for the occasion, as per Manbag's instruction, yet the effect had proved less dramatic, being that he had started from a much lower level than the Project Manager's. Despite the hungry enthusiasm displayed about them by those truly deserving of the free sustenance, Manbag and Mighty were in receipt of occasional questioning looks; dubious eyes were raised from steaming bowls and cast subtly in their direction. Jason was desperate to take his camera from his bag and capture their faces. He refrained, however, lest he should jeopardise the project.

Manbag's spoon paused at his lips with the trepidation of a discerning eater, which threatened to blow his cover. Jason rolled his eyes. 'Do you want me to blow on it for you?' he said. Manbag's eyes reacted wryly to this as his mouth opened finally to sample the honest fare. They ate in silence as they both observed the obstructed man at work. He seemed to be very much in his element, sleeves rolled up, aproned, and sharing smiles and small talk with his fellow volunteers between servings; his greeting of several regular patrons by name reaffirmed the shared opinion Manbag and Mighty had already formed. The obstructed man was good, decent and, all things considered, obviously in possession of great strength of character.

'I feel bad about how we kind of glossed over the whole issue of his daughter,' Jason said. Manbag looked at him and sighed.

'I didn't really see it as a glossing over,' he said. 'To be honest, I think he shared as much as he wanted to, probably more, in fact.'

'Maybe,' Jason said.

'At some point, when the time is right, he'll want to say more, and hopefully, we'll be able to see that we can ask questions,' said Manbag. 'It's easy to assume, because of his age, that he would be guarded about his emotions.'

'Yes, I guess so,' Jason replied.

'But,' Manbag continued, 'when the conversation led in that direction, he did answer truthfully, and without any apparent embarrassment.'

They continued eating.

'The reason I asked you to meet me today,' Manbag began, 'was to make sure you are fully aware of what to expect, of what might easily befall you.'

'Befall?' Jason said. 'I don't like the sound of that.'

'Nor should you,' Manbag replied, his face changing gravely. He spied a nervous shift in his companion's demeanour. He paused dramatically.

'They will come for you,' he said.

'What do you mean?' Jason asked. 'Who will come for me?'

'Men, serious men,' Manbag replied.

'What are you talking about?'

'Jason, at this very moment, Martha is scanning a large number of your, shall we say, pertinent photos, which she plans to distribute through various avenues of communication. This is phase one.'

'I know, yes, phase one,' Jason said with a hint of ridicule.

'Make no mistake about it, my young friend, this is deadly serious.'

'Ok, I know!' Jason raised his spoon in concession to the seriousness of the matter at hand. Manbag continued.

'Once your photos have gone public, certain elements within my office and others who are already aware of your existence, not to mention your profession and your whereabouts, will come for you, in search of further information, in search of a confession.'

'When you say come for me, what do you mean, exactly?'

'They will take you, they will interrogate you, they will be far more focused than you imagine. I will be involved in this, due to my professional capacity. I will try to protect you…'

'Protect me!? What the fuck? Am I in danger?'

'You can't run. If you run, you will compromise the whole project by making yourself look guilty. It will establish your responsibility for the leak of the photos.' Manbag said, tactically not answering Jason's questions.

'So what are you saying? I should just wait until it happens?'

'That's exactly what you should do,' Manbag said firmly. 'As I said, I will try to protect you, but I also have to avoid any hint at my connection…'

'This is ridiculous!' Jason said, his voice rising beyond Manbag's comfort level. 'Who are these people? It's DISA, not the C.I.A.!'

'Don't assume that the information I have shared with you is the extent of what I know, and please, for your own good, hear me when I tell you that the roots of this project run deep, into the very fabric and through the very corridors of power from which orders are given, in whose offices covert operations are conceived and put into action.' Manbag paused and, with eyebrows raised, took the final spoonful of his stew and the remaining portion of dumpling, which he had saved for the last bite. Jason appeared momentarily unable to react.

'I am telling you this now, face to face, away from our colleagues, because I think it better that we limit information known to all four of us. I will continue to liaise with Martha about her tasks, and I will be in regular contact with our esteemed volunteer, here. From now on, until I am convinced it is safe; the four of us must not be seen together, under any circumstances. You know what you have been entrusted to do. You know when Martha is expecting to hear from you.' Manbag looked at the nervous photographer.

'I just go home and wait to see what "befalls" me?' Jason said.

'Yes,' replied Manbag in a professionally empathic tone. 'I'm sorry you're the one in this position, I truly am. But, for the cause, you have to take what comes. We all do.'

'Yes, we all do,' Jason said. 'It just seems like my end of the stick is the shittiest!'

Manbag smiled at him. 'It's for the greater good,' he said.

'Please,' Jason said, 'you sound like an American movie!'

And So It Begins

With the first clandestine meeting of phase one completed, Jason found himself back on the street. He had said farewell to Manbag who, having insisted they leave separately, had promptly vanished, but not before placing a small piece of white paper under his empty stew bowl. Once he had executed his calculated departure, the obstructed man appeared at their table, retrieved the bowl, lifted the piece of paper and placed it in the pocket of his apron. Jason emitted a puff of air. We've become spooks, all of a sudden, he thought. He made no comment on anything that had transpired at the table. He simply thanked the obstructed man and left.

Outside, he found himself at a loss. He didn't exactly fancy going home after Manbag's warning, although he would have to, at some point, he realised. As he crossed the road in search of somewhere to go, he noticed, emblazoned across a high wall at the end of the street, in multi-coloured graffitied letters, MINISTERS EXECUTIVES JUMP NOW, PLEASE! She's already started, he thought. He read it out loud. He felt shocked, not by its content, nor by the speed with which it had appeared since the previous night's conspiring, but more by the very obvious evidence of their plan becoming a reality. Across a dinner table in a Project Manager's pristine house, it had had enough excitement to keep them talking into the small hours. But now, standing before Martha's handiwork, he suddenly felt confronted by something very tangible. He panicked about how much more tangible it might become once the mysterious visitors came to call.

The Sunday afternoon breeze found its way down the back of his neck. After the heat of the soup kitchen, and the information he had learnt therein, the open air of the street felt unwelcoming. He let out a long, quiet, stew-flavoured burp and set off away from the graffiti. He passed a young homeless woman who was asleep inside a man's coat that looked enormous on her. He considered waking her up and telling her about the soup kitchen he had just come from, but then thought better of it. He wanted to take her photograph, but thought better of that, also. He turned a corner, thinking about her and whether she might one day soon end up in the Contemplation Zone. The new street offered a fresh message. DON'T DIE WITHIN THE ZONE, LIVE WITHOUT IT. More evidence – it was real. He started to think about never having taken the photographs, never having produced something which he now felt to be endangering him. The streets looked dirtier than he remembered. Christmas decorations had started to appear; shop windows were full of tinselled invitations to consume. It amazed him how, year after year, the same establishments would continue to ignore the increasingly shabby premises in which they conducted business, yet once the premature period of festive commercial incitation began, hard-earned profit was plunged into all manner of kitsch adornment.

He continued walking. He passed a litter bin which was crammed full of flyers, some of which were strewn on the pavement around its base. He noticed a man leaning over one side of his electric wheelchair, the chair itself on the verge of teetering under the sudden threat to its equilibrium, as he grasped at the pile of fresh shit his Yorkshire terrier had just deposited in the middle of the pavement. Quick as flash, Jason produced his camera and captured the moment which he thought should shame all those able-bodied dog owners who were too lazy and selfish to stoop for the poop. The wheelchair whirred past the litter bin and the canine leavings were discarded along with the unread flyers. In a moment, both man and beast had disappeared. Jason continued.

The wind wafted smells from various ethnic restaurants. He heard an ambulance, or was it a fire engine? He could never tell the difference. He imagined the number of people who were going to see his Contemplation Zone photographs. The contents of those folders, which had sat in his dark room filing cabinet, unseen by anyone else until the last few days, were about to be seen by the entire population. He was struggling to form an opinion of his feelings on this upcoming turn of events; from the cellar dark room of an insular, proudly protective photographer to the front pages of a nation's rags. For all intents and purposes, such a leap should be a career-defining moment, aggrandising the artist and establishing his name, yet somehow, he couldn't quite suppress the desire for it all to go away. This was day one. At this very moment, as Manbag had said, Martha was scanning, copying, posting, sharing, and doing whatever shady activities hackers do, and all of it, as far as he knew, surrounding the widespread publication of his photographs. He suddenly thought about the documents they had read the previous evening. Manbag's stash of illuminating literature must surely cause more of a stir than the photos, he thought. He felt sufficiently worried and started trying to convince himself that if his photos received less attention compared to the leaked documents, it would be better, safer. But then, he was proud of his work. What they were doing was for the benefit of everyone. What right did he have to want to hide from the inevitable consequences? He would take whatever came his way because their project was virtuous and ethical. I can do this, he thought, as he turned a corner.

Martha Goes Out

Martha was the last to leave the Manbag abode after the drinking had stopped. Jason and the obstructed man had gone home, each with their own role in the grandiose plan outlined by Manbag. The positivity of the occasion had sent them on their way, replete with good intention, food and alcohol. Manbag had arranged a one-to-one with each of his three co-conspirators to take place in the coming days, once their plan had started to unfold.

'You told me that you were studying hacking as part of your degree,' Manbag said to Martha, as they sat alone at the table. 'Are you absolutely sure that you can do what is needed?'

'Yes, I'm sure. If I have any problems, I know people who are much better than me,' she answered.

'Only if absolutely necessary,' Manbag said, 'but I must meet them first before we decide whether they can be included. I had hoped to limit the number of people involved. Fewer people, fewer problems.'

'Of course,' she replied. 'But these people would insist on remaining anonymous. Speak to them if you have to, but I'm sure there would be no need to worry.'

'And the other things we talked about?' he asked.

'I'm getting right on that, now. I'll never sleep after all that food, now's the perfect time. I've already texted someone.'

'Excellent! Take this,' Manbag said, offering her a mobile phone. 'Use it to contact me, if you need to. It's the only number stored in there. If I don't hear anything, I'll see you a week tomorrow at the soup kitchen, ok?'

'Yes,' she said, taking the phone from him.

'Remember to dress for the occasion,' he said. She smiled at him flatly.

After he had given her fifty pounds and put her in a taxi, she set off to meet the person she had texted.

Waiting for her under a railway bridge, as she got out of the taxi, was Stylus. He was Bryan to his parents, or Special Needs Bryan to those at his previous school who had made fun of his shyness and his tendency to appear out of nowhere and then disappear just as quickly. To Martha, he was Stylus, an introvert graffiti artist she had met in her Subversion Studies class. She knew, albeit modestly so, that he fancied her, and she knew that she could rely on his discretion. She was also in awe of his creative ability and fully aware that he possessed the skills necessary to work quickly, and in a neutral style which would be unrecognisable to those in the know, and therefore untraceable. She was going to have to persuade him to create original art, and then not sign it. They would have to leave whatever they produced with no tags. For her, he'd do it.

Her text to him was:

>Meet me under DB in 30
>
>Armed with colours
>
>M

He was leaning against the wall, trying not so convincingly to look nonchalant. She closed the taxi door and it drove off, past Stylus, under the bridge and away into the small hours. She loved that Stylus didn't really look typical. In fact, during several of their Subversion Studies classes, she had observed him. Amongst those pretenders who tried too hard to dress as "subversively" as possible, wearing their desire to be taken seriously like a badge, with about as much originality as a Che Guevara t-shirt, she found that Stylus was refreshingly plain and subtle, which led her to believe that he was probably the only person in the room capable of true subversion. The DB of her text message stood for Dirty Bridge, a name given to the bridge under which they now stood, accompanied by late-night whooshing traffic and distant, thunderous subwoofers. The bridge had earned its nickname due to the frequent sleazy activities that were once negotiated through open car windows as engines ran. Some years later, the council had managed to clean up the bridge's reputation whilst injecting much needed money into the area. The name lived on, however, in the minds of locals. Martha's mother would not be pleased to learn of her daughter's whereabouts.

'You told me to come armed with colours,' Stylus said. Martha noticed his eyes wander as she approached him.

'I did,' she said. 'I'll explain as we go.'

Not Just Another Manbag Monday

Antony Manbag, Project Manager of The Insecurity Security Act, DISA executive and generally respected professional, found a smile broadening his lips as he stood at his blender, awaiting the optimum smoothness of his morning fruit. He didn't expend much thought on the origins of the smile, but merely welcomed its presence at a time when such facial contortions seemed few and far between. Today he would be present as what had taken all his professional verve and every fibre of his expertise began to topple. He would watch as the chaos ensued. He would leap into calculated counteraction, playing his own role in their scheme; one of deflection and avoidance to which he was now looking forward. The fruit was done, optimum smoothness attained. He sat at the kitchen table, smoothie in hand, and went over everything carefully as he sipped.

The previous day, after his undercover rendezvous with Jason Mighty, he had returned home and spent the remainder of his Sunday cleaning up all traces of the conspiratorial dinner. Deciding to listen to all the same records which Martha had made no effort to replace correctly during their dinner, he thought about the discarded brown shoe and how he would have to dispose of his stash of incriminating documents. He considered his colleagues, his superiors, how he could facilitate an ineffective investigation, how he could manipulate, falsify, juggle, fudge, and how he could appear to be totally in control of something which, quite deliberately, would lead absolutely nowhere. This internal process took him several hours, at which point, he chose to reward himself with an entirely different internal process. As his fine, organic coffee was brewing, he retrieved his intimate, lustral itemry in preparation for his preferred ablution. He imagined the plan in terms of an enema. He started to think of himself as the organic coffee; the all-important purifying liquid which, when combined with the integral yet more menial tasks performed by its accompanying accoutrements, would wash away the inner rottenness efficiently. This whole country needs to lie down on the bathroom floor and spread 'em, he thought. That's what we're going to make them do.

The coffee was bubbling. He unbuckled his belt as he turned off the gas. Tomorrow he would go to work and assume the position: the position of a non-conspiring Project Manager. It occurred to him that he would have to pick out a nonchalant tie to wear. Immediately he laughed at the notion that anyone but he would even give such a thing a moment's consideration.

He had awoken feeling revitalised, confident and excited. The smoothie was performing its usual trick. Monday had finally arrived, and with it his first step, their first step, towards a change. The stubble had to go. He no longer needed exterior signs of his inner shift. He could shave them, wash and rinse them away, content in the knowledge that his plan was in place; that their commitment to its facilitation could be done with a controlled, smooth face and a well-chosen tie worn purely for his own amusement. As he shaved, he thought about his wolf cardigan, about how he'd thrown underwear around his bedroom, his unaligned slippers, and his days away from the office. He suddenly thought about the obstructed man's daughter and wondered what his new friend saw when he looked in the mirror. How much of his pain can he see in his own face? Where does it manifest itself? Does he just accept that the pain will always be present, in some shape or form? Are there any facial contortions that might, in some way, make him look less bereft? Manbag saw his father in his own reflection, that paternal line staring back at him passively from the bathroom mirror. He applied one of his metrosexual aftershave lotions to his face and the transformation began. He emerged from the bathroom several minutes later as a new man; gelled, oiled, creamed, crimped, tweaked, tweezed and raring to go.

His journey to work was spent focusing on how likely it was that a connection could be made between his absence and what was about to happen. His professionalism, not to mention his status, would undoubtedly preclude any suspicion from entering the minds of his staff. Workman, however…Workman was a problem. Well trained, ruthlessly efficient, ambitious and in possession of not a small amount of professional jealousy; Workman would have to be managed with extreme care.

As Manbag entered the building, he received looks from various members of staff from which he inferred surprise at his return, as if he had been gone much longer than the few short days he had spent in the field. Perhaps they were just happy to see him; it must be the nonchalance of the tie, he thought with a chuckle.

He had been sitting at his desk for fifteen minutes when there was the customary knock and Workman appeared. Manbag detected a hint of disappointment in the younger man's demeanour. 'Good morning, Sir,' Workman said. 'Good to have you back. I trust your time out of the office was productive?'

'My time is always productive, no matter where I am,' Manbag replied. 'But I'm sure you don't need to be told that, do you?' He surveyed his subordinate for signs of dissension. There was nothing at first glance, although Workman's choice of a red tie was quite bold, indicative of intention, Manbag thought, but what intention?

Workman looked at his watch. Their three minutes of neutral time had almost ended. He considered asking about the weekend but felt it unnecessary.

'Tell me,' Manbag said, taking the lead. 'Where are we with the disposal issue you mentioned last week?'

'We've already extended the camera facilities above the platforms and the track, especially in the impact scope, as that is where the disposal workers are active. We already have footage for the last few days, if you'd care to peruse it.'

Manbag thought about his own visit to one of the Contemplation Zones. He thought about the brown shoe he had retrieved from the platform edge. He knew that it would have been recorded as "unretrieved" in the disposal itinerary. He remembered the shoe's newness.

'If I need to peruse it, I'll have you set it up for me,' he said.

'Very good,' Workman replied.

'Well,' Manbag said, 'as it's Monday morning, I assume there isn't much else to occupy us just now. I have no doubt that you managed everything in my absence.'

'Thank you, Sir,' Workman said. 'I appreciate your faith in me.'

Manbag smiled. 'I shan't keep you any longer. I'm sure you have things to be getting on with.' Workman's phone buzzed in his pocket. He stood.

'Thank you, Sir,' he said as he left Manbag's office.

He answered the phone. 'Give me a second,' he said as he hurried down the corridor, out of earshot. 'He's back…yes, as I told you he would be…he seems back to his normal self…no, I think I should stay on him, for the time being, until I'm sure…ok…yes…later, ok…bye.'

Workman closed his office door and sat down at his desk, sighing as he swivelled slowly in his chair. He opened his laptop and looked at the live feed from Manbag's office. There sat the Project Manager, arranging the few items on his desk. Workman watched him for a few minutes before closing the laptop lid.

Back in Manbag's office, things got off to a slow start, once Workman had been excused. The Project Manager thought about the second phone in his briefcase, he thought about his new team and their allocated tasks. The phone on his desk rang. He answered it and was told that there was a call from Madge Nicholson, journalist from *The Anchor*. It was starting.

Manbag: Good morning. What can I do for you?

Madge Nicholson: Mr. Manbag, this is Madge Nicholson from The Anchor.

Manbag: From The Anchor, indeed. This is an honour. How can I help?

Madge Nicholson: Well, this is nothing more than a courtesy call, Mr Manbag. I wanted to offer you a chance to comment on some rather illuminating information that has come into my possession this morning.

Manbag: Oh, yes. And what information might that be?

Madge Nicholson: Information of a particularly sensitive nature, which paints your Department, not to mention several other prominent entities, in a very unfavourable light.

Manbag: Mrs. Nicholson…

Madge Nicholson: It's Miss, actually…

Manbag: Of course it is. Miss Nicholson, let me stop you there. Accusations, threats and rumours are weekly inconveniences for most operations with a scope and public profile such as ours. However, I think you'll find that the exemplary work ethic of DISA is above all that, and that the mud flung at us just doesn't stick.

Madge Nicholson: If this were your common or garden mud, I wouldn't even be troubling you. The documents I am currently leafing through leave little to the imagination and I think you might be shocked by just how inflammatory this information is.

Manbag: [Smiling] I assume the origin of this information is a secret.

Madge Nicholson: Usually I would say so, yes, but I have no idea where it came from.

Manbag: You expect me to believe that such incendiary documents were left anonymously?

Madge Nicholson: Is that so difficult?

Manbag: [Still smiling] Perhaps you could give me a summary of the worst of it.

Madge Nicholson: I'd be happy to…

Madge Nicholson, journalist with *The Anchor*, went on to describe, over the course of the next couple of minutes, exactly what information currently lay on her desk. Manbag imagined how untidy her workspace was as she spoke to him. The tone of her voice hinted at her realisation of the power of what she had before her, although it didn't sound, to Manbag, as though she had read everything fully. He reacted as planned, as he had rehearsed. He gave a well-considered performance of professional indignation and denial followed by a calculated ploy for time to speak to his superiors in order to gauge the official reaction.

Madge Nicholson: But you understand that we will be running the story tomorrow morning, regardless of an "official" comment from DISA, don't you?

Manbag: I do. I will call you back as soon as possible today, Miss Nicholson.

Madge Nicholson: I shall look forward to hearing from you.

Manbag: Thank you and goodbye.

Manbag ended the call abruptly, smiling at his fake sense of urgency. Time to go upstairs, he thought.

"Upstairs", for the employees of DISA, was a simple word which was used euphemistically to refer to the controlling authority, the details of which were known only by a select few. Manbag was one of those select few, but even he had restricted access. The protocol as regards public statements or comments made by DISA employees extended only as far as one golden rule which stated that no such communiqués should be made under any circumstances. Manbag had long been of the opinion that a "no comment" approach revealed far more than a well-considered, more fully-realised response; when it came to dodging the issue; more words conveyed a greater lack of pinpointable culpability. His intention now, was to inveigle, to convince those upstairs that some comment was necessary, and that a break of protocol was in order.

On the rare occasions that a visit upstairs had been necessary, Manbag had dealt exclusively with The Auxiliary, a menacingly beautiful woman whom he imagined to be around twenty-five years of age and of formidable intellect. She had been the one to interview him for his role as Project Manager. She hadn't laughed at any of his jokes, which he found intimidating, as it made her seem unamusable. The interview's success had lain in his impeccable technique, the greatness of which was even sufficient to stymie the effects of his humour. On each subsequent occasion, she had been the end of the line, providing him with the same paucity of information regarding those at the top of the hierarchical chain and their unfortunate lack of availability. He knew her only as The Auxiliary. Nothing more personal had ever been shared, at least on her part. Her title added to her allure and he had often thought about her. Her real name just wasn't necessary.

His identity card cleared him for access to the top floor as he swiped it inside the lift. During his short journey, he checked his appearance perfunctorily in the mirrored walls. He saw his father looking back at him, again. His tie was getting more nonchalant as the morning wore on. The doors opened and he set off down the long, silent corridor. As usual, there were no other people about. It had occurred to him before that she might be the only person up there, running the entire operation. He had dismissed the notion, more than likely out of professional jealousy; she was far too young to be so powerful in his mind. It was true, however, that he had never encountered any of the so-called "higher ups", those who exceeded even his level of privileged security clearance. The notion that the controlling body was comprised of the brightest, most powerful captains of industry was hearsay and nothing more; at least as far as the regular DISA staff was concerned. Manbag had got further than anyone. He had spoken to The Auxiliary; he had stood outside that big, wooden door, the one he was now approaching, the one that had remained closed on each of his previous visits, a looming vertical presence which provided a palpable reminder to him that he had reached the end of the line. His line stopped here, at the desk of The Auxiliary. If he were to go any further, he would need to get through her.

Adjacent to the door was a minimalist waiting area made up of Spartan chairs arranged opposite The Auxiliary's desk. There she sat. As he approached, she directed him towards the seating area with a commanding hand, without raising her eyes from whatever occupied her attention. He took a seat in silence, his expensive shoes producing no static on the carpet, and waited to be acknowledged. It was so quiet he could hear his watch ticking. He found it difficult to divert his eyes from her, as her head remained lowered over her desk. She couldn't see him looking at her, but somehow, he knew she would know he was.

'I shan't keep you a moment,' she said, finally, as if sensing his discomfort at where to direct his gaze. He'd forgotten the deep tone of her voice, and it was enough to keep his focus on her until she raised her head. She took off her glasses and motioned for him to take the seat in front of her desk. He complied.

'The infrequency of your visits would suggest some sort of problem has arisen,' she said.

'I could always visit more often,' he said with a smirk. She didn't move a muscle. Impervious, he thought.

'Am I to assume something requires attention?' she said.

'Yes, Auxiliary,' Manbag replied. He felt his eyes wandering. Her mousy hair was scraped back and tied, but one strand was resting loosely behind her left ear. The symmetry of her face was startling, the little bump on the end of her nose was endearing. She seemed even more beautiful than before. He recalled thinking the very same thing on his previous visit. Her eyes conveyed the slightest suggestion of impatience.

He explained to her the nature of his telephone conversation with Madge Nicholson of The Anchor. She listened and observed the same body language she remembered from his interview - a consummate display of adept understanding of the topic at hand. His facial contortions were sprinkled with micro innocence to the optimum degree so as not to belie the competence that he needed to project. She had to know that he was in control, but she had to think that he was not the leaker. As his account of the phone call drew to a close, he considered the possibility of their current situation being serious enough that he might finally penetrate the inner sanctum and make his way through that ultimate door. Would she remain his limit, or had he started something which was beyond even her power to restrict his security clearance?

'Go back to your office,' she said as she stood up. He didn't remember her being so tall. 'You shall receive instruction within the hour.' She walked around the desk and approached the ultimate door. He turned with an expectant rush of curiosity. She would not open it while he was still sitting there. She raised her eyebrows in silence.

'Of course,' he said, jumping to his feet. Her eyebrows continued on their upwards trajectory, which he took as his cue to leave. He set off down the silent corridor. After ten steps, he allowed himself a cheeky backwards glance over his shoulder. The Auxiliary had already disappeared through the ultimate door.

Back in his office, his thoughts turned to Martha and he felt a surprisingly exhilarating sense of camaraderie born of his sudden change and his need to feel connected to those who encompassed it. More importantly, she had obviously executed perfectly everything they had planned. He curtailed his enjoyment lest he descend into hubris, which would leave him open to error. Ok, let's focus, he thought. The Auxiliary is, at this moment, going through the motions of damage control. The phone rang again.

'The editor of The Verbose Evening Post is on line one, Sir' said the voice of Manbag's secretary. '…and I have Edmund Kemplar from The Circumlocution waiting on line two.'

'Well, we are popular, this morning,' said Manbag. 'Put the editor through and please tell Mr. Kemplar to hold.' He peered through the blinds of his internal office window at his staff going about their usual business, unaware of the machinations that had been set in play.

'Editor, how can I help you?'

There followed, for the next hour, several more calls from various publications, each claiming to be in possession of documents and, of course, damning photographic evidence of professional wrongdoing and misconduct. As planned, Martha had not sent everything to everybody, thereby fostering the delusion, on the part of editor or journalist that, based on the idea of trans-publication tittle tattle, they were in possession of something approaching a scoop.

Manbag fielded every question, all along relishing his own manipulative role in what was turning out to be more fun than he had anticipated. The exchanges were replete with accusatory vocabulary, such as "plausible deniability", "bamboozle", "subterfuge", "chicanery", "malfeasance" and "political expediency". Never had such words sounded so wonderful to Manbag's ears. He ended each conversation promptly and in the same manner as he had the first. As the hour ticked by, he received news from upstairs. He was to return to The Auxiliary.

As the lift doors opened, he set off down the corridor with the idea in mind that he would now have even less chance of getting a smile out of The Auxiliary. No doubt the last hour had involved rigorous debate across a large, polished table, or perhaps a teleconference of international magnates who had been dragged away from whatever vital undertakings occupy such luminaries' time. Or, as Manbag had previously thought, perhaps her deception had led her into an empty room in which her one-woman show was perpetuated, where she had had to come to her own conclusions as to how to proceed. He came ever closer to finding out as each step took him down the long corridor towards her desk. She wasn't there. He considered sitting down at her desk, especially after noticing the apparent softness of the leather chair in which her alluring buttocks had been ensconced only an hour before. He touched the corner of her desk with a fingertip and was happy to note the absence of dust. The ultimate door made a sudden wooden clunk and it opened. Manbag jumped and let out a tiny fart. He darted quickly away from her desk and adopted what he believed to be the nonchalant pose of a visitor waiting patiently. She appeared from behind the enormous door and approached her desk. She paused and inhaled gently.

'Can you smell coffee?' she asked him. He blushed and replied in the negative. She motioned him forward and he retook his seat, as in the earlier meeting. He had to be as careful as possible, now. Whatever plan she had come up with, or had been instructed to implement, he would need to support it fully, in order to display his continued commitment to the project. He would then put into action the next stage of his plan. 'Well,' she began, as she looked across at him. 'I'm sure I don't need to tell you that any step we take at this moment is concerned purely with preliminary damage control.'

'Of course,' he replied with an ingratiating smile.

'Usually, we wouldn't make any public statement or comment in situations where the Department receives unwanted attention. However, it does seem that these circumstances may prove to be extenuating, to the point of making some response necessary.'

'I agree,' Manbag said.

'So, we would like you to prepare a statement promising our full co-operation, so it looks, at least to the less cynical among us, as if we are not simply and facelessly avoiding the issue out of guilt. The reputation of the Department could easily be sullied greatly by such a leak, not to mention the irreparable damage or even loss of our links to our investors and other Departments, who will vanish if the situation worsens and they are at risk of exposure.'

'I understand,' Manbag said. 'I'll do it immediately.'

'We trust that you know how to manage this debacle. You will report everything to me, obviously, but you will remain the highest point of contact for any outside investigators, basically you are to answer all questions and you are to clean up in any way you see fit. Is that understood?'

'Yes, Auxiliary,' Manbag answered.

'I won't keep you any longer, as I'm sure your attention is needed elsewhere, perhaps now more than ever.' She gave him something resembling a smile, more a show of confidence in his ability, or so he thought of it later, as he descended in the lift, back to his own level.

Time to call in Workman…

'Come to my office in ten minutes,' Manbag said in his text. He wanted to be in the midst of the critical calls when Workman arrived, so the minion would see his mentor in action and witness the passive-aggressive diplomacy, and its wielding, which had made Manbag the leader he was, and to which the minion could only aspire.

Precisely ten minutes later, Workman knocked and entered with his customary leeway. Manbag was reclining in his chair with his feet up on the table. He had the telephone on speaker.

'…well, that goes without saying, Miss Nicholson, of course…' Manbag gestured to Workman that he should sit down. Workman complied.

Faint background noise could be heard from the offices of The Anchor, as Madge Nicholson spoke.

'Mr. Manbag, what we're talking about, here, is a gravely serious exposé of epic proportion,' said the journalist, with a dash of smugness at her possession of the deadly documents. They could hear her leafing through pages. Workman looked puzzled. Manbag continued.

'Miss Nicholson, I don't doubt for a second that what you have is sufficient, prima facie, to have you all rubbing your hands together, totally convinced of the scope of the scoop which lies before you, strewn, with impressive girth, across your desk. But, having studied your papers more closely, will you be so confident, once the wider context has revealed itself?'

'The wider context being…?' she asked.

'The wider context being that, despite the horrors upon which you have stumbled, the general public have stood by, seemingly in complete indifference to what was happening under their very noses. Will you be able to convince your readers that you indeed have a scandal, when they are, in fact, all complicit?' Manbag smiled at Workman.

'Is the wider context not the fact that your whole operation was conceived as a means of managing suicide, and put into play at the behest of the very people who are supposedly charged with the legitimate treatment of those "successful unfortunates"?' Madge Nicholson asked.

'I'm sure it appears so, at least at this preliminary stage,' Manbag said.

'Could you tell me how, after further inspection, it will possibly look any different?' Madge Nicholson asked with force.

'That conclusion is one which you will have to arrive at through use of your journalistic prowess. My instructions are to offer the full co-operation of the Department, but I can't do your job for you,' Manbag said, smiling at Workman.

'Nor would we want you to, Mr. Manbag,' said Madge Nicholson. 'We are not in the business of managing facts so that…'

'I'm sorry, Miss Nicholson,' Manbag interrupted, 'but for a

moment, there, it sounded as if you said that your newspaper doesn't manage facts…'

'You didn't let me finish…'

'What's that tired old phrase about getting in the way of a good story?'

'This is your "full co-operation", is it?'

'I think my professional courtesy only extends as far as giving you a comment before you go to press. The full co-operation is a public statement, a show of general amenability, if you will. That is what goes on the record, our "full co-operation", ok?' Manbag noticed that Workman was watching his every move, studying him, almost. 'Very well, Mr. Manbag,' Madge Nicholson said, after a brief pause which made Manbag think she was probably communicating something to other people in the room with her.

'Well, it is nice to reach some common ground, don't you think?' Manbag said smugly.

'I won't keep you any longer, thank you for your time,' Madge Nicholson said.

'My pleasure, good day to you,' replied Manbag, as he leaned forward.

'Good bye.'

Workman pressed the button to end the call, thereby saving his mentor the effort. With a look of incredulity which he tried unsuccessfully to manage, Workman launched into a barrage of questions relating to what he had just overheard. Manbag, in turn, launched into his carefully planned description of the situation, making sure to emphasise the apparent suddenness with which all this had come to light, the resulting shock, and the difficult task that lay ahead in combatting their detractors from such a vulnerable position. Manbag's phone rang again. He cancelled the call.

'I need you to find two or three of the best people we have,' Manbag said.

'Of course,' Workman replied.

'They need to take all calls relating to this matter for the rest of the day, they will have to say, that due to the circumstances, both you and I are in meetings and are consequently unavailable for comment. They must promise the full co-operation of the Department, nothing more, nothing less. Under no circumstances are they to engage in conversation, comment on anything, or answer any questions directly.'

'Got it!' Workman said.

'Please organise this ASAP, and meet me back here in one hour, Ok?'

'Ok.' Workman, displaying all the necessary urgency, left the room.

Once the coast was clear, Manbag took out his secret mobile phone and hurriedly thumbed a text to Martha which simply said, PERFECT, WELL DONE!

He sent another to the obstructed man which simply said, ALL GO!

He sent one final message to Jason Mighty which simply said, GET READY!

Manbag and Workman spent the rest of the afternoon investigating possible sources of the leak, the young subordinate never once appearing to suspect his superior of any malfeasance, whilst the most trusted below them fielded the incoming slew of probing telephone calls. When Manbag found himself alone at around seven o'clock in the evening, he was able to leaf through the transcripts of each recorded telephone conversation, to be sure of what Workman's top people had said.

In Workman's office, his computer displayed a diligent Manbag at work. The second in command spied on his Project Manager with what appeared to be frustration, perhaps even dismay at the apparent ordinariness of the goings-on within. Workman reached for his phone.

'He's just…working!' he said after a few seconds. 'Yes…so it would seem…He really does seem calm…No…No…I guess it's just…I know, patience, trust me, I know…fine.'

He hung up and continued to watch his conscientious boss.

Happy with what he had read, Manbag's mind drifted towards Enema Fanatics Anonymous. Today was Monday, and not a scheduled meeting night. What was he really getting from being a member of the group? This was the dominant question that seemed to return after each attempt at finding positive benefits gained from his membership. His current project was flushing through him, rinsing, purging and sluicing his very being. DISA had given him his professional focus. It had been the perfect receptacle for the many well-written attributes which leapt from his superbly laid out curriculum vitae. But this; this covert deconstruction was truly purifying, more so than any support group populated by desperate fanatics and those living in fear.

He began writing an email to The Auxiliary, detailing the afternoon's events, keeping her abreast. Abreast, he thought; still amused by that word at forty-six years of age. He thought about her aloofness and how it seemed at odds with her obvious assiduous work ethic. He was still enchanted by the idea that she was running the ship from behind the closed ultimate door. He considered adding "kind" before the "regards" he had used to sign off the email, but then thought better of it. She didn't really deserve it, she never laughed at his jokes. If he ever managed to get one laugh out of her, then she might get a "kind" out of him. Until that time, she would receive plain "regards". He left his office thinking about what information was likely to surface next, what he would be dealing with tomorrow. The car radio came on loudly as he turned the ignition.

"…and copies of these photographs have just appeared, sent anonymously?"

"Apparently, yes. There has been speculation all day as to the origin of the images. Is this a leak of some sort, or have they come from a third party outside of DISA? Either way, it's not looking good for the Department."

"No, absolutely not. But then leaking documents is of course very fashionable, these days, isn't it?"

"It certainly is, yes. But this doesn't seem to be one of those disposable stories which can be used as a distraction for a few days."

"You mean one of those stories with no substance that are presented as dramatically as possible, don't you?"

"Those are the ones, yes; style over substance."

"But these photos, if our listeners can use their imagination, are decidedly graphic in nature and they depict an all too familiar part of everyday life."

"*...a part of everyday life which, until now, had been pretty much ignored by the general public.*"

"*That's true, yes. I think that there'll be a lot of people reassessing the Contemplation Zone project after seeing these images.*"

"*But then, isn't that hypocritical? Like a dead refugee child can suddenly make us pay attention? We only start caring when we have good photographs of something that should have horrified us from the beginning?*"

"*You make a strong point.*"

"*I think whoever took these photographs is making the strong point, don't you? I mean, here we are, discussing something that has been ignored, more or less, because it is suddenly presented to us from a different perspective.*"

"*You may be right. Well, listeners, keep your eyes open for what will obviously be making news headlines tomorrow...*"

"*...and for some time after that.*"

Manbag smiled as he put his foot down. He wondered if Jason was listening, too. The image of the young photographer cowering in his dark room caused Manbag to frown and hope that Jason didn't feel that he had been forced into it, in any way. In a way, they had all been forced into it, in fact, had it not been for Jason's photographs, Manbag might easily have continued to champion the cause. But, he thought, there had been a period prior to his first encounter with Jason, where he had almost convinced himself that he was in a state of paralysis regarding his career. He had suffered the symptoms of what he later determined to have been nothing more than a clichéd crisis of doubt about his professional value. He had brought his own worth into question one night a few months ago, when he had decided to buy and then smoke some very expensive weed that a casual acquaintance had assured him would be good for him because of its high THC content. Preferring to indulge in the privacy of his own home, he had managed to persuade himself that Project Management was a total waste of time, and that his life and his skillset demanded thorough examination and re-evaluation if he had any hope of professional fulfilment. He had then decided that he should reorganise everything he owned into such detailed systems of tidiness, the profundity of which only he, the master of categorised orderliness, would be able to understand and appreciate fully. He then realised that this was indeed a project, and he was managing it. There was no escape, he concluded.

Messages Received

Having received Manbag's PERFECT, WELL DONE! message, Martha smiled and deleted it, as per his instructions. It seemed as though the Project Manager was pleased with the preliminary results of her fruitful hours of exposing the precious information which he had shared with them over their Saturday night dinner. Free from the glow of homemade food and alcohol, away from the cosy irony of knitted cardigans and home-baked tea bread, the sheer weight of the documents' provocative contents, which she had absorbed during the process, now had the added seriousness of a Monday, a working day whose harsh reality tainted the ghastly pages even further.

She had stayed out most of the night after the dinner party. With Stylus's expertise, she had managed to cover various neighbourhoods of the city centre, and the graffiti they had left emblazoned across various doors, walls and fences had been the first thing to greet many an early-riser on the Sunday morning. She had snored through the majority of it, much to the frustration of her mother, who, generally speaking, took her daughter's absence from the common family areas of the house as some sort of personal insult. When Martha finally appeared, bedraggled, yawning, and with the imprint of bed sheet wrinkles across her left cheek, the effrontery was amplified, as her mother's desire for her daughter to take pride in her appearance went unsatisfied yet again.

'You missed almost all the unveiling, you know,' her mother said.

'I should've tried harder,' Martha said, 'and I could've missed all of it!'

'I would say it's too early for sarcasm, but as you can see, the afternoon is already upon us,' her mother said.

Martha sighed as she opened the fridge. 'Is there anything I can do for you, Mother?' she said impatiently.

'Well, you could try dragging a brush through that mop that used to be your hair, how about that?' She reached out to her daughter's unkempt head in a half-hearted attempt to restore some sense of control, as if her once precious little girl could be rediscovered simply by making some minor adjustments. Martha dodged her mother's hand - an abrupt reminder that the little girl was gone forever.

'Is the thought of my touching you so terrible?' she asked her daughter.

'Frankly, yes, I'm still half asleep and you want to give me a make-over,' Martha replied.

'Why won't you let me help you?'

'Because I don't need any help!'

'That's a matter of opinion, young lady.'

'I've been in here thirty seconds, and you're already calling me "young lady".' She drank orange juice from the carton. Her mother didn't rise to the bait.

'Everyone was very impressed by the photographs,' she said.

'That's useful for you, at least you know whether to like them or not, now!' Martha replied.

'Why do you have to talk to me like that?'

'Because you displayed photos of my dead grandfather for all your friends to gawp at whilst sipping sweet sherry,' Martha said forcefully.

'He would have been very proud!' Her mother's face was reddening.

'Really!? Are you sure about that?' Martha said.

'Why not? It was very tastefully done.'

Martha didn't answer. She couldn't answer. She just couldn't.

The obstructed man had received the ALL GO! from Manbag, which he had deleted, as per his instructions. As he switched on the television, he was feeling more or less back to normal, Monday's seriousness finally curing him of Sunday's hangover. The dinner party at Manbag's had been his first social event since the loss of his daughter. He had hit the wine quite hard during and in between courses, and that was after mojitos. Despite the terrible state in which he had awoken the morning after, he could still remember everything they had discussed, planned and then vowed to execute. He could also remember finally revealing to his three new friends what had originally brought him to the Contemplation Zone, where he had first met Jason.

Having washed away as many dregs of his overindulgence as possible with tea and bacon sandwiches, he had set off to the soup kitchen, determined to help the less fortunate, not only by serving them with stew and dumplings, but by embarking on the first stage of a plan which would put some sense of closure hopefully within his grasp, and provide others with the attention they were sadly lacking.

His wife had made no comments on his whereabouts the

previous night other than to ask if they had enjoyed the tea bread. He had answered in the affirmative with a forced smile which did little to cover his sadness. She was becoming invisible.

    The vigour with which Jason Mighty had attacked the morning after the night before had, of course, all but disappeared in light of Manbag's Sunday morning soup kitchen pronouncement. Having avoided his house for as long as possible, the pre-Christmas coldness of city centre wandering, plus the seemingly omnipresent results of Martha and Stylus's nocturnal daubings, had finally sent him home in search of warmth, tea, and reading material, which he hoped would provide some much needed distraction from what was rapidly snowballing in his mind. He had confined himself to the darkroom with War and Peace, having turned up the central heating and brewed a pot of Ceylon. He laughed to himself at his need to seek solace and protection in his darkroom. Who would think to look for a photographer there!? He jumped at every noise coming from his neighbours, however familiar the sounds were. Was it the old water pipe next-door that always clanged when someone flushed the toilet, or was it shady, government henchmen turning his house upside down, looking for him? 'I'm in the darkroom!' he shouted. 'Isn't it obvious?' He thought about switching the red light on, so they wouldn't enter. However much he tried to amuse himself, he still couldn't get rid of the niggling dread which Manbag's words had put into him. "They will come for you." It rang in his ears like a ghastly refrain, like the stew and dumpling indigestion which still bubbled within him. He made very little progress with War and Peace, which he had been chipping away at for several weeks now, mainly because he only picked it up at certain times of the day, and in the last week not at all. The tea provided some comfort. He'd often imagined the simplicity of a life in which nothing would be bad enough or that serious that it would prevent his enjoyment of a good cup of tea. Up until that very moment, he might even have been able to say he had managed it. However, he realised that the pot was half-empty and he hadn't yet marvelled at the sublimeness of it. He had reached that point where his immediate circumstances were proving to be too much of a distraction, and he lamented briefly the loss of simplicity.

The toilet next-door flushed again. The pipes clanged. He couldn't stay down in the darkroom for the rest of the day. Why should he feel like a prisoner in his own house? As he got to his feet, he suddenly thought about his time studying Muay Thai and wondered if his memory of the art of eight limbs would serve him well when it came to defending himself against unwanted visitors. He spun his hips and lolloped into something approaching the start of a roundhouse kick. He stumbled into the table, which spilt tea over his discarded Tolstoy. He regained his balance, gathered his things and took them upstairs, where he set about trying to dry out the unread tome. He spent the following hours busying himself in the darkroom, making prints of the most graphic of his Contemplation Zone images. He had tried to read again before going to bed, but War and Peace was still moist and stained. He had lain awake for a couple of hours, just thinking about his life's trajectory, trying to remember the things he had done which had most surprised him. It was then that he had returned to the darkroom.

He awoke suddenly in the leather armchair. The red light was switched on. He had no idea of the time. His neck ached and he had drooled on his t-shirt. He couldn't remember sitting down. His freshest prints hung above his head. They were dry. He went upstairs, and as he opened the door, he saw that it was daytime. He was supposed to be meeting Martha. He went to his bag and found the disposable phone. One new message was waiting for him. It was from Manbag, and it said simply, GET READY! Jason deleted it, as per his instructions.

He went to meet Martha at the university library, as they had arranged. She introduced him to Stylus, who actually complimented him on his photographs. Jason looked surprised by the compliment.

'You haven't seen any news today, have you?' Martha said.

'No,' Jason responded. 'I've been asleep most of the day, why?'

'Why do you think?' Martha said with a puzzled look.

Stylus pulled a smart phone from his pocket and proceeded to show Jason various news headlines, flicking from page to page rapidly.

'They're everywhere!' Stylus said. 'It's great work!'

Jason was silent. His Contemplation Zone photos were suddenly all over the news, spread across the internet, out there for all to see – indelible evidence of his own creation. It wasn't as if he hadn't known this was going to happen, but, seeing the full extent of it made him all too aware of what they were doing, not to mention the fact that his visitors would soon be calling.

'Are you ok?' Martha asked him.

'Yeah,' he said vacantly. 'It's just so much, that's all... Can we talk alone for a minute?'

'Stylus, give us a minute!' Martha said. Stylus left them alone.

'How much does he know?' Jason asked, once they were alone.

'Keep your voice down, will you,' Martha said. 'This is a library, after all!'

'Since when did you worry about following the rules?' Jason said, lowering his voice to a whisper.

'Don't worry about Stylus, he's ok.'

'Is he? And what does Manbag think about involving someone new?'

'He gave me the go-ahead to ask for help, if necessary.'

'Really, and we need help from someone called Stylus, do we?'

'What's the matter, the name's not mighty enough for you?' Martha said with a sneer. Jason didn't respond. 'Look,' she continued. 'He only knows the minimum. He would've known your name eventually, anyway. You're on the verge of becoming a well-known photographer. I asked for his help because he is a brilliant graffiti artist.'

'I've seen a lot, you've been busy.'

'Yes, we have. As far as he is concerned, we were just protesting on a few walls. You're here because I told him I knew you and I was helping you with materials, that's all. He's the one who got us in here and able to use all the facilities without a trace. You should be thanking him!'

'Ok, ok, I'm sorry. Let's get on with these copies and then we can get out of here.'

Talk Time Radio

"…*you're joining us here, on Talk Time Radio, it's Tuesday morning, and it's time to talk…*"

"*That's right. We're discussing the big story of the moment, the DISA leak which, I have to say, is proving to be very interesting.*"

"*Why's that?*"

"*Well, for a start, it's not just your typical run-of-the-mill scandal we're talking about, here.*"

"*Oh no?*"

"*No. We find ourselves in a particularly uncomfortable position due to these really quite remarkable photographs which have been circulating.*"

"*That's right. Why don't you explain for those listeners who might not have seen or heard about them?*"

"*Ok. The photos in question are graphic images of the Contemplation Zone, which is rapidly becoming the most controversial government installation in recent years.*"

"*Why's that, then?*"

"*Well, we all know what the Contemplation Zone is, of course, but what we're only now starting to realise, in light of these photos and the accompanying leaked DISA documents, is that we're all complicit in some way.*"

"*That's right, isn't it?*"

"*Yes!*"

"...and we really have to draw attention to the fact that several of these documents shed a very negative light on the so-called testing which was conducted prior to the CZ scheme's inception."

"Well, this is where I have to jump in, if you pardon the expression [audible background sniggers], and say that really, we can't get annoyed and offended by the testing just because all it did was prove that we are heartless and apathetic. We have ignored it without question until now, when we have documentation we somehow have the right to be indignant. It's really quite ridiculously hypocritical, if you think about it."

"Well, that's really the key phrase, isn't it - If you think about it? Now, because we've been nudged into awareness, we're being forced to think about something that we don't want to confront."

"That's true. Anyway, back to the photos. They are apparently the work of one Jason Mighty."

"Is that his real name?"

"So I'm led to believe. Anyway, he has been producing high-quality analogue prints of his funeral photography and he decided to turn his hand to capturing the Contemplation Zone."

"It gives a whole new meaning to a dying art."

[Groans and laughs]

"Oh dear...!"

"Sorry, I did think twice about that."

"Yet it still came out..."

Manbag laughed out loud. Even in this situation, he thought, people still can't control themselves. His journey into work was proving more enjoyable, especially considering he was responsible for the whole thing.

"So these photos are what's really making people sit up and take notice?"

"Of course, what do you think? Nobody has time to read full articles anymore. If the photos provide the context, why should people waste time filling in the details?"

"It seems like something that is worth reading about, though, doesn't it?"

"I know that, our devoted listeners of course know that. But come on, everyone knows that the majority of people never read beyond the first paragraph, these days."

"So this is why the photos are so important."

"Exactly! They are a true representation, a document of what is really happening. The news is the news!"

"What do you mean?"

"I mean that we can't trust what we read, but we can't argue with the photos, we can't dispute the photographic evidence. The only problem is, is that the photographic evidence shows us, the whole country, to be a bunch of unfeeling zombies!"

Manbag smiled as he stopped at some traffic lights. In front of him, on the other side of a roundabout, he could see an enormous print of one of Jason's photographs. Martha, Jason and Stylus had fly-posted it on a billboard the night before. Manbag looked at it. It showed one Disposal Team Technician scrubbing what appears to be human tissue off the front window of a train with a long brush, whilst another Technician stands behind him holding a severed foot. Manbag imagined the brown shoe, and the foot that had been inside it just moments before he had collected it from the platform edge. He didn't notice that the traffic lights had changed, and suddenly horns were beeping behind him.

He accelerated, passing the poster, glad to be away from its clutches.

"... so, what comes next, then?"

"Well, I assume, as ever, that social media will tell people what to think; once this story and its shocking photographic accompaniment have had sufficient online coverage, which could already have happened, considering the buzz its generating, well, then people will know what they think about it."

"Are we going to see people changing their profile pictures into different colours, or something, by way of showing support for the "successful unfortunates"?"

"Well, that one never gets old, does it?"

"...and what else do we know about this photographer?"

"Very little, at this point."

Manbag pulled onto the street of the DISA building and was immediately confronted by television trucks, journalists, photographers, and a multitude. He slowed down as he approached the gate of the building. He was glad of his tinted windows as he arrived at the security hut. He was waved through in a second. The standard security procedure had been put into action in light of the attention. There were extra guards with dogs on patrol inside the gate. The bullet-proof shutters were down on the whole ground floor of the building. This was the first time that these security measures had been activated. Manbag welcomed the sight. He didn't really need any further motivation for what he was undertaking, but seeing the building look so vulnerable, and just knowing that he and his secret accomplices were responsible, made his sphincter twitch and he pulled into his parking space with a screech of tyres.

"So at this early stage, he seems like some kind of anonymous vigilante, documenting humanity's inertia."

"Well, that's a nice way of putting it but let's not forget that we do know his name, so he's hardly anonymous."

"Oh come on, can't we make the most of the idea, just for a while, at least until his face is everywhere and Sunday supplements start telling us everything about him that we don't need to know."

"Ok, let's stick with it…"

Manbag switched off the engine. He sat quietly, thinking about every possibility that the day might throw at him. It had to be the A game all the way. He couldn't afford to make any mistakes. He had to be at least two steps ahead of Workman at every moment, and he had to manipulate every single item of information that he shared with The Auxiliary. He got out of the car, straightened his new tie, put on his jacket, and set off inside to begin another day of tampering.

Who Is Percy Harrison?

Having postponed the usual morning meeting with Workman in favour of an early one-to-one with The Auxiliary, the Project Manager found himself in the lift, going up. There was his father again, staring back at him from the mirrored walls of the lift. What would he think of all this? Manbag imagined the old man's typically taciturn approach to everything wouldn't be interrupted, even by his son's involvement in something as big as what was happening. The lift stopped, the door pinged open, and Manbag set off down the long corridor towards the ultimate door.

There she was, sitting at her desk in readiness, looking as immaculate and phlegmatic as ever. He gave her a smile, which she did not return. He felt a brief moment of gladness at having withheld the "kind" from his regards.

'Please,' she said, gesturing for him to sit down.

'Good morning, Auxiliary,' he said.

'You sound very positive, I must say, given the circumstances.' She peered at him curiously.

'The circumstances are indeed grave, I admit, but I have every confidence in this operation, not to mention the ability of my people…'

'There's no need to perform for me, Antony,' she said. That was the first time she had ever called him by his first name. Dare he hope for a sudden injection of familiarity?

'I'm simply trying to reassure you, Auxiliary, that we are up to the challenge that has befallen us.'

She took off her glasses and leaned forward in her chair, intertwining her fingers on the desk. 'You know, I'll never understand you corporate types,' she said.

'Why's that?' he asked, anticipating an insult of some kind.

'Well, you chunter on about brainstorming blue-sky ideas and joined-up thinking, then you're saying the "challenge that has befallen us"!'

'I don't see your point, Auxiliary.'

'I'm telling you that your bullshit is unnecessary.'

'Bullshit?'

'I've heard it all before, but never with such variety, I have to say.'

'Thank you, Auxiliary.' Manbag smiled.

'You're thanking me for pointing out the extent of your bullshit?' she said.

'So it would seem, yes,' Manbag said. 'Aren't you a corporate type, yourself?'

She bellowed one second of laughter. Manbag jumped. She calmed herself but her face remained redolent, as if she would carry his ridiculous suggestion around with her for the rest of the day. Her voice became serious.

'This challenge that has befallen us,' she said, 'are you handling it?'

'I most certainly am, Auxiliary.'

'…and the photographer, he needs to be brought in.'

'Yes, I'm making those arrangements this morning. It will happen soon.'

'Be careful to distance yourself from whatever befalls him,' she said coldly.

'I will.'

'…and the investigation?'

'I have the perfect person in mind for the task,' Manbag said.

'I assume this person comes highly recommended.'

'He does indeed, Auxiliary. All inquiries will begin officially on Monday of next week, and of course, a comprehensive report will be produced. His name is Percy Harrison.'

'I suppose it's too early to shed any light on the origin of the leak, is it?'

'At this stage, yes, unfortunately.' He gave her a well-considered smile of optimism, the subtlety of which he had practised whilst shaving, after his breakfast smoothie.

She sighed and said, 'At this point, there seems little more for us to discuss.'

'I agree. It's always nice to come and visit, though,' Manbag said.

She sat back in her chair, removing her hands from the table and replacing her glasses astride her proud nose. She didn't reply to his banal remark. A moment of silence, which he eventually took as his cue to leave, forced him up onto his feet and back down the corridor towards the lift without further word from her highness. The lift doors closed and he descended back to his own level, where people were less strange.

'What did she say to you?' Workman asked, as he took his usual spot on the visitor's side of Manbag's desk. The Project Manager looked at him quizzically.

'You know hierarchical protocol strictly prohibits me from sharing any details of my visits to the higher ups,' he said sharply.

'Of course, Sir, forgive me,' Workman began, his face reddening slightly. 'Maybe the circumstances have got the better of me.'

'Let's put it down to your enthusiasm for the task at hand, shall we?' Manbag said, giving his assistant a magnanimous smile. 'Now, I assume our telephone team is still going strong?'

'Of course, Sir, they are fielding several calls as we speak.' Workman said.

'…and all with the established MO in place, I take it?' Manbag asked, even though he knew that the team would never deviate from his instructions.

'Absolutely, Sir, without a doubt,' replied Workman.

Manbag paused. On his desk, symmetrically situated, was a plain, black file. Workman had glanced at it several times since entering the room, curious as to its contents. Manbag lifted it and passed it across the desk.

'What we have, here, is a directive, which I wrote during the preliminary stages of the project, as a fail-safe. Your security clearance entitles you to read this, and indeed, to play a part in its implementation.'

Workman took the file and opened it carefully. The first page inside bore the title:

DISA INTERROGATION PROTOCOL & DAMAGE LIMITATION DIRECTIVE.

Manbag continued. 'You will see, if you turn to the final page, that there is a clause which stipulates that those participating in the employment of this protocol, and all the methods listed therein, will be held accountable for the efficacy of its use.'

Workman's face displayed a glimmer of pride in the elitism he thought his inclusion in this process afforded him.

'Now, turn to the contents page,' Manbag instructed.

Workman complied. He ran his finger down the list as he skimmed such titles as:

1) PREPARED LOCATION
2) SUBJECT APPREHENSION
3) FORCE BOUNDARIES
4) PLAUSIBLE DENIABILITY

He looked up from the file and cast a glance at Manbag, who raised his eyebrows. By including Workman in this, he was manoeuvring him into a position where the assistant would feel more powerful, more trusted by his boss, and perhaps slightly more vulnerable because of the vanity such an increase in stature would inevitably foster. Manbag knew how to control his staff and this was a classic tactic which he had utilised in the past with very beneficial results.

'You may take this back to your office and read it thoroughly before returning it to me after lunch. It goes without saying, that under no circumstances are copies of this file to be made,' Manbag said.

'I understand, Sir, absolutely, without question,' Workman replied, as he thumbed through the pages.

'The other pressing item which requires our attention is the official investigation,' Manbag said. 'I am to initiate whatever measures I see fit, so, with this in mind, I have organised an independent investigator, who will be here first thing on Monday morning.'

'…an independent investigator, Sir?' Workman seemed surprised.

'Yes, so as to eliminate as much possibility of internal politics impeding the proceedings,' Manbag added. 'Nobody likes being investigated, and this way, we'll hopefully avoid unnecessary tension in the office.'

'And who is this mysterious investigator, Sir?' Workman asked.

'His name is Percy Harrison.'

'Who is he?'

'He's not widely known outside of investigative circles, but he has, over the years, achieved notable successes under quite unfavourable circumstances,' Manbag replied.

'I see.'

'His references are superlative, and he comes to us also on the strength of numerous glowing recommendations.'

'Well, it'll be interesting to have a new person's methods with which to attack the problem, Sir,' Workman said.

'I'm glad to hear you say that, as you know, you and I are also under suspicion, until proven otherwise, of course.' Manbag winked at Workman. Never had such an informal gesture been cast across that desk. In fact, Workman was unsure how to take the sudden dip in formality. Manbag continued. 'I think that's it, for now. Take the directive and read it thoroughly. We'll reconvene here this afternoon and discuss the procedure for the interrogation of Mr. Mighty.'

Workman left, holding the directive close to his chest as he went through the door. Once Manbag was alone he sat back in his chair.

'Who is Percy Harrison?' he said to himself. 'They'll see…'

Anonymous Support

All preparation, every plan, each scheme, and several contingent episodes over the following day and a half couldn't possibly have gone better for Antony Manbag, Project Manager. He was experiencing a professional high, manipulating the ultimate private project - the covert destruction of DISA. Despite his thriving morale, not to mention the untold glee at being the one pulling the strings, he felt in need, once Wednesday evening arrived, to attend his E.F.A. meeting, where he hoped to escape momentarily and find some relief from the situation that, whilst thrilling him, was also tiring him.

There was no new business to discuss and for once there was no guest speaker. This paucity of typical group formalities meant that the floor was soon open to free discussion, and without any delay, the conversation turned to the DISA scandal. None of the members knew Manbag's profession, nor he theirs. He was free to listen to their opinions with no chance of a link being made.

'I've always thought it was a quick way out,' said one of the Carcinophobes. 'Perhaps that's what we could all do with…'

'Oh come on,' said one of the Holistics, 'you can't just look at it so simplistically. You have to look at the bigger picture.'

'…and what might that be?' said one of the Gersons, as she peeled a banana.

The Holistic continued. 'It's not just people jumping to their deaths because they suffer from mental health problems…'

'I don't think anyone thinks it is just that…' said the Gerson.

'What about our friend, here?' said the Holistic, motioning toward the Carcinophobe.

'Well,' began one of the Klismaphiliacs, shuffling uncomfortably on his chair, 'I think these people should come forward, don't you?'

'Which people?' said the Gerson.

'The people who leaked the documents,' said the Klismaphiliac.

'Do we really need to know who they are?' asked the Holistic.

'I just don't like the idea of them hiding in the dark, as if they're ashamed of what they've done. They should be more forward, more proud…'

Manbag chuckled. Everyone turned to him.

'Something amusing you?' asked the Klismaphiliac.

'Sorry,' Manbag said, raising his hands. 'I was just thinking that perhaps these people have no need for the limelight, perhaps they're just doing what they think is right.'

'And what about that young photographer?' asked one of the Carcinophobes. 'Everyone knows who he is…'

'Yes,' said Manbag, 'but that's because his photographs are excellent, shocking, but really fantastic. Really, though, they don't care who he is. Do you even know what he looks like?' They all shook their heads.

'But isn't giving him credit at the expense of those poor people?'

'You mean the "successful unfortunates"?' said one of the Klismaphiliacs.

'Call them whatever you want,' said the Gerson woman, having finished her banana, 'I think the fact that somebody is doing something is long overdue.'

'Why's that?' asked Manbag.

'Because I never liked the idea of The Contemplation Zone, not from the start,' she said. 'And all those people in the newspapers who are saying that we're all responsible because we ignored it…'

'It's true though, isn't it?' said the Holistic.

'No, it's not,' the Gerson replied. 'I never use the trains.'

'Are you kidding?' said one of the Klismaphiliacs, laughing at the Gerson's comment.

'What's wrong?' she said, taking umbrage.

'We're only responsible if we use the trains. Is that what you're saying?'

'I think so, yes.'

'So if you never use the trains, you should be able to ignore the fact that people who do use them ignore the fact that people are jumping to their deaths?'

'Erm…yes, I guess.'

'…and you therefore have no obligation to be outraged and fight against it?'

'All I said was that I wasn't responsible, I've been against it from the start…'

'So against it that you did what?'

'Well what did you do?'

'Nothing, just like everybody else!'

'Aha!'

'...but I'm not claiming to be free from responsibility, am I?'

Manbag intervened. 'I think that we're getting slightly off track, here.'

'Why?' asked the Klismaphiliac. 'Don't you think we all have some responsibility?'

Manbag gave a wan smile. 'Trust me,' he said, 'when it comes to dishing out blame, some of us definitely deserve more.'

'See!' said the Gerson.

There was a brief pause which she claimed childishly as some kind of victory.

'I have to say,' said one of the Holistics, 'I think these people have done something fantastic. They're toppling a cold, heartless system. They're bringing down executives who usually never fall from their ivory towers.'

'I agree,' said a different Gerson. There were murmurs of agreement from the group.

Manbag went home for his coffee-before-bedtime treat, replete with positivity. He had seen the light and it had turned him against his office, his profession and, most significantly, against his project. He was the one doing the toppling, bringing down the privileged and striking back against the system that had shaped him.

And Come They Did

Martha and Manbag had exchanged various carefully worded text messages throughout the course of the week. He found that he was extremely happy with her whole approach to the project, and thought, despite her age, she would be a valuable asset for him to have on any future team. Martha, with the help of Stylus, had continued to venture out each night on graffiti jaunts, spraying the city with anger. Jason had accompanied her on various other flyposting operations, also, which he had found both rewarding and uncomfortable. He knew what they were doing held great importance, but he found that seeing his work at such an enlarged size, spread across the city's bus stops, billboards and walls, evoked a nausea in him, not merely from the images' contents, but the excessive personalisation of the whole process, like he was flinging his muck around for everyone to see. If they were someone else's photographs, he would be more detached and capable of covering the city in death-laden imagery.

Much to his relief, the graphic nature of his work had taken all the attention away from him as a person. He had been able to avoid any unwanted contact with journalists by virtue of the fact that, even in such times of vacuously desperate celebrity, his being involved in a serious news story made him less interesting to the general public. The theme of mental health and its gross mismanagement wasn't sexy enough for the population to want to know who he was. As soon as his photographs had been published by the majority of newspapers, they became so common that it was almost as if the people themselves owned them. Looking at them was like singing Happy Birthday. Nobody cared where they came from and who had created them. Apart from in the most serious of all elitist publications, of course, whose contributing writers and editorial staff managed to scrape the entire barrel of possibilities; every cliché imaginable was trotted out in honour of what he had achieved with his camera, "what reality his eye had captured". On Tuesday and Wednesday of that first week, he had received various offers, invitations and requests from such niche market publications, that the money they were offering him seemed incredible. He couldn't believe that such money would be available when the magazines in question seemed so pointless that their readership must have been miniscule. He turned them all down, choosing to remain aloof.

Martha was now on her sixth consecutive night of graffiti and flyposting activities. She had spent much of Thursday at home, sleeping and trying to avoid her mother. When it came time to venture out into the night, she found herself more animated than the previous day. She couldn't remember the last time she had felt so enthusiastic to be part of something, let alone something such as this. Her appreciation of their project was growing with each passing moment she spent in the field, spray paint in hand, under the watchful eye of Stylus. It was very cold and they had wrapped up with extra layers under their black covert operation clothing.

When Jason explained to them just how many offers of lucrative employment he had had, they remained cynical until he actually started mentioning a few of the accompanying numbers.

'Why don't you just say yes?' Stylus said from his position atop an electricity box.

'Why would I do that?' Jason asked him, managing to sound realistically horrified by the very suggestion.

'The way I see it,' Stylus said, 'is that you could risk the people closest to you calling you a sell-out; sucking Satan's cock for extra zeros…'

'Nicely put,' Jason said, his forehead wrinkling.

'…or you could just think, fuck it! I'm gonna milk the opportunity for all it's worth. If they want to throw money away, why shouldn't it land in my pocket?' Stylus said all of this whilst spraying a wall with what might look, to the untrained eye, like erratic movements; short bursts of colour executed rapidly and simply to deface a free, unprotected surface. Jason stood below, holding his rolled-up posters which they were yet to get around to.

'He's right,' Martha said. She was standing next to Stylus, holding on to his belt as he leaned out over the street to spray. 'Why shouldn't you get something for all of this?' she added.

'It wouldn't feel right, that's why,' Jason said.

'Do you think you'd be the first photographer to make money out of death? Besides, you're already doing that with your funeral business,' Martha said.

'That's different,' Jason said.

'How is it different?' she asked. 'You're taking photos of dead people who are not in a position to refuse, and getting paid for it.'

'That's true, but we're not trying to expose the origins of the funeral photography industry,' he said.

'Maybe we should!'

'Thank you, I'm familiar with your opinion of my work.' He paused as he watched Stylus at work. 'There is a big difference between photographing dead people peacefully at rest, surrounded by loved ones, and capturing the last moments of hopeless people before they end up mangled and dismembered,' he said.

'Of course there is, yes,' Martha said, 'but you could take this ridiculous money and do something worthwhile with it.'

'What, you mean invest it?'

'Invest it?! Yeah, right, that's so worthwhile. Would investing it sensibly eventually make you feel any better about taking it in the first place?'

'No, I guess not,' Jason said.

'Exactly, you could give it away; you could use it to help the very people you've been photographing, so they never end up in front of your camera in the Contemplation Zone.' Stylus could feel Martha's grip on his belt tightening as she spoke. Jason went quiet. The prospect of being able to do more, of making an even greater contribution, appealed to him.

'I could do that, I suppose,' he said.

'Just take the fucking money!' Stylus said.

'Yeah,' Martha added.

'Ok, ok,' Jason said. 'Maybe we should be a bit quieter,' he added as he saw a light go on across the street. 'Jesus, it's cold! If you don't need me, I think I'll go back to that 24-hour place we passed and get us some tea.'

'Ok,' Martha said. 'Don't be long, we can't hang around.'

Jason smiled at her bossiness, as he set off in search of hot beverages.

'He really should consider what we said,' Stylus said to Martha, once Jason had departed.

'Yeah, you're right,' she said, 'but I can see why he would feel uncomfortable, too.'

'But if he does something positive with the money, something that reflects on the cause and benefits those who've suffered, or even helps to prevent further suffering…'

'Yes, I know. Maybe he'll do it,' she said. Yanking his belt, she pulled him back towards her and into a safer position. They stood for a moment and surveyed the multi-coloured freshness of their creation. Stylus tilted his head into the various positions he used to assess his own work. He exhaled mild disappointment as he clutched a spray can and began adding more finishing touches. She watched him work in silent admiration.

By the time it was finished and they had packed up their stuff, Jason had been gone for almost an hour.

'Hey, what happened to the tea, anyway,' Stylus asked.

'I was just wondering about that,' Martha said. 'He should've been back ages ago. The place was only around the corner.'

They picked up their belongings and set off in search of the missing photographer. When they arrived at the 24-hour place, the night shift assistant said he had served tea to someone fitting Jason's description, that he had drunk it, and then asked for two more to go. That was about an hour ago and nobody had been in since. Martha and

Stylus set off back in the direction they had come, as per the night shift assistant's account of how Jason had left. The street was very quiet and so cold. Stylus considered suggesting he wait inside with the stuff, while Martha looked for Jason, but then thought better of it.

'Look!' Martha said. They crossed the road and came across what appeared to be the rolled-up posters Jason had been carrying, just dumped on the pavement. Next to them lay two take-away cups, as if dropped.

'I guess he thought better of it, and went home instead!' Stylus said.

'No,' Martha said. 'He wouldn't do that. Something's wrong! He wouldn't just dump the posters like that, and he certainly wouldn't waste tea!'

'Well, he's not here, is he?' Stylus said. 'Let's go back to the café and you can call him.' They picked up the posters and went back.

Rules Are Meant To Be Broken

…and suddenly, he was awake. He kicked his legs to no avail. His torso and arms would have flailed about desperately, but for the bindings which tied him to a chair in the centre of a room. His emotional reaction to his regained consciousness was stymied by the thoroughness of his captors. From beneath the gag, his mouth could only emit a fraction of the noise which emanated from within. What use were his screams if they went unheard? Through whatever material was covering his head, he could see a faint light which seemed to be moving, perhaps a single, suspended bulb which had been knocked by whoever had left him in the chair, bound, gagged, and unsure of what to expect. Manbag had said, "They will come for you". The words had scared him at the time but now he was starting to panic. Was he going to be one of those people who just disappeared after somehow becoming involved with a shady clandestine organisation so tenuously linked, probably unprovably so, to a government agency? The light finally stopped swaying. He tried doing what people do in Hollywood movies. What could he hear, what could he smell? What was the temperature of the room? Would he make it through this and be able to give discernible, salient details to whichever gruff yet empathic investigator was assigned to ask sensitively worded yet probing questions?

He had learnt this ability for distraction through his work as a funeral photographer. Of course, at several of the funerals he attended in his official capacity, he would encounter suffering and genuine bereavement. Capturing that emotion was what he was paid to do and sometimes it took its toll on his own emotions. He wasn't an automaton. Anyway, back to the matter at hand. He couldn't hear anything, there were no obviously recognisable smells, and the temperature was quite low. He had been tied expertly and the tightness of his bindings made it almost impossible for him to move even an inch. His right foot was starting to cramp. He needed to pee. A full bladder was another inconvenience that one learnt to control whilst working as a funeral photographer. Were they watching him, aware of his consciousness, yet letting him stew alone? They had to take him after he'd drunk all that tea, didn't they!? He supposed that if someone appeared with a bucket and a toilet roll, it would be some indication of their intentions and how long they might be going to keep him, assuming that toilet necessities featured in what was probably a very limited amount of compassion.

He heard a distant noise, like the muffled closing of big industrial doors. He thought about movies again, and how there never seemed to be a shortage of abandoned industrial buildings in situations like the one in which he found himself. *If they don't come soon, I'm just gonna have to pee. At least it'll be warm for a few minutes.* Suddenly, he started thinking about all the things he had never asked Manbag when they had last met in the soup kitchen. He really had no idea what was going to happen. Why hadn't he demanded more information? There was that sound again – big industrial doors. Did that tell him anything?

As he tried to visualise closing his urethra, he felt grateful that there was no water in the room, no dripping sounds typical of abandoned buildings. He realised that his brain was tricking him into thinking of things that would make him want to pee – *subconscious self-sabotage, really!!?* His bindings meant that he was unable to cross his legs. He would have to try to imagine. *But, what good is mind over matter if my mind is working against me?* He felt a faint rumbling sensation beneath him, the underground train, perhaps? *Well, if it isn't, what else could it be?* Within the sound he could identify staccato variations, like train tracks beneath heavy wheels.

He was unsure how long he had been in the room. He tried revolving his foot and clenching his toes to get rid of the cramp. Big industrial doors again. There was a draught coming in from somewhere. He wondered why draughts always seemed to coincide with full bladders. His was getting so desperately close to emptying itself now, that he couldn't sit still on the chair. The limited facility for movement permitted the smallest amount of jiggling, but unfortunately, not nearly enough to prolong his bladder's fullness. Finally, and somewhat ecstatically, he let go. Despite his predicament, it was a comforting release. He wondered where his urine would appear first. The area around the left pocket of his jeans darkened with wetness. The smell was strong, as if from dehydration. The underside of his left thigh was warmed as the wetness spread. He thought about movies again and the number of times he'd seen a pool of urine form between the feet of an unfortunate victim of bullying, a berated child, or an incontinent relative. As his flow ceased, there was a loud metallic clunk, the same loud noise of industrial doors, but this time it was just in front of him. *Now they arrive, just after I've pissed myself!*

He could hear the doors open. The draught suddenly increased;

it was almost a breeze. He worried about the speed of its cooling effect on the wet warmth of his trousers. The doors closed again and the draught decreased. Through the material which covered his head, he saw the movement of shadows and he sensed that somebody was very close to him. The hood was suddenly pulled from his head and the light hit his eyes. He readjusted with a blinking squint as his gag was lowered. By the time he could open his eyes normally, he couldn't see anybody. The bulb above his head produced a circle of light, in the centre of which he was sitting, on a stone floor. Beyond the circle it was pitch black.

'Who's there?' he said. Nobody answered. 'I know you're there,' he added, 'or did that hood magically lift itself?' There was no response. 'I don't really see the point of bringing me here if you're not going to talk to me!'

'We will talk to you, Mr. Mighty,' said a voice from the darkness beyond the circle.

'Your attempt at intimidation won't work,' Jason said, lying through his teeth. '...and, in case you're wondering, I drank a lot of tea before, that's all!'

'I wasn't wondering, but thank you. All information is useful,' said the voice.

Jason sat up as straight as his restraints would allow, as if proud of his wet patch. After a moment's silence, the voice continued, but this time from behind.

'I have to say, your photos are very impressive,' said the voice from the darkness.

'Well now,' Jason began, 'I think you really have to take some of the credit, don't you?'

'Why's that?' said the voice, this time from the left. The speaker was circling him. He tried his utmost to refuse to be intimidated, but he did find it sinister.

'You provided such an impressive location, didn't you?' Jason answered.

'The Contemplation Zone?'

'Exactly, it would be difficult to go wrong, really.'

'Come now, Mr. Mighty, let's not allow that to diminish the beauty of your achievement,' the voice said.

'Those images are beautiful to you?' Jason said.

'Depending on one's definition of beauty, wouldn't you say?' said the voice.

'Have you any idea how many laws you've broken, taking and keeping me like this?' Jason asked.

From the right now, the voice replied, 'Have you any idea how little I care about that?'

'I'm starting to realise,' Jason answered. His trousers had started to cool, the process bringing with it a hint of shame at being in this position, not to mention the creeping suggestion of the greater vulnerability caused by being in pissed pants. He would undoubtedly be a less dignified injured subject now that the evidence of his empty bladder had discoloured his crotch.

'I suppose I shouldn't expect too much compassion from a bunch of suicide peddlers!' he said.

'Nice!' replied the voice. 'That's a new one.'

'I'm sure people are going to be calling you all kinds of things in the coming months,' Jason said.

'No doubt!'

'But I'm sure, also, that you don't care!'

There was no reply to this. The person he was speaking to didn't even care enough to comment. It seemed as though the phrase "no comment" was one of the most common utterances, issuing forth from the mouths of countless shameless individuals in the public eye. This person couldn't even be bothered with that. Jason considered his status.

His wet patch was really starting to cool down.

'I suppose I don't really need to explain why you're here,' the voice said, again from behind him.

'You like tying up young men?' Jason said.

'When they're a threat to all that we've worked for, yes.'

'Whereas kidnapping and imprisonment pose no threat whatsoever to your status.'

The voice laughed. 'We can do whatever we want, don't you realise that? How do you think something like the Contemplation Zone was approved in the first place?'

'Oh, I don't know,' Jason began. 'Maybe because we live in a soulless system which thrives on indifference and dissociation, where empathy is long-gone and the compulsive oversharing of nothing fuels our time.'

'That's a very bleak outlook,' the voice said.

'You're calling ME bleak!' Jason said. '…and the Contemplation Zone is a fucking holiday camp, I suppose!'

'For some of us, perhaps,' the voice said.

'How can you possibly justify that opinion?' Jason asked.

'Do I have to?' the voice replied, now from the front. 'Isn't the justification of my opinions pointless at this juncture?'

'Unfortunately for this entire country, nothing you do is pointless, and what you do seems to be perfectly executed.'

'Thank you,' said the voice, 'but, perhaps, not quite perfect or we wouldn't be here right now, would we?'

'Are you going to tell me what you want from me?' Jason's voice had taken on a confrontational edge which seemed risky, considering his position. His control was dwindling and his intended sense of caution was giving way to something approaching an inner fearlessness which surprised him.

'I would've thought it was obvious,' said the voice.

'Well you could at least do me the courtesy!'

'Alright, let's keep this as civilised as possible, shall we?' The voice had stopped moving. 'How is it that a large collection of your photographs suddenly finds its way into every publication and onto every television screen in the country, not to mention onto the lips of every armchair philosopher who works in broadcasting, in the very same week that highly sensitive information pertaining to DISA activities is leaked?'

'Happy coincidence?' Jason said.

'Happy for whom?' the voice asked.

'Anyone who isn't a total fuckhead, I should imagine!' Jason said. 'A select few, you might say.'

'That's really quite amusing,' said the voice.

'Thank you!' Jason replied.

'Oh, don't misunderstand me. I wasn't referring to your comment.'

'No?'

'No, I was referring to the stupid risk you're taking, insulting a man who has you tied to a chair in a darkened room,' the voice said.

'Is that right?' Jason said, not backing down.

'It certainly is, especially as you have no idea who else is in here with us!'

Quickly, from the blackness of the room, a man rushed forward and pressed a cattle prod into Jason's stomach. The electricity filled his body; he writhed and thrust in agony. In a couple of seconds, it was over and the man disappeared. Jason recovered momentarily from the shock; at least enough to see that he was once again the sole inhabitant of his circle of light. He was speechless. It had been so fast he had barely seen his attacker. He'd expected an interrogation; probing questions designed to weaken him, but not to be shocked like an animal.

'What the fuck are you doing?!' he finally managed to squeeze out of his dry mouth.

'Making a point,' the voice said. 'You're here to answer questions, and you will do so with the utmost respect for the authority I hold over you.'

'You hold no authority over me!' Jason replied.

'Is that right?' the voice said.

There was a moment of silence broken only by Jason's futile attempt at shuffling himself into a different position. The cramp was setting in. His stomach hurt where the cattle prod had made contact.

The voice continued. 'So, you were about to tell me about your happy coincidence, or your collusion, however you care to describe it.'

'I don't imagine I'll be telling you anything,' Jason replied. He assumed naively that his interrogator wouldn't go much further, should his subject prove unwilling. The cattle prod had been a shock, but how much more would they risk, really?

'That's what they all say,' replied the voice.

'Don't tell me you're an old hand at this,' said Jason, trying to convey some sort of professional insult.

'Does it really matter at this point?' the voice said from behind.

'Well, I would like to feel that I warranted an interrogator with at least a modicum of expertise, and that I hadn't been fobbed off on any old covert henchman who knew barely nothing more than how to keep his mouth shut,' Jason said. 'Perhaps if I could see your face, then maybe we could connect.'

'I'm afraid that is out of the question.'

'Ah, come on, it can't be that bad!' Jason replied.

'That's not what I meant.'

'Don't feel bad, at least your mother must love you!' Jason said.

'My mother is no concern of yours!'

'She must be very proud!'

The cattle prod appeared again from the darkness. Its bearer came and went again in a flash, striking more or less the exact same spot on Jason's stomach. He cried out, shaking in the chair, the bindings digging into his flesh. His head dropped, his chin rested on his chest. He breathed deeply as he spied the moist patch in his crotch. He regained his faculties.

'Was that really necessary?' he asked, short of breath.

'The necessities are for me to decide,' the voice said.

'I assume that it's not you who keeps appearing out of the dark,'

Jason said.

'I can say with conviction that our little gathering here will prove more effective for me and less traumatic for you if you make less assumptions,' the voice said.

'Fewer,' Jason replied.

'What?'

'Fewer assumptions, not less; it's a countable noun,' Jason said.

'Is that right?' asked the voice. '...and what about "slap", that's countable, isn't it?'

From behind, Jason felt a heavy hand slap him across the side of the head.

'One, two, three,' the voice said angrily, counting the slaps as they were administered. Jason was getting angry now, but he managed to restrain himself, preventing an outburst.

The voice continued. 'How about we forget the grammar lesson and focus on why we're here?'

Jason didn't answer.

'What do you know about DISA documents and their sudden appearance in various newspaper offices?'

Jason remained quiet.

'How did your photos get passed to so many places?'

Jason was tight-lipped.

'What is your connection to DISA? Who is responsible for circulating your photos with these documents?'

'One, two, three!' Jason said.

'Excuse me?' said the voice.

'Slap me again, I'll still have nothing to say!' Jason said.

The cattle prod appeared again from the darkness. He managed to get a quick glimpse of the perpetrator before it made contact. Once, twice, three times in the stomach. He managed to keep his eyes open long enough to see a hooded man, faceless yet big and muscly, like a rugby player. He withdrew the cattle prod, punched Jason in the face and then disappeared. Silence from the darkness was broken only in the circle of light by Jason's heavy breathing. He tasted blood; the metallic flavour from a cut lip. He was really angry now. He spat out blood into the darkness.

'All this for some photographs,' he managed to say. He spat again. The blood trickled down his chin.

'It's not just some photographs, though, is it?' the voice said.

'To me it is,' Jason said.

'You expect me to believe that?'

'You can believe whatever the fuck you want!'

There was another pause as he caught his breath. The pauses were difficult. He didn't know what to expect, but he could really see how serious they were, now.

'I'm sorry,' the voice said amenably. 'I didn't offer you a drink. You must be thirsty.'

From the darkness, two hooded men dashed at Jason, grabbing him from either side and pushing his chair backwards so he fell into a horizontal position with a thud. One of the men rested his foot under Jason's head, keeping it from banging the stone floor. A third hooded man was suddenly upon him. He threw a small towel over Jason's face, and then the water came; cold water, cold as ice, through the towel, into his nose, his mouth, flooding his throat, into his lungs; he shook violently, his bindings digging in further with each thrust; five seconds, ten seconds, and then it stopped. His chair was lifted and the towel removed. He coughed explosively, gasping desperately. His nose burned. He blinked the water from his glistening eyes and saw nothing but the now familiar circle of light.

He was dumbfounded, though he couldn't quite make a sound which would in any way express it. Waterboarded, for taking photographs. As his breathing subsided; the intensity of the situation losing barely an iota of its immediacy, he could finally see just how serious a predicament he was in, not because of what he had done, but because of how far they were willing to go to extract what they wanted. Up until that point, he had tried to mask his nervousness with blasé off-handedness, but waterboarding! *Fuck me*, he thought. *DISA motherfuckers!*

'Now, I'm guessing,' said the voice, 'that you're not that keen to repeat that, as I'm sure it's very painful.'

'Untie me, give me the water, and I'll show you!' Jason said. Where was this coming from? He couldn't quite believe the things he was saying. If he were watching this happening to someone else, he'd be thinking, "Woooh, legend!" but it wasn't someone else, it was him, and he was fighting back in a way he would never have imagined himself capable of, despite being at a distinct disadvantage.

'I'm sorry, you're obviously not taking this seriously,' the voice said.

'I'm taking it just as seriously as you are, trust me!' he replied.

'Then isn't it about time to answer the questions, and all this stops?'

'I can't give you the answers you're looking for,' Jason said.

'Can't or won't?'

'Can't AND won't!'

'That's a shame.'

The water came again – the same procedure. This time it was more aggressive; five seconds, ten seconds, fifteen…more shaking, spluttering, burning, and it stopped. The chair went back up, the towel and his tormentors disappeared. His clothes were soaked; the wet patch in his crotch was no longer an issue. He couldn't breathe. There was water in his ears this time. He coughed and they popped, one after the other. He was alone again in his circle.

There was obviously no question of them recognising the fact that the photographs were his, his intellectual property, to do with as he pleased. At no point since he had first woken up tied to the chair, since he had first inhabited his circle of light, had he considered telling them what they wanted to know. He had taken the photographs; in his own way, he had started this whole thing, his eye, his lens, his presence in the Contemplation Zone; all of it had formed the catalyst. They had come this far and arrived where, exactly? He was being tortured by men hiding in the darkness. He was in agony, his lip was busted, he was bleeding, he had been shocked and almost drowned, and he had pissed himself. There was no reason to back down now.

This intimate gathering of close enemies remained inactive; for several minutes Jason was left untouched, unharmed and free from further questioning. Was that it? Was it over? Had he defeated them? It seemed unlikely, he thought, then again, after electricity and water, where else could they go, thumbscrews? These and other thoughts merged in his mind like incomplete, overlapping ideas. Martha, he thought, what about Martha? *I just disappeared.* He suddenly considered Manbag's role in it all. Was he there, in the darkness? How far would he let them go? Perhaps they were acting on his orders; maybe the electricity and water were his idea. Panic rose within him as he wondered about the gravity of his situation. Perhaps he was being set up for something; a patsy for a government agency manipulator who'd used the photographs for his own end, and was now dropping Jason in the shit. No, it's too Hollywood, he thought, surely. *Focus on what we're doing here, trust Manbag, I have to trust Manbag. What else have I got?*

The silence quickly became intimidating. He was suddenly blasted with intense white light from crime scene spotlights. His eyes darted around the room, trying to find a spot on which to focus in order to avoid afterimages. He didn't want to close his eyes, despite the intensity. He remained like that for what seemed like a long time. He couldn't have said how long, exactly, but then he was losing all sense of time. He really had no idea how long he had been there, since he'd pissed himself just before his captors had arrived. Was Martha looking for him? Did he have a funeral to go to? He couldn't be sure of anything, only the lights. He started to imagine himself as if seen from above, in his circle, now highly illuminated, sodden, shocked and soiled – a pathetic prisoner.

The lights went off, even the bulb above his head. He was now in absolute darkness. Instead of light, he was now blasted with death metal music. The volume was incredible. He'd never heard anything so loud. He didn't recognise the song but he could feel its vibrations. It finished and then started again, and then again, and so on. During what he thought was the fifth playing of the same song, he felt a heavy blow to the face, like he was being punched. He shouted out, his expletive-filled pain and anger lost in the music, and then again, another punch. He felt his lip split further. He could taste more blood. He screamed in abject indignation. 'You fucking bastards! You can't do this to me, I'm just a photographer!'

The music stopped. The lights came back on; the same intense brightness as before. He spat more blood out as he writhed in the chair. The voice spoke from beyond the spotlights. 'We can do whatever we want, Jason. You already know this. The more you resist, the more you receive. How much can you take?'

'How much can you take, you cunt!?' Jason replied loudly. 'It's very easy, hiding in the darkness!'

'It is, yes, you're right. But why shouldn't this be easy for us, we're not the ones being questioned?'

'I'm not being questioned either, I'm being tortured!'

'All part of it…'

'Part of what…' He spat again; the blood seemed to be coagulating quickly in the dryness of his mouth. '…part of your plan to extract information which I just don't have?'

The lights went off. The music started.

This time, it was reggaeton; loud, pulsing, irritatingly present reggaeton. He felt its force in his chest, pounding and grinding him down. He had to raise himself above it, try to imagine he was listening to something else, look for an escape from its dominant rhythm. He was punched again, this time in the stomach, hard, two, three, four times; flying fists from the darkness pummelled his ribs, his gasps lost again in the music. He found himself screaming out repeatedly, his throat ached with the effort as it competed against the musical onslaught. He stopped as the dryness got the better of him. The same song, again and again; this time he didn't count how many times. What was the point?

The punches had landed in the tender spot left by the cattle prod. Everything hurt, everything landed not only physically, but as an insult, extreme in its force and its weakening of his tolerance. But he would not talk. Their goal was too important. He couldn't sit on his arse, surrounded by his cache of photographs, proud of them yet never capitalising on their potential, but he could be forced into a chair, tied, beaten, shocked and almost drowned for the sake of his seditious images, for the idea that somebody had to be capable of provoking change. He would never have considered himself that type of person, until now, until he found himself willing to take whatever they threw at him, to bear the brunt and resist, bloody-mindedly, until some sort of end was forced upon him.

The music was really starting to get to him. It was what he often heard young people blasting from their phones; shit music, distorted and thrust in the faces of submissive train passengers by socially inept teens. He wondered about the many situations in which one was forced to listen to music, and why it was never music one would choose.

The punching had ceased. The music stopped. The lights came on. He screwed his eyes up tightly. The brightness of the lamps was making him sweat and his forehead felt hot, despite having been doused in ice cold water only moments earlier.

'I have nothing to tell you, so what are you gonna do, kill me!?'

'I could, believe me,' said the voice, 'but it would be a shame to have to go to such lengths, wouldn't it?'

'Is killing me here really any different from killing me in The

Contemplation Zone?' Jason asked.

'You don't actually think we kill people, do you?' the voice replied.

'Oh, yes, that's right,' Jason said, 'you just make it easier for them to kill themselves, my mistake. It's a "humane push" before a jump!'

'I like that,' said the voice. 'Do you mind if I use it?'

'I'm not really in a position to disagree, now am I?' Jason replied. 'Do you think I could have some water?'

'I would've thought you'd had enough already,' the voice said mockingly.

Jason didn't reply.

'Tell me what I want to know and you can have as much water as you like,' the voice said promisingly.

'I can't tell you what you want to know, because I don't know anything!' Jason said forcefully.

'Do you really expect me to believe that?'

'Seriously, I don't give a fuck at this point!'

'You see, I think you DO give a fuck, and I think you have a very strong connection to this whole operation.'

'What operation?'

'There are no coincidences…'

'Oh, God…'

'…this is not a coincidence, and you are part of it.'

'Part of what, what are you talking about?'

'You are working with whoever is behind this leak, they are using your photos and you are in cahoots.'

'In cahoots!' Jason laughed and then frowned with pain. 'Have you considered, for even one second, that even though it seems to you as if there might be a connection, really it *is* just a coincidence, however much you like to believe that there's no such thing?'

'I believe it because it's true, you're up to your neck in it…'

Jason let out a deep sigh.

'…you're up to your neck in it, and I'm going to prove it!'

The owner of the voice was wavering in his control and Jason could hear the frustration in its tone. From behind his chair, the hood was placed back over his head. The spotlights were turned off. The death metal came back.

The absolute darkness with the addition of the hood made him feel more vulnerable. The music was so loud. He sat there, during several plays of the same song as before, anticipating more punches or shocks, expecting something new, but nothing physical was forthcoming. They had left him there to imagine the worst. He tried not to. The song continued on repeat. He imagined they had left the room. Why would they put themselves through this? Perhaps they'd expected him to crack before now, and they have to rethink their strategy, he thought. He had surprised himself. He had never thought of himself as a resilient person. His life had never forced upon him any condition in which a sense of his own stamina might have been gleaned. For that, he had to be grateful; grateful that he was learning things about himself, that such things were surprising and not obvious due to painful experience. And just as that thought presented itself, the punches returned, faster, harder, the face, the stomach; it was all too much. He was fighting a losing battle against the threat of unconsciousness.

Part Four

Rip It Up And Start Again

Since their daughter's suicide, the obstructed man and his wife had not eaten breakfast together. She had faced a struggle in dragging herself out of bed every morning, and usually appeared downstairs long after any suggestion of sharing the breakfast table had passed. He knew that she was awake, lying in bed with her eyes wide open yet unfocused. He couldn't quite manage to shake off the idea that she was simply waiting for him to be finished before surfacing, in an attempt to avoid any interaction that might conceivably occur due to proximity and the need to eat. Consequently, he had grown accustomed to eating his porridge alone. She didn't even complain about the smell of his occasional kippers anymore. There was no tension between them, indeed nothing that would qualify as an atmosphere as such. Their existence was too empty for that. They spoke only when necessary. He would say more, if only she gave him some sign that whatever words he chose would not be spoken in vain. He often blamed himself for not trying hard enough to get through to her, but then he could also see that she was incapable of forming any sense of a new normality. That was their life now – childless former parents who shared a space and nothing else.

He kept his eye on the clock as he ate. The early morning wind blowing outside accompanied its ticking. He looked at the shirt he had ironed the previous evening. Today would be the first day he'd worn a suit since the funeral. He'd been reminded of this as he was ironing, and would be reminded of it again later as he was tying his tie. He finished the last spoonful of porridge and thought of the disgusted expression his daughter had pulled the first time he had made her try it for her breakfast. She was just a little girl and couldn't believe anyone would want to eat "that stodge" for breakfast. That girl didn't exist anymore. Neither did the woman she had become.

He opened the door to the bedroom and glanced across at his wife, who was, as he had suspected, awake and staring at the ceiling. She exhaled, possibly in recognition of his presence, probably with no real awareness of anything. He slipped off his pyjamas and stood naked before the bed. She didn't move a muscle. He caught sight of himself in the mirror - a full-frontal reflection which made him feel his age.

When he returned from the bathroom after his shower, she was still in the same position. He had no problem assuming she could stay like that all day. What more was there for her do, he thought? Tea bread? She had her crossword puzzles and enough silence to sink her spirit. It seemed as if that was all she required. He would buy her a new puzzle book while he was out.

'I'll be going soon,' he said. She exhaled again. Over the weekend he had attempted to explain his part in the proceedings; she had actually responded with something approaching an opinion, at least she had expressed misgivings over what he had told her. When he had pressed her for more; seeing a glimmer of light in the surprising fact that she was suddenly using words that weren't purely related to practical domestic necessities, she simply responded, 'I can't.'

Without mentioning too much about Manbag's plan, he had tried to convince her that what he was doing was for their daughter and for them, as grieving parents; for their sake he had to do something before they disappeared completely and they ceased to exist as a family unit. She had cried at the mention of their daughter; the idea that their dead child had any connection to anything that was happening in the present tense was overwhelming. She had begged him to have nothing more to do with any it, perhaps out of fear that he too might suddenly be gone, irretrievably lost.

He had lost control. She was finally talking yet it was only to try to prevent him from doing what his convictions were telling him was vitally important. He had raised his voice, implored her to see reason, to consider why he must act, with the two of them in mind; with the three of them, he'd said, after correcting himself. She'd looked at him with the broken eyes of grief that she hadn't cast in his direction for weeks, beseeching him not to use their child as a means of justifying his actions. He'd picked up her crossword book and ripped it up whilst shouting that there had to be more they could do, that they couldn't fill the empty hole in their lives with gardening and puzzles. They needed more; something with a tangible link to what they had lost. Something had to be done.

They were the last words they had exchanged. Now, the morning after, she was staring at the ceiling in her customary fashion. He was dressing, preparing himself. Before leaving the room, he kissed her forehead. She looked at him briefly but made no final attempt to dissuade him. In his eyes she could see his determination. He left.

He decided against listening to the radio during his car journey. He probably should've made the effort to listen a little, considering his destination, but he felt a better use of his time was the reflection of his current position. He thought of his daughter. She had always been present in his thoughts since the moment she had ceased to be present in his life. He and his wife had been thrust into that dreaded position which no parent should ever have to face. If he simply sat back and let this opportunity pass them by, he would never be able to forgive himself. He owed it to the three of them. He owed it to himself.

Having been waved through the barriers on arrival, he parked his car and submitted to a thorough frisking on entering the building. He was then ushered towards a very polite receptionist who gave him a white-toothed smile.

'Good morning, Sir, how may we help you this fine Monday morning?' she asked the obstructed man.

'I have an appointment with Antony Manbag at nine o'clock,' he replied.

'Very good, Sir. May I take your name, please?'

'My name,' replied the obstructed man, 'of course, yes. My name is Percy Harrison.'

Grilled Manbag

'He'll be ok, trust me,' is how Manbag had replied to Martha's frantic messages. He couldn't say much more than that, as the intention was to avoid the oversharing of information. What she doesn't know can't be used against her, is how he thought of it. In fact, this had been one of his key considerations throughout. They each knew enough, that's how it had to be. Of course, she had no idea where Jason was, but she had realised quickly after his disappearance that it wasn't as simple as just going home because he had been bored. Something had happened to him, she knew that much. She hadn't been absolutely convinced by Manbag's sanguine responses and accepted, very reluctantly, that her help wasn't needed. Consequently, when it came to the arranged Sunday morning meeting at the soup kitchen, she was combative and less than cordial. She had had to take Manbag's word that he would locate the missing photographer, and against her better judgement, she had had to stay away from Jason's house and not make any further attempt to contact him. All this had been done in accordance with Manbag's instructions and she had consequently spent most of the weekend in a bad mood, frustrated that she had no choice but to comply, and also worrying about Jason's welfare.

As per the previous Sunday's brief, extreme dress-down attire was compulsory. This was more than acceptable to Martha as she saw it as an opportunity to annoy her mother, who had turned white with consternation at the sight of her daughter's apparel. Timing her departure perfectly to coincide with the typical pre-church preparations, she appeared next to her mother at the bottom of the stairs. The surly teen checked her reflection (oldest, most ripped jeans, her father's old decorating jumper which she had rescued from the rubbish bags a couple of years previously and usually only wore around the house during her period) in the hall mirror to be sure that her hair was just about as wildly messy as she could possibly make it, slipped her feet into a pair of tatty boots which her mother hated, grabbed her parka and her green hat and said, 'Goodbye, Mother!'

As she was closing the door behind her, she heard her mother shout out, 'You know boys aren't interested in girls who look like that.'

'…and girls who look like this aren't interested in what you think!' she shouted back.

Manbag was actually happy to see her when she arrived at the soup kitchen. However, considering how much effort he had gone to with his blending-in disguise, he was a little put out that she walked straight to his table and sat down opposite him.

'You saw me immediately?' he asked.

'Is that a joke?' she said, sighing as she looked around.

'Don't you want anything to eat?' he said. 'Nice outfit, by the way.'

'You should speak to my mother,' she said. 'So how does this work?'

'How does what work?' he replied.

'This,' she said, nodding at their surroundings. 'Are we safe here?

Surely you must be under suspicion, too. What if someone is watching you?'

Manbag gave her a reassuring look with an accompanying gesture demonstrating his faith in the efficacy of his disguise.

'Oh, my God, I spotted you in a second!' she said. 'I need something to eat.' She stood.

'I'll keep the table,' he replied.

Martha lined up behind two middle-aged men who seemed to be debating something with which she assumed only they were familiar. When her turn arrived, she gave the obstructed man a warm smile, which he returned with a subtle wink in the spirit of their escapade. She thanked him for the stew and dumplings with a giggle at the size of the portion he'd given her.

'I think he thinks I need fattening up,' she said to Manbag when she sat back down.

'I'm sure he just misses having somebody young to care about,' Manbag replied.

Martha gave him a wan smile. 'Just because you're being sensitive, doesn't mean I'm not pissed off,' she said, '…waiting all this time to find out what's going on!'

'Ok, let's just remain calm, shall we?' Manbag said, looking around them. 'Eat your food, and I'll tell you what you want to know.'

'I want to know where Jason is, and I want to know what happened. Why did he just disappear?' She picked up her spoon and started eating.

'You eat stew with a spoon?' Manbag said in a bemused tone.

'Yes, I do. Don't tell me my cutlery choice is jeopardising the mission!'

There was that tone again, he thought. No wonder her mother gets annoyed. He decided a smile was his best option. She chose a grimace in return.

The obstructed man appeared at their table. 'I've brought you some coffee,' he said.

'Thanks,' Martha said, nodding at Manbag, 'but I don't think he's brought his equipment with him.'

Manbag's mouth opened but he was cut short by the obstructed man who raised a hand between the two of them.

'At these tables,' he said calmly, 'we speak in a civilised manner, or we don't speak at all.'

'But…' Manbag said.

'Shh!' the obstructed man said. Manbag shut up. Martha grinned across the table at him. He frowned back at her.

'Martha,' said the obstructed man, 'be nice.' He placed the cups of coffee on their table and returned to his duties. She raised her eyebrows, which Manbag took as a cue to begin.

'First of all,' he began dulcetly, 'let me say that the extent of your individual roles in our little operation is known only by you and by me. Jason has no knowledge of the part played by our esteemed waiter here,' the obstructed man glanced across at them, 'who in turn knows nothing of your activities, and so on. For the safety of each of you, I have withheld certain facts so as to limit any perceptible culpability, should things go…'

'Tits up?' Martha said.

'A vital part of project management is a comprehensive

contingency plan.' He gave her a superior nod in recognition of this fact.

'You love saying stuff like that, don't you?' she said with her mouth full of stew.

'I won't apologise for loving what I do,' he said.

'...despite conspiring to destroy the whole thing!' she said. She smiled, this time in what appeared to be a genuine manner. He sipped his coffee.

'Now, Jason and I spoke last Sunday, at this very table, about an unfortunate inevitability.'

'Please,' she said, 'we're in a soup kitchen, supposedly incognito. Let's speak in plain English.'

'Ok,' he said. 'I knew that once Jason's photos went public, they would be everywhere very quickly, mainly thanks to you, of course. Anyway, this meant that certain questions would need to be asked, he would be interrogated because of the leaked documents.'

'Interrogated?' Martha said. '...by your department?'

'Yes, well, this is where I have to take responsibility,' Manbag said. 'You see, I thought that if I gave my assistant the task, it would keep him in a favourable position, because really he would be acting above his station and, well, the problem is that he took too much initiative and acted without my final all-clear.'

'What do you mean, exactly?' Martha asked. She looked worried.

'It seems that the power I gave him went to his head, brought something out of him that I just hadn't predicted.'

'What happened?'

'They took him from where you said, where you texted me from, after you'd found his posters. They took him to one of our safe locations, and…tortured him.'

'What?!'

'They tortured him. It seems that my assistant took it upon himself to hire a discreet team of, shall we say, "experts", who don't like it when people don't talk!'

'Is he ok?'

'He will be. I have him in a safe place, with a doctor and security, and really, don't worry, he'll be ok. He just needs time to recover.'

'But we have to go to the police!' Martha said.

'No, we can't do that.'

'Why not, so your colleagues can get away with more and more crazy shit?!'

'We can't do anything, right now. We have to be patient.'

'Patient?!'

'I'm afraid so. That's all I can say right now. When the time is right, I'll let you know where he is, and you can visit him, ok?'

She looked at him angrily and put her spoon down loudly. A few heads turned in their direction.

'What choice do I have?'

'You always have a choice, Martha,' Manbag replied. 'But right now, I urge you not to act, but rather to remain calm and trust me when I say that Jason will be fine. He's safe, and he's being looked after.'

'And your assistant, what happens to him?' she asked with a sneer.

'He is being dealt with, don't worry about that?' Manbag replied.

She exhaled. 'What does that mean? He'll be arrested, or you'll just slap his wrist?'

'It means he's being dealt with, as I said,' Manbag replied seriously.

'How do I know that's what's really happening? Maybe you're just trying to cover your arse!'

'Welcome to project management,' he said. They both fell silent for a brief moment. She filled her mouth with stew. After a moment she looked at Manbag.

'Did they see us, Stylus and me? Jason was with us. They must've seen us doing the graffiti!' she said.

'Don't worry about that,' Manbag said. 'Even if they did, there's no reason to make a connection. Besides, Jason was their target. He could've been just chatting to two graffiti artists, for all they know.'

She didn't look too pleased by the possibility, but there was nothing to be done about it.

As he spooned out food into bowls clutched in hungry hands, the obstructed man looked across at Manbag and Martha and wondered about the nature of their discussion.

Back at the table, Martha sighed. '…and Jason agreed to all this?' she said.

'Not exactly,' Manbag replied. 'But really, what could he do? He had to play the part, he wanted us to use his photographs; how could we not have used them? They're so provocative. He understood the importance of not speaking. He saw that he would be the obvious choice when it came to where to look for information. I told him they would want to speak to him, and he knew they were coming for him. What he didn't know, unfortunately, is that they would do it in that way; that their approach would be covert.'

'They were never going to knock on his door,' Martha said.

'Exactly,' Manbag said. 'That's not the world in which we are operating, and it certainly isn't the world in which they function best. They do what they do behind closed doors, out of earshot.'

Martha looked more worried. She put down her spoon and looked at Manbag.

'Look,' he continued gently, 'what we're doing is very dangerous. I have a pretty good idea what might happen to me, were I to be exposed, but, that's not going to happen. Nothing is going to happen to you or the rest of us, Jason is quite safe now, trust me. I'm very good at what I do.'

'I don't doubt that,' she said, 'I guess I'm just worried about the extent people will go to…'

'That's a good thing,' Manbag interrupted. 'It's vitally important that we don't underestimate anyone. When we stop worrying, we are at our most vulnerable. By all means, keep worrying, but don't let it stop you from believing that we can do this.'

She smiled at him. 'And as soon as it's possible, we can visit him?' she asked.

'Yes,' Manbag replied.

For the next hour or so, the Project Manager and the teenager spoke secretively, in hushed tones, as many a hungry person came and went, and the movement around their table continued. She explained to him in great detail her comings and goings and her nocturnal graffiti jaunts with her humble yet grumpy assistant, Stylus. He complimented her on everything she had done, asked about her blog, the videos and the hacks, he asked her if Stylus was more than just a friend, to which she responded with a puff of air before telling him to mind his own business. By the time the obstructed man came to clear their table, they had all but concluded their business for the day. It had been an unusually busy Sunday session, with the highest number of people fed during the obstructed man's tenure as willing server. He cleared their bowls away and then returned with a smile. He pulled up a chair and joined them for a well-earned break. Manbag explained Jason's situation as concisely as possible. The obstructed man listened with a pained expression on his face and proceeded to make similar noises of protest to those made by Martha, although he quickly saw that Manbag's intention had in fact been admirable and correct.

As the soup kitchen began to empty, once serving had ceased, they soon found themselves alone but for the other serving staff. It was at this point that Manbag indicated subtly that Martha should be making her way out, as he needed to talk with the obstructed man about something.

'Ah, more bloody secrets,' she said sardonically.

'I'm afraid so,' Manbag replied. 'But...'

'Yes, I know,' she interrupted, 'it's for my own good!' She stood and placed a hand on the obstructed man's shoulder as he raised himself slightly. 'Lovely food,' she said. 'This place needs someone like you.' They exchanged smiles as she put on her hat. She turned to Manbag. 'I'll keep my phone on,' she said.

'Ok,' he replied.

She left them alone.

'So,' Manbag began with a smile, 'Percy Harrison, your first day back at work tomorrow...'

The obstructed man smiled. 'That's right,' he said.

'Are you nervous?' Manbag asked.

'You know, I thought I would be, but no. I've been thinking about it a lot. I've read the notes about your staff members that you gave me last Sunday; nice touch, by the way, putting them under the stew bowl for me to find when I was clearing up.'

'Jason was very amused by that,' Manbag said.

The obstructed man sighed. 'Is he really alright?' he asked.

'He will be. I won't lie to you; they gave him a really good going over. By the time I got there and managed to stop it, I thought, for a second, that I might've been too late.'

'Really, it was that bad?' the obstructed man said.

'I have two trusted men,' Manbag said. 'I've had them on call for the last week, and I took them with me to Jason's location. We had to take control of the situation by force…'

'I know, it's probably better if I don't know,' said the obstructed man.

Manbag smiled. 'Let's just say, for our own peace of mind, that he's alive and in the best medical hands I could find. He'll recover and eventually he will appreciate that what he did was very brave and integral to the cause.'

'Well we certainly appreciate it.'

'We do indeed,' Manbag said.

They spoke for half an hour until the obstructed man had to return to his duties. It was almost closing time and the Project Manager made his excuses and left them to it. It was time to return to the Manbag abode, where it would soon be time for coffee.

His return home had taken some careful consideration. He didn't want to be seen driving whilst in his soup kitchen disguise, so he had walked there wearing his normal clothes with the disguise in an old rucksack. En route to their scheduled meeting, he had made a stop in a shopping centre toilet, where he had made his transformation into soup kitchen patron.

En route back home, he made another stop in a different public toilet, so as to avoid suspicion, where he proceeded to transform himself back into his suburban Sunday casuals, and back into the guise of Project Manager. Having stuffed his old clothes back into the rucksack then flushed the toilet without having used it, also to avoid suspicion, he exited the stall and found himself standing in front of the mirror. He saw his father again. There was disapproval in his reflection. He dropped his rucksack and ran back into the stall where he threw up into the toilet. He had known all along that Jason would be in serious danger, perhaps not to such an extent, but he had known, from the moment they had agreed that they should use the photographs, on the day he had visited Jason's house and been grilled by Martha and the obstructed man. Since that moment he had known that Jason could be used as bait, but it was only whilst he was busy in his dinner party preparation and during the dinner itself, as he had been formulating his plan, that he had seen the potential concatenations laid out before him. He had been privy, on occasion, to Workman's fast temper, usually by being silent and observing his assistant's behaviour in his treatment of other people in the department. He had overheard how he spoke about people. In short, Manbag had deduced that there was, lurking inside his assistant, a seething, which was perhaps closer to the surface than its bearer might care to admit. The cold professionalism, which Manbag himself exhibited, seemed colder still in Workman. The Project Manager knew that Workman's opportunity to impress, his fierce loyalty to the DISA cause, the seething which he worked so hard to supress: all of it, when combined with a sudden career boost and his signing on the DISA INTERROGATION PROTOCOL & DAMAGE LIMITATION DIRECTIVE dotted line, would inevitably lead to one victory; that of Workman's vanity.

    Wiping his mouth with the back of his hand, he spat the last remnant of disapproval into the toilet bowl. As he retrieved his bag, he looked once more into the mirror, but this time he saw no paternal ghost; just a man with a burden, who had destroyed a colleague and almost killed a friend, a man who refused to feel guilty for fulfilling the demands of the project. He leaned forward, and with his hands flat against the mirror to take his weight, he flexed until his back cracked. Newly aligned and freshly attired, he left the toilet and began his walk home.

Not Just Another Obstructed Man Monday

Present and correct, as agreed, at nine o'clock in reception, the obstructed man was greeted by Antony Manbag. The two men shook hands firmly.

'Percy Harrison, welcome to DISA HQ,' said Manbag affably.

'A pleasure,' replied the obstructed man with an officious tone.

'I thought we might take a little walk together so you can get a feel for the place,' Manbag said. 'By the way, here is your ID badge; it carries sufficient clearance for your needs.' He gestured away from the reception and they set off. The obstructed man noticed his photo on the badge as he took it.

'Well, I guess it's official, then,' he said quietly, as they walked.

'So it would seem,' Manbag replied. There was an air of excitement between the two of them. This next stage was to be an exercise in misdirection. Their activities had to look like a legitimate internal investigation, which, as they had seen so often in countless news reports, would continue beyond the scope of people's interest so that when it was eventually announced that the whole process had been a fruitless waste of time and money, nobody would care enough to really make a fuss. They wanted it to become one of those stories that television news viewers would talk through whilst waiting for something more sensationalist. People's thumbs wouldn't hover over the headline out of curiosity before scrolling down.

They passed various open-plan offices and walked the length of numerous corridors, during which the obstructed man's overall impression of his surroundings was that everything seemed to be made from glass. It was very light; everyone could see everything, almost as if the whole place were transparent. Of course, they were currently touring the lower level, where the staff was constantly monitored.

'I would like to start by talking to Workman,' said the obstructed man. 'I have to say, I was surprised when I read your message.'

'It has been deemed more appropriate to keep him in our midst, whilst the investigation continues,' Manbag said.

'Rather than risking getting rid of him, you mean?' the obstructed man said.

'Not my decision,' Manbag said, 'but it does make sense, from the point of view of damage limitation.'

'But he's not likely to act against the department, is he? I thought you said he was fiercely loyal.'

'He is, as far as I can tell,' Manbag said. 'But we would be unwise to assume anything.'

'I see. Is he here?' asked the obstructed man.

'Of course he is,' said Manbag. 'We wanted him where we could always be sure of controlling him. His conscientiousness will be fervid in light of his recent deviation. He is expecting you.'

They took a lift up a few floors, Manbag looked for his father's reflection, but it wasn't there. He saw only himself and the obstructed man, starting his first day as Percy Harrison, Consultant Investigator.

The lift opened onto a more intimate form of interior design. There was less glass, more real walls, and everything looked more expensively decorated and arranged for executive staff.

There were several extremely well-dressed people moving about efficiently in what could almost be choreographed precision. Seeing this place took the obstructed man back to his days as a full-time investigator. He had been in so many offices, in so many buildings, populated by attractive professionals, vying for esteem with covert aggression. This one, at first glance, seemed to be a hub of activity; its inhabitants glided about the place dynamically and productively.

'Everyone, a moment, please!' Manbag said loudly. The whole place ground to a halt. All eyes were turned to the two of them. 'May I introduce Mr. Percy Harrison. We are very fortunate to have him here as a Consultant Investigator. I'm sure that we are all aware of the seriousness of our current situation. He is here to make sure nothing obstructs the successful completion of the investigation, and I ask you all to accommodate him in any way. What he wants, he gets.'

The obstructed man bowed his head as a murmur of greetings filled the room.

'Ok, thank you, let's get back to it, shall we?' Manbag said. He ushered the obstructed man across to his office and they entered.

Inside, the obstructed man inspected his new surroundings. The office of Antony Manbag, Project Manager, was more or less as he had imagined. He was glad to note the absence of antique enema paraphernalia. They sat at the desk and a moment later, a Manbag minion arrived with coffee, and then left hurriedly.

'So this is where it all happens, is it?' the obstructed man asked.

'You could say that; I suppose…'

'But maybe it's better if we don't, considering what we're talking about,' said the obstructed man.

Manbag smiled as he poured the coffee. The obstructed man noticed the emptiness of Manbag's desk. The lack of papers or files would suggest a lack of work, but he knew that couldn't be the case. Manbag stirred his coffee and readjusted the pen holder on the corner of his desk by a millimetre before leaning back in his chair.

'I thought we could take a moment to clarify a few things before we talk to Workman,' he said.

'As you wish.'

Having signed an addendum, which amended and modified his DISA contract, at the time of agreeing to participate in the interrogation of Jason Mighty, Workman, in light of his conduct, had been subjected to the consequences of the addendum's "curtailment clause", by which he was held under house arrest and obligated to comply with any counter-measure necessary as a result of what the literature called "injudicious interrogation". His conduct had seriously jeopardised the already severely weakened public opinion of the department. In order to protect themselves from any further weakening as a result of gross misconduct, the addendum allowed DISA to detain the culprit, debrief him, and ultimately protect him and themselves from the temptations of outside influence.

In the subterranean depths of the DISA building was a purpose-built facility, which in the brief duration of the project had not been used. Workman's situation was the first to merit such a necessity. The facility included five sparsely furnished cells, plus an interrogation suite, as Manbag chose to call it. In addition, there were audio-visual monitoring facilities which recorded everything from the moment the "subject" became a resident. Since Workman's instalment after Jason's interrogation, his stay had been recorded and later perused by Manbag at various points over the weekend. He had noted the subject's apparent ease with his new surroundings, and got the impression that he was fully aware of the consequences of his actions and was simply riding them out, perhaps under the impression that his unwavering resolve would ensure his full reinstatement and his slate wiped clean. Manbag had set his trusted men the task of debriefing Workman. He considered it better for him to keep his distance, to leave Workman in unfamiliar hands. He didn't want to make it easy for him in any way. Of course, Workman had insisted on seeing Manbag, but the trusted men were to deny any such request.

'…and you can keep him here like this?' the obstructed man asked.

'I can indeed,' Manbag said, 'and I have signed paperwork which confirms it.'

They had both finished their coffee. Manbag noticed how comfortable the obstructed man looked in his suit and he approved of his choice of a blue tie for entering a hostile environment as a Consultant

Investigator. They made calculated small talk which could be overheard as they journeyed down into the DISA depths. The obstructed man wanted to tell Manbag about his wife's disapproval of his being there, working again. He wished he could explain, at least try to arrive at something resembling an explanation of how doing this was so important to him. He assumed, after the little information he had shared during their dinner at Manbag's house, that his intentions would be clear, that any father suddenly thrust into a position of actually being able to do something to make a difference would do the same. In spite of their brief association, the obstructed man, Martha, Jason and Manbag all seemed to intuit a lot, indeed, more than in any previous circumstance that their differing lives had thrown at them. Suffice it to say, Manbag simply didn't need the obstructed man to go into great detail, at least at that point it just wasn't necessary. Today he was Percy Harrison, Consultant Investigator, and that was all anybody needed to know. He would be the one demanding information.

Once seated in the observation area, on the other side of a one-way mirror, Manbag and the obstructed man spent half an hour listening to Manbag's trusted men as they debriefed Workman.

Excerpt from transcript entitled, "Curtailment Clause Debriefing" session 4, Monday 9.50am:

    Subject: How many more times do you need to hear it?

    Trusted Man 1:   Until there are no variations.

    Subject: I'm not lying to you, what would be the point?

Trusted Man 1:   Our job is not to determine whether you're lying.

Subject: What is it, then? As far as I can see, you're interrogating me about how I interrogated Mighty, presumably while he is off somewhere, free from scrutiny.

Trusted Man 2:   What makes you think that?

Subject: Look! I was getting somewhere; he was about to break...

Trusted Man 1:   You were about to kill him! How was he supposed to tell you anything then?

Subject: I was given responsibilities. I was given control.

Trusted Man 2:   Now we're back to control. That really is the key word.

Subject: Is this your idea of control? Punishing the good guy!

Trusted Man 1:   You see this as a punishment?

Subject: Being trapped in here with you two, going over and over and over what you already know? No!

Pause

Trusted Man 2:   What you fail to realise is that this is being done for your own good.

Subject: And it benefits the department in no way whatsoever?

Trusted Man 2:   Of course it does. The department doesn't do anything from which it can't benefit in some way. But this is more for your protection. You have just been through a highly emotional situation, and you need to be 100% sure that the events of Thursday night are crystal clear.

Subject: What makes you think it was so emotional?

Trusted Man 1: You nearly killed a man. You tortured him.

Subject: And?

Pause

Trusted Man 1: Are you saying that there was no emotion involved?

Subject: For him there was, undoubtedly, but I was just doing my job. I did what I had been entrusted to do, I don't know how many times you people have to hear this before it sinks in.

Trusted Man 2: And you stand by that statement, that you were just doing what you were entrusted to do?

Subject: Unequivocally!

Trusted Man 1: Now you see why you are still here.

Subject: Do I?

Trusted Man 1: If Mighty goes to the police and makes a formal complaint, are you really going to give them the I-was-just-following-orders speech? That's the extent of your originality?

Subject: You know as well as I do; nobody does anything original these days. I got every technique I used on Mighty from an app I downloaded.

Trusted Man 2: Really, a torture app?

Subject: Don't knock it. Perhaps if you'd thought ahead like I did, we might have been finished in here by now.

The obstructed man found the whole process fascinating, but he also grew impatient with Workman's arrogance. It certainly wasn't difficult to see what type of person they were dealing with. He imagined that DISA and its connected organisations, those responsible for the Contemplation Zone, were only populated by such callous individuals. He felt that Workman epitomised the worst kind of corporate automaton; one that had the power to override its programming and act of its own volition. He thought about Jason and how these trusted men of Manbag's seemed to be accusing Workman of almost killing him. Until that point he had not imagined the necessity for further convincing of the worth of their plan, but here it sat, on the other side of a one-way mirror, preening and spouting. He turned to Manbag and they shared a silent look of affirmation.

Manbag found himself wondering about the obstructed man's reaction to finally being there. They had prepared, and Percy Harrison, Consultant Investigator, was certainly not lacking in professional experience. However, to suddenly be granted access to the secret offices of those responsible for the creation and implementation of the facility which had taken the life of his daughter; to be rubbing shoulders with the very team who had made the Contemplation Zone happen - that would certainly be a challenge even to the resilient man sitting next to him. Undeniably, she had jumped; having made the decision to do so, she had leapt to her death, but her father was now sitting in the heart of the headquarters whose staff, figuratively speaking, had put the gun in her hand. What that felt like, Manbag could only imagine.

The obstructed man found himself wondering about the scope of Manbag's planning abilities, and the significance of the facility in which they were ensconced. The Project Manager had envisaged the potential necessity for interrogating his own staff about their misconduct, and not only had he conceived the "Curtailment Clause" for the purposes of mitigation, but he had also custom built a state of the art detention facility to cater to the demands of such an unsavoury task. It all provided yet more proof that their trust in Manbag's skill was entirely justified.

When it was finally time for the obstructed man to enter the interrogation room, he was ready to go back to work. Manbag's trusted men left the room as he entered. Workman looked curiously at his new visitor.

'Good morning, Mr. Workman. My name is Percy Harrison,' said the obstructed man, taking a seat opposite the detainee.

'Percy Harrison,' Workman said, 'well, we've been expecting you. Apparently, an external investigator is necessary.' He smiled; his face lighting up with sarcastic effusiveness.

The obstructed man sat nonchalantly, his legs crossed, resting his clasped hands on his plumpish stomach.

'Did you leak those documents?' he asked.

'I'm sorry, what?!' Workman replied, nonplussed.

'Did you leak those documents?'

'You think I'm the whistle-blower!?'

'Aren't you?'

'This is ridiculous!'

'It's a perfectly simple question, Mr. Workman, and one that you still haven't answered.'

'No, I didn't leak the bloody documents. Why would you think I did?'

'Why would I not think that?'

'What?'

'I'm just trying to ascertain the facts based on the available information as it is laid before me,' said the obstructed man.

'Is that right?' Workman said aggressively. '…and what facts lead you to think that I am the culprit?'

'I'm struggling to comprehend why, in the course of what should be a routine interrogation, an entrusted, protocol-savvy participant goes so far over the top in employing aberrant information-extraction methods, that he has to be prised away from his subject and ends up here, talking to me.'

'Ah, so that's your approach, is it?'

'What approach is that?' asked the obstructed man.

'I must have been using excessive methods to cover up my guilt. I wanted to deflect any suspicion under which I may have fallen by assuming the role of staunch employee.'

'Am I right?' asked the obstructed man.

Workman didn't answer.

The obstructed man paused in his questioning; leaning forward, he brushed the surface of the table with his fingertips, as if removing dust. He looked around the room.

'You see, the thing is,' he began, 'you're about the most obvious choice at the moment.'

Workman sighed deeply. His forehead exuded frustration.

'I mean, look at it from my point of view, for just a moment,' the obstructed man said. 'You're in the inner circle; you have very few restrictions when it comes to access to documentation, and, well, your performance on Thursday night reeks of overkill. Let's be honest, if there were ever a case of someone trying too hard…'

'You listen to me, old man!'

The obstructed man appeared totally unruffled by Workman's outburst.

'I have given my life to this project, to DISA, to Antony Manbag. I fought for the cause against a pretentious photographer who still, and this can't be ignored, STILL hasn't explained the "coincidental" appearance of his photographs in the same week as leaked documents find their way into every journalist's inbox!'

'The lack of an explanation from Mr. Mighty does nothing to deflect the attention away from you,' said the obstructed man.

'Ahhh, for FU…' Workman managed to catch hold of himself.

'Ooh, should I be careful? Am I in danger of receiving the cattle prod?' the obstructed man said. Workman's face changed, like a switch had been flipped. He stared right inside the obstructed man, as if in search of the inner-most depths, where the most exploitable vulnerabilities lay.

'And there it is,' said the obstructed man.

'There's what?' Workman asked him.

'There is the change, the look which tells me one simple fact.'

'You really do love a slow build-up, don't you?'

'The one simple fact being that you did what you did to Jason Mighty because you enjoyed it. You knew it wasn't necessary, but you just wanted to, that's it. Tell me I'm wrong.'

'I imagine you stopped listening to people who tell you you're wrong years ago.'

'So you really did just want to do it, didn't you?' The obstructed man said.

'Whether I *wanted* to do it is irrelevant. I still believe Jason Mighty is connected; I did what I did because I believed he had information. While we're in here, going through this pointless sham…'

'Oh, so official DISA protocol is nothing more than a sham, is it?'

'…while we're wasting time here, he could be…'

'What, leaving the country? He's a funeral photographer; he has a simple life, by all accounts.'

'Which means what, exactly? He can't be involved because his life is unremarkable?'

'No less remarkable than yours, Mr. Workman.'

'Look! This is just stupid. I have the other two guys in here telling me I have to remember every tiny detail so nothing is left to chance, in case Mighty files a report and I have to create a solid "account" which contradicts his version of events. And, then there's you…'

'Don't forget I'm external…'

'That's right; you're separate from all of this…'

'I am, yes, and I'm going to complete the task I've been assigned…'

'And you think I'm your best bet, do you?'

'If I didn't consider all possibilities, I'd be remiss.'

'…and we wouldn't want that, would we? What, with us being so used to efficient, cost-effective investigations.'

The obstructed man smiled at Workman. 'I'm sure you're about ready for a break,' he said, standing up. 'Thank you, this has been most illuminating.'

'If you say so,' Workman replied as the obstructed man left him.

Returning to Manbag in the observation room, the obstructed man retook his seat. 'Consider that the first official piece of time wasting,' he said.

Manbag looked at him and they both smiled. The two of them then looked through at Workman, sitting alone. Throughout the course of his first day, the obstructed man interviewed several members of Manbag's team. DISA's elite were brought in to a special office space which Manbag had arranged for the purpose of such one-to-ones, and during their brief sessions they were asked open questions, leading questions, loaded questions; they were guided expertly in various contradictory directions until they left feeling somewhat unsure of exactly what had happened, but sure of their liking for the newest addition to the office. The obstructed man had pulled out all the stops and his charm offensive had left him feeling invigorated. After the last interviewee had closed the door, he sank back in the chair and exhaled the first emission of satisfaction in what felt like a very long time.

After a successful final meeting with Manbag, during which they summarised, foresaw and planned, he tried not to let the negative anticipation of returning home to his wife and their stagnant domesticity ruin the high which had accompanied his departure from the DISA headquarters. His arrival was met with an approximation of the typical torpor but somehow diminished, as if a change had been made. To his surprise, his wife greeted him in the hallway as he entered the house. He gave her the customary perfunctory kiss on the cheek, which unless he was mistaken, she actually received with a pause, meaning she was in the direct vicinity of his lips for longer than either of them could have conceivably remembered. It was a momentary hint at closeness, brief in length but certainly not insignificant. He welcomed it and a sudden suggestion of warmth between the two of them presented itself as he followed her into the kitchen in silence. This sensation was enhanced by the heat of the room and the realisation that she had been cooking for his return. He was suddenly transported back to older, happier times, when he would arrive home to find his daughter doing homework at the kitchen table, when she would look up and smile at him as he kissed the top of her head. That could never happen again, and he had begun an attempt at acceptance, which he had started to assume he would continue to do alone, but now, as he looked at his wife, as she approached him and picked some fluff off the lapel of his jacket, he saw hope, which he dared to imagine was not doomed.

As they sat and ate, she asked him timidly, as if recovering the ability to speak, about his day at DISA. He revelled in the opportunity to discuss everything with her, to emphasise the importance of his being there, of his decision to come out of retirement. He didn't mention their daughter as it hardly seemed necessary. The empty chair at the table meant her absence was always present. They ate more than they had done for weeks. He found himself sharing the entire story of his association with Jason, Martha and Manbag. It was the first time he had spoken to his wife about visiting the Contemplation Zone. She winced at its mention, but rather than commenting, she continued listening with interest. He thought he saw the beginnings of a smile at the corners of her mouth as he told her about playing Jason's camera assistant, about

Martha's sharp tongue, and about Manbag's antique enema syringe. She explained that she was worried about his involvement in the project, but that she could see, having thought a great deal about it, why he was doing it. She told him that she admired his strength, and that if anyone was going to fight for what was right, she knew he was. He smiled at her and retrieved the new crossword book he had bought on the way home. His smile widened as she took it and put it in a drawer. He told her to go and sit down as he would wash up and make them a cup of tea. As he heard the sound of the television, he started running the water and clearing the table; he was feeling strangely pleasant, perhaps even happy.

Auxiliary Hospitality And The Minister For Avoidance

When the obstructed man arrived at his new office for his second day within the DISA walls, he found Antony Manbag already there waiting for him. They exchanged greetings. The Project Manager watched as his Consultant Investigator removed his coat, scarf and gloves before advancing upon him and laying a lunch box upon the desk.

'What's in there?' Manbag asked.

'Leftovers.' The obstructed man smiled in addition to his response. He had woken up refreshed having spent the previous evening making more progress in communicating with his wife than he would have imagined possible. However, what really fuelled his smile was the fact that she had awoken with him, they had breakfasted together and, after promising him she would accompany him to the soup kitchen that coming Sunday, she had packed his lunch as he had been preparing to leave. There, before him and Manbag, lay a Tupperware symbol of change, of fresh hope for long-awaited improvement.

There was a knock at the door and a Manbag minion appeared bearing coffee, which was quickly served before said minion disappeared again.

'Do people just follow you around with coffee?' the obstructed man asked.

'If I want them to,' Manbag replied with faux superciliousness.

They laughed as the obstructed man took his seat behind the desk where, as Manbag observed, he seemed to belong, despite its being only his second day. They proceeded to sip their coffee as they discussed the important meeting scheduled for later in the morning. In addition, Manbag explained the intricacies of the "curtailment clause" that Workman had signed, which included a statute of limitations whereby the detainee would be released after seven days of debriefing detainment. Of course, this meant that if Jason Mighty were to suddenly decide to make a statement to the police, Workman would be out and available, which might lead to journalists having yet more mud to sling around. They were careful not to mention any of this out loud, for fear of being overheard, but from the look they shared across the desk, Manbag could see that the obstructed man was aware of the ramifications of Workman's release. Once free from containment, he would be a conveniently available scapegoat. Instead of denying everything, as was their standard procedure, they would throw Workman under the bus, or the train, as it were, and finally, for the first time ever, they would say YES, THIS HAPPENED!

The hour of the important meeting was upon them, and Manbag, rather than influence his new colleague's opinion in any way, decided to withhold any information about the Auxiliary, in order to observe what he hoped would be a true and honest reaction to their first meeting.

In the lift, Manbag looked for his father's reflection in the mirrored walls. All he saw were two serious men: A Project Manager and a Consultant Investigator, ascending with purpose and determination.

Again, he wondered what the obstructed man usually saw when he looked in the mirror and hoped that he was able to see at least some of the positivity he generated.

The doors opened and they set off down the corridor towards the ultimate door. As they drew closer, they saw that the Auxiliary was seated at her desk. She gave no reply to their greetings, but gestured to the waiting area without raising her focus from her work. Manbag and the obstructed man sat down and waited patiently in silence for her to finish. With thirty seconds to spare before the start of the meeting, she stood, drawing the obstructed man's attention away from the painting behind her desk. Both men stood and moved closer.

'Auxiliary, may I introduce Percy Harrison, our Consultant Investigator?' Manbag said.

The obstructed man extended a hand. The Auxiliary came around from behind her desk and with a smile, the likes of which Manbag had never seen issue from her face, she shook hands warmly.

'Welcome, Mr. Harrison,' she said, the tone of her voice leaving Manbag nonplussed and slightly jealous. He had always tried so hard. Nevertheless, his confusion soon dissipated as she gestured politely towards the ultimate door and asked them to follow her. His face lit up with something approaching childlike excitement at finally being given the chance to see beyond its allure and perhaps meet the true higher-ups. The Auxiliary grasped the door handle firmly and slowly it began its heavy movement. Light from whatever lay beyond fell upon their faces as they followed the Auxiliary through to the other side.

The first thing that Manbag noticed on entering was the floor to ceiling window which ran the length of the far side of the sizeable room.

Adjacent, a long table accommodated three women and three men, each of them pallidly staid; conservative in their attire and economical about the face. Manbag recognised them all from various preliminary meetings and progress updates, which had always been held in other locations. However, the obstructed man was at a loss, as the gentleman sitting at the head of the table, The Minister for Avoidance, was the only person he recognised. As they approached the table, The Auxiliary introduced the other two men and two of the women as four chief executives, each one from a hospital participating in the Contemplation Zone project. The remaining woman was a legal representative from the Ministry of Health.

'…and of course, last but not least, The Minister for Avoidance,' said The Auxiliary. He smiled smugly as the obstructed man bowed his head in deference to them all. The names she had just said sounded strangely ordinary and forgettable to the obstructed man, as if, considering what they were responsible for, he had expected outlandish corporate monsters. In fact, he was almost disappointed by their ordinariness. He and Manbag took seats next to the executives as The Auxiliary took the head of the table, opposite the Minister for Avoidance, whose smile had transformed into something approaching playful, perhaps even flirtatious interest in her.

'Ladies and gentlemen,' she continued. 'Antony Manbag you all know, of course, but please let me present Percy Harrison, our Consultant Investigator.' The obstructed man smiled passively as all eyes were cast in his direction.

'Percy Harrison,' said the Minister, 'the Percy Harrison who brought down the POVAK group in 2001?'

'Guilty!' said the obstructed man, smiling.

'...and cracked the insider networks at Bishop's?' added the Minister.

'...as charged!' the obstructed man added, slightly embarrassed.

'Well,' the Minster continued, 'I feel considerably more comfortable now, I must say. Of course, I'm only here as a favour to Jennifer,' he said, winking inappropriately at The Auxiliary. 'I don't usually get my hands dirty, you see.'

'Well, quite,' said the obstructed man, playing along with the Minister's fatuity. 'What more could a man with your job possibly do?' There was a pregnant pause, after which, the Minister for Avoidance was the first to laugh. The others followed suit, albeit with far less gusto. Manbag, who was opposite the obstructed man, conveyed a glow of approval as his new friend smiled unassumingly at those around him.

The Auxiliary cleared her throat authoritatively, thereby closing the brief window of frivolity. All heads turned in her direction. Manbag, the obstructed man and The Minister for Avoidance all gave their own impressions of being calm and collected. The legal representative from the Ministry of Health was wearing her finest poker face, whereas the hospital executives were showing obvious signs of being ill at ease, each of them holding the firm belief that he or she had the most to lose, given their current situation.

'Well,' The Auxiliary began, 'for the purpose of continuity, and for the benefit of Mr. Harrison, I would ask that we go around the table for some concise updates.' She gestured to Manbag, who was first up.

'Good morning. As you know, I am Antony Manbag, Project Manager; currently providing assistance to Mr. Harrison, as well as continuing as normally as possible with everyday operations.' He looked to his left with a professional smile.

'Janet Smith, CEO from St. Bart's Hospital; currently struggling to understand how all this is possible.'

'Ian Kendall, CEO from The Royal; currently worried about paying my children's school fees.'

'Alison Brown, Legal Representative for The Ministry of Health; currently looking to bolster my career, whilst giving the questionable impression of ethical concern.'

'The Minister for Avoidance, of course. You all know what my department does; it hardly seems necessary to go into it again.'

'Brian Walker, CEO from Christ's Hospital; currently considering a career change.

'Joan Baxter, CEO from Murgatroyd General; currently in the process of cancelling the staff Christmas party.'

'Percy Harrison, Consultant Investigator; currently accepting the gracious assistance of Mr. Manbag.' He could have said more, indeed, he could easily have lost his temper, jumped up and berated the whole foul lot of them for what they had done to the mental healthcare system, for how they had manipulated and schemed; how they had basically ruined an already crippled rail network. But the image of his daughter, despite their providing the means of her death, kept his bum on his chair. The sweetness of her voice; the sense of the sound which he had struggled to maintain, despite trying to convince himself that he could never lose something so precious: that sweetness had returned as a result of the previous day's breakthrough with his wife. Ever so slightly it had crept back out of the deepest recesses of his grief to the extent that the idea of it, if not the actual sound itself, was subtly audible. He feared that giving in to his anger would mean losing it again, perhaps for good. As a child she had always hated raised voices, and would resort to silence, often not speaking to her parents for days after they had argued. This is what kept him still. This is what allowed him to control his behaviour when confronted by a boardroom of people who really deserved to be shouted at more than anyone he had ever met in his entire life.

'Thank you,' said The Auxiliary. 'Now, we've a lot to get through, so I suggest we…'

'Really, Jennifer,' said The Minister, receiving a less than favourable look from The Auxiliary. 'I was hoping not to have to go through a long list of items,' he continued. 'What we all want to know is what is being done.'

'Yes,' said Janet Smith, 'the public hates us!'

'Come, Janet, one mustn't take it personally,' said the Minister, 'the public has no idea who you are.'

'That's as may be…' she replied.

'Our staff hates us, too,' added Joan Baxter.

'We've had to take on extra security guards to patrol our offices after the number of complaints and threats of violence we've received from all types of people in the last week,' said Brian Walker.

'My car was covered in paint!' said Ian Kendall.

Manbag and the obstructed man shared a subtle look of silent amusement as the room erupted in a barrage of petty complaints. The obstructed man suddenly thought of the stories from his childhood about Nikita Khrushchev's shoe-banging incident. He even looked down at his feet beneath the table.

'ENOUGH!' shouted The Auxiliary. The room was plunged into silence. Once again, all heads turned in her direction.

'Really, Jennifer…' said the Minister.

'Don't "really, Jennifer" me!' she said. He looked shocked by the vigour of her response. 'How do you expect any answers?' she asked, addressing them all. 'What do you hope to gain by complaining about such trivialities?' Nobody responded. 'We have vital items to discuss, and I don't want to hear a single gripe out of anybody!' Still nobody responded. 'Very well, Antony, if you wouldn't mind…'

'Thank you, Auxiliary,' Manbag said. 'Ladies and gentlemen, I won't patronise you by attempting to convince you that this isn't a major setback. We have suffered an attack on our department beyond even my foresight, I have to admit. Documents have been exposed, documents whose revelations have coincided with the publication of the extraordinarily compromising photographs taken by Jason Mighty. Never have we found ourselves at a lower point.'

'These photographs,' the Minister began, 'are they really that incriminating? I mean, to be honest, all they really show is a well organised facility operating at full efficiency.'

'But that isn't all they show, is it?' said Alison Brown, Legal Representative.

'You don't mean the "unfortunates", surely?' said the Minister with a sigh.

'That's exactly what I mean,' she replied. 'The public are experiencing a shift in their perception of the entire facility, and the ethical quagmire it has provoked now has photographic ammunition; faces of desperate people, to whom they can attach themselves, with whom they can identify.'

'Well, bugger me!' said the Minister with a sneer. 'They shouldn't even have the bloody right to just "attach themselves". We did extensive testing, spent a significant part of our budget on quite conclusively proving that the general public was fuelled by indifference.'

'Of course,' Alison replied. 'But your testing placed people in simulated physical situations, the repetition of which forced them to acquiesce, no, not even acquiesce; they just accepted everything, initially out of embarrassment, shame, discomfort. But now, with the benefit of retrospect and sublime photographic documentary evidence, they have mutated and become an entirely different beast.'

'So this Mighty has created a national shitstorm of collective hypocrisy; is that what you're saying?' he asked.

'Pretty much, yes,' she replied. 'Of course, we can't forget the leaked documents, also.'

'I have to say,' began Janet Smith, 'St. Bart's Hospital has experienced no security breaches of any kind.' Similar declarations of innocence were expressed by the other CEOs at the table, culminating in what appeared to be a guilt-free solidarity. The focus was then shifted back onto The Auxiliary and Manbag. The Project Manager stood up as he began to speak.

'Let me offer a modicum of mollification, please,' he said, walking slowly around the table. 'There is no insinuation of responsibility and no doubt is being cast in the direction of the hospitals. Nevertheless, I'm sure you appreciate that, for our investigation to be as thorough as possible, and with the interest of propriety in mind, a rigorous visit must be made to each premises by our investigation team.'

Sighs of reluctant acceptance accompanied his return to his seat. The Auxiliary invited the obstructed man to take the floor.

'Ladies and gentlemen, I shall begin by telling you nothing,' he said. They looked confused. 'What I mean by that is that I am not going to share any information with you today regarding my methods. I will not explain my approach to solving this problem. This lack of information works as reiteration of Mr. Manbag's comments regarding thoroughness and propriety. What I do requires the utmost sensitivity, and I promise you I will act to the fullest extent of my abilities. I will find your answers. I ask only one thing, and that is that you take my findings as truth, wherever this investigation leads us, I will not deceive you and I expect the same professional courtesy in return. If you don't like whatever truth emerges, that is not my fault. I will not put my name on any falsehood and I will not play any part in deceiving the public further. I will not be used and I will not be the next Dr. David Kelly; dying an implausible death in a field would be something my wife would never forgive; I can assure you.'

A sardonic glimmer flashed in the eyes of the Minister for Avoidance, but he refrained from commenting on the obstructed man's reference. Manbag cast a professional smile at his friend as all eyes turned to The Auxiliary.

'I assume this is the point where you tell us there is no other business, and we all go home?' The Minister for Avoidance said. 'Jennifer...?' She winced at his mentioning her name yet again.

'Frankly, yes,' she said to a table of dissatisfied visitors. 'Go back to your hospitals,' she added, gesturing towards Manbag and the obstructed man, '...and entrust my people, both internal and external, with the task at hand.' There followed various murmurings of dissatisfaction from the visitors around the table, with the exception of the Minister, who avoided making any further comment.

Despite the exemplary conduct which he had shown since making an entrance, Manbag was experiencing a tinge of disappointment at the room's sparse ordinariness. Indeed, he had left far more salubrious surroundings downstairs, namely his own office, in order, finally, to make his way through the ultimate door into what appeared to be nothing more than bland soft tones and, quite honestly, uninspired furnishings. Moreover, there was nothing to suggest that this was the end of the line. He still had no idea whether The Auxiliary was it. The room contained absolutely nothing of substance, nothing personal like her usual area where their meetings normally took place. There were no sinister "even higher-ups"; no pallid, pinstriped, pre-pension baby boomers, who had made their underhanded money from having fingers in long-term pies and their feet under the tables of covertly corruptible captains of industry. The anti-climax would plague him for the rest of the day, long after the hospital CEOs had scurried off back to their understaffed hellholes, and the Minister for Avoidance had declined to comment as loudmouthed reporters pursued his car from the DISA front gates to the end of the road, whilst beneath its tinted windows, he attempted instead to convince Alison Brown, Legal Representative, that she was wearing too many clothes and a trip to his flat could soon rectify this oversight. 'I now know why you are called the Minister for Avoidance,' she said, and then asked the driver to drop her at the next corner.

Wednesday's Child

Martha sidled into the kitchen to find both her parents seated at the breakfast table. It was early and their mere presence provoked a sigh from their sullen daughter. During the last few years, her mother had often found herself wondering just what had happened to the sweet girl for whose adorable pre-pubescent cuteness she had taken credit. Her husband was frequently held responsible for Martha's current moodiness, and several of their turbulent parental debates included the unimaginative accusation, "She gets it from you, you know!" He was often amazed at his wife's ability to wander through family life, blameless and blinkered, consistently unaware of their daughter's desire and potential to be much more than her mother would ever imagine possible for such a "difficult girl". He admired Martha's spirit and often found himself awash with vicarious pleasure, as he was told tale after tale by his wife about the girl's combative and begrudging approach to the everyday functions of the family unit. Martha had it in her to disagree, to challenge, to reject; to have the strength and need to create an alternative which suited her own version of how her young life should be played out, and certainly not according to her mother's twee ideas of clichéd femininity. Perhaps the saddest element at play within the home was his inability to do any of the things which he so admired in his daughter. Martha saw it more as apathy on his part, as if any type of familial intervention just didn't interest him enough. Despite loving him, she resented his wetness, and for every instance in which he didn't participate, she respected him a little less. That left her mother free range to impose and to criticise; to dictate the darkening domestic underbelly whilst filling their shared life with facile mores and passive aggression.

'…and anyway,' her mother began, as if the subject had already been established; 'they're not going to achieve anything, are they?'

'Well, it seems as though they might be already,' her father responded.

'Quite frankly,' her mother continued, as she looked at her sleepy-faced daughter, 'I'm in favour of anything that streamlines the Health Service. These interlopers are putting a strain on resources, and then where will we be? Queuing at the Doctor's behind a plague of depressed ditherers!'

'You already queue at the Doctor's, Mother. It's called a waiting room and you sit down, that's all,' Martha responded, as she tipped a large helping of cereal into a bowl as noisily as she could.

'Ah, it speaks!' her mother said. 'And yet again, only to correct her poor mother!'

'Not really a correction,' Martha said, 'more of an addition to an incomplete thought.'

Her mother let out the subtlest breath of indignation which garnered no attention. Her mood fluctuated and she leant forward to touch Martha's hair as the teen sat down at the table. Turning up the television and slurping her cereal, she moved her head away from the intrusive hand; a movement which she knew would precipitate one of the customary comments about her appearance.

'Your hair could be nice,' her mother said. And there it was.

'Always could be, but never is - right?' Martha responded, without turning her gaze from the television. Her father's tablet kept his eyes away from the touching scene.

The television news was running a report on DISA documents and their scandalous contents. Jason's photographs were mentioned. 'That can't be his real name,' said her mother. They showed the DISA headquarters; the footage focusing mainly on the growing number of protesters and press camped outside. They showed the Contemplation Zone. Another slurp of cereal made her mother wince. They then showed some of the graffiti that Martha had done with Stylus just two days earlier, as a matter of fact, very close to where Jason had been abducted. She wondered how he was. She thought about Manbag and the obstructed man.

The news reporter, talking directly to camera from outside DISA headquarters, made some asinine attempt at expressing a thinly-veiled opinion, which made Martha cringe and her mother nod in agreement from her vastly different standpoint. The teenager longed, between slurps of cereal, to inform them of her involvement in the rapidly escalating scandal that was unfolding before them. She knew that was impossible, of course: Manbag's orders.

'He always wears such nice ties,' said her mother. Martha sighed. Her father paid no attention. 'Oh, have I offended you again, dear?' her mother added. Martha wiped a dribble of milk from her chin with the sleeve of her hoodie.

'I'm not offended,' she replied. 'I'm just surprised that your only reaction to all this is to admire the reporter's tie.'

'Maybe I think this is all getting a bit too serious,' her mother replied, 'maybe things need lightening up a bit.'

'This *IS* serious,' Martha said, 'and it can't be lightened up!'

There was a pause before her mother said, 'You're so full of woe, aren't you?'

'Oh, for...!' Martha said, putting her spoon down in the cereal and throwing her head back. She closed her eyes and then opened them again, only to see the same dull patch of ceiling which always accompanied such moments of frustration.

'Well, it's true,' said her mother pettily.

'Ok, whatever you say. If understanding how serious this is makes me full of woe, then yes, I'm full of woe; rather that than...' She stopped. She refused to be pushed into saying something nasty. She looked at her mother, who seemed surprised, all of a sudden, to be in receipt of her daughter's attention, to the point where she actually started to feel a little uncomfortable, as if Martha might do something dangerous. She looked down at the teenager's hand as it grabbed the spoon again. Neither of them said a word but the look, from Martha's point of view, conveyed the dry-eyed refusal to buckle under the crushing weight of insidious maternal niggling. From the niggler, herself, came coy, disingenuous eyebrows, but little else. A woman who should never have become a mother, her reluctant daughter and a father who was there in body only; there they sat, to the sounds of highly significant news being reported badly.

The DISA report was followed by a story about the year's most successful android app designers, whose latest triumph was called Personal Updater, an app created for ambitious professionals who are pressed for time but wish to remain socially active. 'Basically, it provides status updates based on calibrated data and GPS location, enabling users to maintain an online presence whilst focusing on their work,' some boffin explained smugly.

Martha sighed. 'Don't you like that either, dear?' her mother said. Martha sighed again. Her mother continued, 'It seems like a nice idea to me, you know, for people who work hard.'

'What'll it be next?' Martha blurted out. 'Selfie generators which create a picture of you doing something you're not actually doing? A composite image drawn from previous photos with added activity background?'

'That's actually a very good idea,' said her father, finally deigning to enter a conversation. 'You should hang onto that,' he added, 'in case the law on happy images changes.'

The report finished with the designer explaining that the app would be modified in the near future to include the special feature which they were currently working on, whereby the calibration would be extended to the point of the app gaining a true insight into the mind of its user and trawling the daily news in search of items which would be in his or her interest, whereupon it would be able to generate an apposite opinion, even mimicking the user's particular turn of phrase and vocabulary, and then update their social media status. This would allow users to express an opinion without having an opinion, and without lifting a finger. Apparently testing had been going well, and initial concerns over the app generating invalid opinions, perhaps even manipulating the user, were being ironed out.

'It's just incredible!' Martha said.

'It is, isn't it?' her mother added, quite deliberately ignoring the obvious incredulity in her daughter's voice.

'But it's being used for all the wrong things,' Martha said.

'What is?' her mother asked.

'Technology!' Martha said. 'Why not use it for education or medicine? No, that would actually be useful, let's make a machine that expresses an opinion for you, so you don't have to. I mean, how stupid are we?'

'If we can create this technology, we can't be that stupid,' her mother said.

'Mother, if you type "what are the things that…" into Google, on the list of suggested ends to the question are "eat trolls" and "God hates"!'

'What's your point, dear?' her mother asked.

'My point is, yes, there are very intelligent people capable of producing great things, but look how they use that intelligence, Personal Updater, when internet search predictions clearly imply that some of that intelligence could be spread around, perhaps even used to educate people.'

'Well,' said her mother, 'I can't say that I have any opinion at all where trolls are concerned, but I do know that I wouldn't want to live in a world in which asking questions about God is considered unintelligent.'

'Well, luckily for you, your local train station is very accommodating. If things become too secular, you can always line up with the depressed ditherers!' Martha said. She stood and carried her cereal bowl to the dishwasher before leaving the room.

'That's how she talks to me,' she said to her husband. 'So full of woe; she gets it from you, you know!'

Wednesday's Manbag

Martha spent the rest of that day plodding grumpily through three lectures on the themes of White Hat Hacking, Ethical Discrimination, and Politics & Gender. Her mother's breakfast table commentary on the world as she saw it: did she really see it? Martha wasn't sure; however, she was in a bad mood for the rest of the day as a result of what had been yet another excruciating visit to the kitchen.

In the DISA camp, though, things had progressed entirely to plan, i.e. slowly and covertly obstructively. The obstructed man had risen to the challenge and proved himself to be a worthy team member for the third consecutive day. Manbag was somewhere approaching elated. The two of them had managed to exploit the minutiae of each unfolding development with quintessential ease. Percy Harrison was even more than the true professional Manbag had hoped he would be.

It was this sense of exhilaration which he carried with him into his weekly EFA meeting, determined not to allow any of those usually irritating members to get under his skin. As he entered the room, the gentle hubbub of activity diminished and he suddenly found himself the centre of attention. Being the last to arrive meant that the attention came from a full representation of the usual suspects. Manbag certainly wasn't unfamiliar with the sensation. As a Project Manager of some prominence, he had often found himself in the position of being the last to arrive at a meeting; a meeting at which bad news was anticipated by those lower level attendees who in some way thought that their punctuality would mitigate the outcome. Manbag liked to call it "tactically tardy" or "professionally late": a way of instilling gratitude in those who survived the meeting, and a way of encouraging painful self-realisation in those who didn't.

EFA eyes were on him. Brows furrowed and sphincters twitched. The Gersons, the Holistics, the Carcinophobes, the Klismaphiliacs; all factions, all eyes, all brows, all sphincters were alert and awaiting the Project Manager. He looked at his watch. He wasn't late. He wasn't being tactical. He was always professional.

'You were seen today,' said a Gerson as Manbag took an empty seat in the gathering.

'By whom?' Manbag enquired politely.

'I was just sharing with the others before you arrived,' the Gerson continued. 'My brother-in-law has a little sandwich van: all organic. We saw the protestors and the press down at the DISA building on television and thought we could make a killing. The crowd's been growing since last week. Anyway, we were down there this morning trying to get some breakfast business, and who did we see arriving and being waved straight through by the security? Only our friend, Antony, here,' he said, gesturing impressively towards Manbag, who noticed the knowing expressions on each of the EFA faces that surrounded him.

'Oh come now,' Manbag began. 'If we were friends, you'd have known that already.' The Gerson tried to suppress his peevish reaction. 'So, you work there, in a high position, I assume, judging by the way you were welcomed.'

'Am I to assume that the A in EFA doesn't really stand for ANONYMOUS?' Manbag said.

There were mumblings from the circle as the peevish Gerson raised his hands in faux deference.

'I do apologise,' he said with a smirk. 'I just thought it'd be interesting to have one of us working at the place which is on everyone's lips.' There were sounds of agreement from the group.

'It's hardly why we're here, though, is it?' Manbag asked. 'I mean, now that you've shared information about your brother-in-law, can we really call ourselves EFA anymore?'

'You're right, Antony, of course,' said one of the Holistics, that week's designated chairperson. 'Everybody, even if Antony does work at DISA, it's none of our business, and it certainly doesn't pertain to tonight's programme. Now, let's get back on TRACT, shall we?' He laughed alone at his own joke as the rest of them groaned.

'Yes, yes...' said one of the Carcinophobes wearily. 'And no doubt we have a lot to DIGEST, too. This happens every time you chair the meeting.'

'What's wrong?' said the Holistic. 'Are you gonna tell us that humour is carcinogenic, now?'

'No, but your attempts at it might well be!' the Carcinophobe responded, to cheers of agreement from his fellow members. At this point Manbag stood up.

'What's wrong with you?' asked one of the Klismaphiliacs.

Manbag looked around the group. 'You know,' he began, 'I just don't want to be here.'

'Oh come now, Antony, there's no need to be rash,' said the

chairperson.

'I'm not being rash,' Manbag replied. 'I just don't need this anymore.' He turned his back on them and, to the outflow of their umbrage, he walked out. As he went, he thought of all the things he could have said to them, all the cleverly-worded shaming he could have spewed on their jejune grasp of the group ethos. But why should he have shared anymore? Let them continue with their arseholes in the sand!

More Talk Time Radio

"…*and of course, it'll come as no surprise to our listeners that we're starting off this morning with the latest events in the DISA story.*"

"*Really!? Are people not getting sick of it yet?*"

"*No, in fact it seems as though the interest is only increasing as the days pass by.*"

"*Yes, well, we're only in the second week of it, I suppose.*"

"*That's right, and most of us are still getting used to the idea of being outraged by something we were ignoring only a couple of weeks ago.*"

"*Indeed! So, what is the latest, anyway?*"

"*Jason Mighty! Jason Mighty is the latest!*"

"*He's the photographer who may be connected to all this.*"

"*Well, come on, he's obviously connected, isn't he?*"

"*You tell me. Why is he the latest?*"

"*By all accounts, he has disappeared!*"

"*Disappeared?*"

"*Vanished!*"

"*That's interesting.*"

"*It certainly is interesting. You see, it seemed plausible, at least to some people, that his only connection to all this was his selling the photographs. Perhaps they were stolen, and he had absolutely no part in any of this, we just don't know. But now, he has disappeared…*"

"*...and you're thinking he's been...*"

"*...I'm thinking he has BEEN disappeared!*"

"*Ah come on, really?*"

"*Yes, really. Can we just keep on calling everything a coincidence? Is nobody going to stand up and say, hang on a minute?*"

"*Maybe he just went to visit his mother...*"

"*...and maybe he's at the bottom of a river somewhere with his cameras...*"

"*What?*"

"*...silenced for what he knows!*"

'Why do we listen to this crap every day?' said the obstructed man to his wife.

'We don't,' she answered, referring to the fact that, until the last couple of days, they hadn't had breakfast together since their daughter's death.

'Well, I didn't really mean us, specifically, I meant in general. Why do people listen to this crap?' He sighed.

She looked at him. 'I guess if everything is crap, you don't really notice the crapness of individual things, you just accept them.'

'Well that's a depressing thought,' said the obstructed man.

'Yes,' she answered, 'but probably true.'

"*You're joining us here on Talk Time Radio. It's Thursday morning...*"

"*...and we're running through the top stories, but of course, the DISA story is still dominating the news and looks set to continue well into the new year.*"

"*That's right. Even if there were a few human interest stories, they probably wouldn't get a look-in.*"

The obstructed man switched off the radio. His wife looked at him.

'This situation doesn't seem very fair on the young photographer, does it?' she said.

He sighed. 'Not really, no,' he replied. 'But it was the only way to do it. He agreed to let his photographs be used. He knew that they'd attract a lot of attention.'

'But why?' she asked.

'What do you mean?' he said.

'Well, as they keep saying; until a couple of weeks ago, nobody cared. In general, it was only people like us, who'd been directly affected. Suddenly everyone is up in arms about it, just because of some photographs,' she said.

'But it's not just the photographs, is it?' he replied. 'It's the leaked documents, it's the connections between hospitals and government; it's the idea that controlled suicide can be put forward as a solution for mental health issues.'

'None of which changes the fact that nobody cared two weeks ago,' she said firmly. 'We can't just suddenly do a U-turn now that we don't have to make an effort to understand a situation.'

'Ah, because that never happens in this country,' he said with a smirk.

'Whatever,' she said. 'Now that we're bombarded with it, and we don't have to go to the trouble of looking for information, and can just lie back and have it thrust upon us, we're suddenly outraged.'

'Because it was so much easier to ignore before,' he said.

'Exactly, that's it,' she replied.

They smiled at each other in silent recognition of the extent of their conversation. Only a few days earlier he had ripped up her crossword book in a fit of pique, for which he had rebuked himself. He had finally lost control of the slow burning frustration which had dominated their domestic life, and it would take him some time to forgive himself. But now, just look at her, he thought; she's coming back, slowly but surely she's coming back. He stood, kissed her cheek and left the kitchen to prepare himself for another day inside DISA. She switched the radio back on once he had gone upstairs.

"…and every day it looks more and more like an embassy in a war-torn middle-eastern country. There are protestors, their numbers increasing with every new revelation. There are placards stretching the full length of the street. The DISA top brass must surely recognise this public outcry and may, dare we say it, even worry slightly about the potential escalation of what seems, for now anyway, to be only a mildly peaceful protest."

Sunday Best

Under most circumstances, the soup kitchen could be an assault on the senses for a first-time visitor. With the incongruous additions of nervous excitement, pride and deep sadness, the obstructed man's wife made her first appearance. He had tried his best to provide her with an accurate description of the various smells and sights which would greet her, but the overall effect was compounded by physicality. It was the nervous excitement that had propelled her; getting her up, dressing her and preparing her, finally, to take an active interest in something outside the confines of her crossword book. She realised, on arriving, that she had in fact been proud of her husband's ability to throw himself into his benevolent volunteer work all along, since he had first told her of his intention. She'd been unable to convey any such thought to him at the time, of course, but now that she could actually observe and, better still, participate; she found the pride more definable in her mind – as if fundamental functions were suddenly graspable again. The deep sadness which accompanied the physicality was not only brought on by the obvious suffering and evident neglect on the faces, in the clothes, in the voices of those who came there to eat, but also by the situation she now shared with her husband – that it had taken the loss of their child, arguably the profoundest human experience, for them to become truly aware of others.

Having been fully apprised by her husband, she knew what to expect while being introduced to Manbag and Martha, and was consequently able to suppress a smile at seeing Manbag's soup kitchen disguise and the resulting sneer it drew from Martha.

'This is Harriet,' the obstructed man said, 'my wife.' He presented her at the corner table which Manbag seemed to have made his own during the last month.

'It's very nice to meet you, Harriet,' Martha said, offering her hand politely. Manbag made a covert gesture with minimal oral accompaniment; the utmost limit permissible under the circumstances. He had already instructed the obstructed man to apologise on his behalf for any apparent rudeness, which also took a substantial weight off his shoulders in terms of approaching the minefield of talking to the mother of a "successful unfortunate". The ruse provided circumvention. Harriet was the only name used at the table.

'It's great to see you here,' Martha said, taking the lead.

'It's great to be here, I think,' Harriet replied, a thin, self-conscious smile playing on her lips.

'You might be the first person to ever say that about this place!' Martha said.

Harriet looked at her warmly, their meeting already proving palliative. She hadn't spoken to a young woman since the death of her daughter. She turned to her husband after a moment of reflection.

'Well, dear,' she began, 'that shepherd's pie isn't going to serve itself, now, is it?'

The obstructed man raised his eyebrows. He shared a smile with Manbag and Martha before accompanying his wife to the serving area.

The lines of people were filling up. Steam rose as lids were lifted. Plates clattered. Cutlery scraped. Hungry mouths blew on piping hot food. The Project Manager and the teenager sat in silence for a moment.

'You look ridiculous, by the way,' Martha said finally.

'What do you mean?' Manbag asked; a little offended.

'These disguises are getting a little...'

'Inspired?' he said, interrupting his fiercest critic, proudly.

Martha gave one of her finest harrumphs.

'I know you're a teenager,' Manbag said. 'But you should try and cheer up!'

'That's the stupidest thing you've ever said!' she responded.

He sighed. She spied her chance, stood and joined the shortening queue for the shepherd's pie. She rolled her eyes as Manbag gestured for her to get him some too.

On her return, they ate their food and discussed their next moves. She had insisted on knowing about Jason's condition, of course, and the Project Manager had had to offer as much information as possible before the brusque teen would enter into any discussion relating to the project. The obstructed man brought them some tea during their meal and also enquired as to the progress of the missing photographer.

'All being well,' Manbag said reassuringly, 'you'll be able to visit him soon. He seems to be doing very well, by all accounts.'

'Does he have any idea how much attention he's been getting in the news?' The obstructed man asked. 'They've mentioned him on the radio practically every five bloody minutes over the last few days!'

'He knows very little, as far as I know,' Manbag replied. 'He's still a long way from...' he paused and sighed deeply. The obstructed man placed a hand on his shoulder. Even Martha's face displayed a tiny glimmer of compassion.

'It's not your fault,' the obstructed man said.

'Really, isn't it?' Manbag replied. 'I'm the one who put him in that position.' He lowered his voice, never losing the grip on his professionalism.

'Look,' said the obstructed man. 'If there's one thing I've learnt over the last few weeks, it's that punishing yourself for what you should or shouldn't have done, whilst it may be necessary, can also be destructive. We have an objective here. Let that be the focus. We have an investigation to fudge. If the boy is getting better, like you said he is, than let's get on with delaying the most pointless enquiry of my career, ok?' He smiled at the two of them. Manbag sighed again then nodded.

'Alright, then,' said the obstructed man, and returned to his duties.

Harriet had found her way quickly and soon fell into a comfortable rhythm which allowed her to serve whilst smiling and offering words of welcome. Seeing her busying herself had given the obstructed man a great deal of pleasure, as he again felt, in a similar way to how he had felt as he'd walked into the DISA headquarters on that first morning, suited and booted and ready to tamper, that their being proactive whilst continuing to remind themselves why they were doing it, would be the way to get through it all.

As they lay in bed later that night, having just switched off the light, she commented, whilst watching the moving shadows on the ceiling cast by the street lamp and the trees outside their bedroom window, that she wouldn't allow herself to feel guilty for not having thought about their daughter for part of the time they had spent at the soup kitchen. She had enjoyed the work and, more than anything, she had needed the interaction. Since the moment their lives had changed forever, she had barely spoken to anybody other than her absent daughter; her empty chair at the table, her empty bed - even the photographs of her which now seemed to display a discomforting hollowness – to these objects she had spoken private words of anguish and turmoil. But that day, with those poor hungry souls, she had reconnected and started to feel again.

Even More Talk Time Radio

"You're joining us on a crisp, clear Monday morning."

"Well, what certainly is clear is that action is necessary to defuse the DISA situation."

"That's absolutely right, isn't it? There has been a steady, well, perhaps steady isn't the right word; there has been an increasingly vocal movement of people arriving outside the DISA headquarters."

"Yes, and they are of course joining the already sizeable gathering which has built up over the last few days. Increasingly vocal and somewhat aggressive, wouldn't you say?"

"Well, we can't really blame them, can we? As the debate on whether this really is social cleansing rages on, the public is becoming exponentially indignant."

"Add that to the frustration of being refused treatment at two of the city's busiest hospitals due to revenge attacks leaving equipment vandalised, and you have some idea of how people feel at this precise moment, in what is being described as a dark period in our recent history."

"That's true! It seems that facilities at two hospitals were damaged in what the newspapers are calling counter-productive retaliation, as the result means that people in need of treatment are being turned away due to those healthcare institutions' lack of functioning resources."

"So these indignant protestors have sabotaged the hospitals in retaliation; to fight back against their neglect of the mentally ill. Now, when other people need *medical attention, the hospitals are incapable of providing it."*

"Result!"

"If you cut your nose off to spite your face, don't expect to have it sewn back on at your local hospital!"

"Exactly, and this is the same health service that the public thought they could rescue by voting us out of Europe!"

"The very same, and now look..."

"Well, it's time to go over to our reporter who is joining us live from outside the DISA building. Judith, are you there?"

"I'm here, yes."

"Tell us — what is the mood like, there, this morning?"

"Well, as you might expect from such a large number of angry and disappointed people, it's tense. The police are here in much greater numbers than last week, and the public seems to be working on rotation. My colleagues who were here during the night said that the same people have returned this morning, ready to protest again after doing a full day yesterday. In fact, in the park nearby, people have pitched tents and parked vans, and they are here for the long haul. Were it not for the serious purpose of their protest, their makeshift gathering would resemble something along the lines of a festival; indeed, I'm told that the band Empty Threat performed an impromptu acoustic version of their rather controversial song, Suicide Backlog, last night, for those choosing to show their solidarity under the stars."

"Not exactly festival weather, is it, Judith?"

"It certainly isn't, no, but I think that people feel strongly enough about this issue that they can withstand the cold."

"...and is there really a sense of solidarity, do you think?"

"There seems to be, I have to say. In fact, there are various groups, perhaps not your typical bedfellows, but they seem to be united in their indignation."

"But this solidarity you're referring to, Judith; it doesn't extend to the police, obviously."

"Absolutely not, make no bones about it; these people are fighting together against all factions of the establishment, and the campfire mentality is soon thrust aside when it's time for them to state their case and make their voices heard. As you can hear in the background, there are various chants already underway and the general tone sounds considerably more aggressive than yesterday. In fact, we've had to relocate at a slight distance from the main procession, for our own safety and because the volume of people has increased greatly since we arrived an hour ago."

"Well, thanks for now, Judith. We'll be back with you shortly."

"You're listening to Talk Time Radio, bringing you the latest DISA news in the moment, as it happens!"

A Mere Public

People gather; amassing indignation, false or otherwise, beneath placards of angrily worded umbrage, shouting in unison as they go, their voices just on the wrong side of peaceful protestation. More Police uniforms become visible, as if the decibels demand them. Smart phones outnumber television cameras on every corner; every angle is more thoroughly covered by amateurs, poised and ready to post, repost and share anything and everything which television would, politically, have to avoid. Mental health workers, long frustrated with the system, release their professional gripes in well-timed chants about the various deficiencies at play. Government failures are the chief targets. Along the procession of people, one chant merges into another, as various groups combine efforts in an amorphous din. In the centre of the group, the chant is clear. Vitriolic verses, rancorous refrains; preparation is certainly not lacking. Homeless people join the procession at certain points along its length, appearing from doorways and side streets; motivated by a sense of solidarity, they soon catch up with the rhythm of their respective chants. "LEAVE THE ZONE, GO HOME!" "STICK YOUR GOLDEN WHISTLE UP YOUR ARSE!" Along the line, people are shouting the words of *Suicide Backlog*. The members of the band are at the front of the procession. Musicians playing at politics, in line with ordinary people - workers, patients, neglected by the system and left to consider the final jump. Helmets with visors, German Shepherds, armoured cars. Journalists shout above the melee. "DON'T JUMP! DON'T JUMP!"

DISA office workers appear at office windows as the procession fills the street outside their building. There is pushing and shoving as more people appear.

The noise level increases as traffic is forced to detour. Disgruntled motorists beep and shout about inconvenience. Police lower their visors.

Office windows are full, noses up to the glass, smart phones poised, office phones ring.

More chants begin. "SUICIDE BACKLOG, SUICIDE BACKLOG!" "WE ARE A MERE PUBLIC!"

People inside check news updates. News tickers are awash with sound bites, incomplete information, sound nibbles.

A strong wind blows, making an impression on the placards as they sway above the heads of grimacing shouters.

Those inside turn back to the window, having been unsatisfactorily updated by facile reporting; one or two consider joining the procession and protesting against journalists.

Bags of rubbish line the streets. Thousands of footprints overlap each other in construction dust. Traffic cones do little to contain the procession's widening girth. "SEE THEM FALL UNDER FURTHER!" At the front, walking alongside the members of Empty Threat, is a small group of opposition politicians, namely those most in need of conveying the idea of being in possession of a conscience. Their presence is not accepted negatively, despite their vying for the most opportune positions as photographers and television cameras appear. Minor television celebrities, the desperately semi-famous, who these days make up the majority of the country's inhabitants most in receipt of unwarranted attention, are dispersed around the edges of the procession's front, hoping that a magazine cover showing their serious side will detract attention away from the cellulite, stretch marks, prescription painkiller addiction, sex change, leaked porn video; their hierarchical statuses, or lack thereof, their need for a cause making even the mildly cynical salivate.

The number of people continues to grow beyond what was expected, beyond what was predicted by so-called knowledgeable experts, whose research informed police, officials, news teams, local business owners and all participants. As numbers swell, so does the variety of demographics represented. With this comes further diversity, both in the appearances of the marchers, and in the levels of aggression they employ in the chanting of their chagrin. Numerous religious denominations are represented along the procession, striding with purpose within the confines of their paradox, attempting to blow on the Assisted Dying hot potato by turning up with a show of faith. They can neither condone the all-important assistance, nor condemn the use of it, thereby promoting anguish, pain and suffering. The schism in which they are trapped provides sufficient space to walk about, shouting about untenable points which their fellow, secular marchers shout down. Anglicans, Catholics, Church of England - they all rub shoulders with the Muslims. The sacred human life given by Allah must not be taken by suicide-control puppet masters from government departments and hospital boardrooms. None of the denominations can decide amongst themselves, not one congregation can say definitively, "this is our stance", but they can all jump on the bandwagon to wax lyrical when they realise that adopting a side of the dichotomy will serve them well, until the window of opportunity closes, and their paradox envelops them. Their chants are more blandly compassionate than the others which fill every pocket of air around the ever expanding edges of the procession.

Office windows are smeared with consternation expressed in close proximity to the tinted glass. In the distance comes the sound of ambulance sirens; closer and closer. People start to separate, forming a narrow space along which the blaring ambulances approach the DISA office grounds. Protestors continue to cheer and chant over the sirens. Police usher them away from the advancing vehicles as delicately and peacefully as possible; batons are lowered so as not to incite misunderstanding. The ambulances grind to a halt, four in total, their sirens switched off but their lights still flashing urgency, calling for the attention they already have. In what appears to be well-rehearsed unison, the back doors of each vehicle open. From each door, one balaclava-wearing paramedic emerges followed by one suited person, head covered with a black hood, hands tie-gripped at the crotch. A second similarly disguised paramedic exits after each hooded captive. Protestors quickly become aware of the four hostages and eight paramedics, and the noise dies down, the chanting stops. Ambulance p.a. system feedback screeches for attention. In more well-rehearsed unison, the four ambulances broadcast the following recorded message.

"DISA executives:

Standing before you, hooded and bound, you will see four

hospital executives, your fellow conspirators, or representatives thereof, chosen because of their role in what you have perpetrated. If you do not send out your top people, those that have so far remained nameless, these four hooded executives here will be taken and forced to use the Contemplation Zone for its primary purpose, the disposal of undesirable elements. We will begin our own social cleansing, and we will begin at the top. These four will be the first of many."

People look to the police at various points within the gatherings of protestors, assuming that some movement will be made, some action taken towards stopping what is potentially a very dramatic turn of events. The police remain still, however, listening for the next threats from the paramedics. Television cameras are poised as the inactivity of the police causes a sudden silence to descend across those gathered around them.

Inside the DISA offices, and on millions of television screens across the country, live footage of the ensuing neglect of one emergency service, as they refuse to intervene in the extreme actions of another, is broadcast to bemused viewers.

Amongst the crowds there is a hubbub of muttering bewilderment. Why aren't the police making a move? What are the paramedics going to do next?

The two emergency services seem locked in a silent stand-off. There is movement from behind the police as a ripple of pushing, which starts from the edge of the gathering, finds its way to their cordon. The paramedics make no move whatsoever, unlike their trembling captive figures, whose quivering hoods suggest less ease with their immediate surroundings. The cordon undulates in response to the public's force. Inside the DISA office building, more people gather at the windows, asking the same questions as the people outside. Live feeds of the situation continue to fill television screens, laptops and smart phones.

'So it seems,' says one reporter, 'that the police are here to control the people who are protesting against the Contemplation Zone, but not to intervene as officials from one of their fellow emergency service crews threaten what is, for all intents and purposes, the murders of four kidnapped hospital executives.'

'…if indeed they are really from the ambulance service,' says another.

'…the identities of the four captives is yet to be confirmed, of course,' says another.

'…for anyone just joining us, what you are watching is live footage of a stand-off between eight paramedics and the police force, who have cordoned off an area and are dressed in full riot gear,' says another.

Shaky camera movements provide the situation with further verisimilitude, disorientating the viewers inside in a way that could easily be mistaken for clichéd filmmaking, were it not for the real event happening outside their very window. Office workers turn away from the television screens and back to the real thing, the office windows providing a fuller widescreen effect that embellishes any episode of rubbernecking, their aspect ratio providing the self-assured belief which will inflect the affirmations made in later eye-witness accounts of the incident which is now unfolding before their aesthetically accommodated eyes.

After what appears to be indifference displayed by the police, the paramedics move rapidly, pushing their hooded prisoners back into the ambulances. The crowds start shouting and jeering and pushing. As the ambulance engines start, the sirens screech back into action once more. The crowds start to push more and more. As the ambulances begin to move away from the area, a glass bottle smashes in the middle of the road and suddenly there is fire, and then another bottle, thrown from the edge of the road, smashes at the feet of the police cordon, directly in front of where the ambulances had been parked. Hands are raised, batons brandished…pushing…pushing…the fire burns, people run, plenty not wanting to get caught up in a riot…cameras shake even more, as intrepid journalists stay the course. Sounds of disbelief usher from shocked mouths as office window witnesses observe the furore. Direct contact is made as police strike protestors, batons aloft, shields raised against makeshift missiles. Lazy journalists, at a loss for spontaneous vocabulary, make Miners' Strike comparisons, as injuries occur against the indignant unarmed. People run and fall and get up again. People lose those they were marching with, and run in all directions, desperately looking for escape routes. Water cannons appear, finally having been permitted into the police arsenal. The most outraged protestors venture forward, unfazed by the potential force of their imminent drenching. The water appears. Protestors go down. The fires are out; a secondary benefit which enables frontline police to retreat. People scatter, having seen the force of the water, shouting, screaming and swearing about excessive force, some slipping on the wet tarmac.

    People inside are already uploading videos, tagging them with outrage and incredulity. The TVs continue spewing…

       '…the police resorting to water cannon, here, as you can see the very palpable tension between them and the protestors…'

'...the four ambulances are completely out of sight, now...'

'...we interrupt this weather forecast to bring you breaking news...'

'...where we hope to have a few words with the members of Empty Threat, once they have all been located...'

The asinine comments are accompanied, incongruously, by very graphic images of bloodied faces; hobbling, limping, running, falling protestors, trying to escape the mite of a provoked police force, some not quite fast enough to avoid the blows as batons connect with limbs and heads. Live feeds are lost intermittently, airtime being returned to bereft presenters who are forced into mumbling apologies for the spontaneous interruptions, before being interrupted, themselves, by fleeting returns to live action captured from skewed angles on cameras clutched in resilient hands. Determined to capture the truth, an occasional camera operator, perhaps in mind of their time at university spent studying Soviet Kino-Pravda, ignores the direction in their ear, and chooses to focus instead on the blood in the water.

'...and the streets seem to be clearing, finally, as the full force of the police is felt...'

'...for those viewers who've just tuned in and are wondering what's happened to the golf, we'll be back there in...'

'...we have to take a quick break, but stay with us, please...'

Part Five

Jason

…is that music? It is; it's that song, again. Why won't my legs move? I know how to move them, after all, don't I? Am I paralysed? Did they do this to me? Is someone holding me down? I don't know why they don't turn it up; how am I supposed to hear it? I'm lying down. Am I in bed? Ah, there's the music; they must've heard what I said. Did I say it? Maybe I didn't. I'm struggling to breathe. If nobody is holding me down, why can't I move? The music is very muffled, like I'm under water, but there is no water, but I'm wet. Why am I wet? Ah, I pissed myself, didn't I? But why is my hair wet, and everything else; how much tea did I drink!? I'm asleep. I'm asleep. I'm asleep. I can't wake up. Get off me! I can't move! I have to move! WAKE UP! Stop hitting me! STOP! WAKE UP! WAKE UP!

'Jason.'

Who is that?

'Jason, wake up.'

Help me, please, they're drowning me!

'Jason, you're dreaming. Wake up.'

So much water…

'Jason, you're ok, you're ok. Try to calm down.'

Who is that?

'Jason, you were just dreaming; you're ok, you're safe!'

Martha

…why was he there? He should've been in class with the rest of us. It's just… Who was he with? How can this be happening? How…?

'Martha! Are you listening?'

He never said anything to me about going…I could've gone, too.

'Would you like us to call your parents? Martha…?'

I stayed away because Manbag told me to, and now my friend is dead…

'This has been a big shock for all of us, Martha. We're cancelling the rest of today's classes and everyone is being told to go home. Martha, can you hear me?'

'Yes, I can hear you.'

'Good, you had me worried there for a moment.'

'Sorry…'

'There's no need to apologise. You've had a shock, we all have. There were several absentees yesterday, far more than a typical Monday. It's safe to assume that most of them were at the protest, but, well, erm…so far, Brian, erm, Stylus is…was the only…'

'…dead one?'

'I'm afraid so.'

'You'd rather there were more?'

'No, of course not. That's not what I meant. Look, I think you should go home.'

'I have to go…'

Manbag

It's not quite cool enough, yet; five more minutes.

That poor girl; will she cope with this? Water cannon death at eighteen; for something we started.

Still too hot – patience…

Thank fuck she followed my warning, and stayed away. We couldn't have handled that, not after everything else. It's been years since I've lost a friend, and I was much older than Martha is…but my friendship was most certainly deeper, there was definite love involved…

She'll be ok, in time; it'll make her stronger…listen to me – so profound! She'd kill me if she heard me.

Perfect temperature, finally…I need this…

Jason

'Thanks for calling….no, he's asleep. He seems to be settling a bit more easily than last week. He hasn't really been able to speak much, of course. I'd say he's going to need another week or two before he's up to anything more than rest…yes, that's right…Of course, I'll call you if there's any change, but I wouldn't worry, he just needs rest and peace.

Percy & Harriet

'…all these young people, Percy, it breaks my heart…'

'I know, dear, I know.'

'And what is this going to do to that poor girl?'

'That poor girl is very strong, dear.'

'Maybe, but she's only eighteen, Percy, only a child…'

'That's as may be, but we shouldn't underestimate her. She has a strong head on her shoulders, in spite of her parents.'

'What's wrong with her parents?'

'Let's just say they don't appreciate what they've got, perhaps they don't even understand the value of having a child like that...'

'Well we have to help her, don't we?'

'We will, dear, we will, don't worry about that.'

'I'm not worried, really. I just want to be useful, again.'

'When did you stop being useful?'

...

Martha

www.onlyonebrownshoe@blogpit.com

This is my first post in a few days and, to be honest, I'm not sure if there is really anything for me to say. On Monday this week, I lost a friend: a talented, intelligent friend, who had joined those who stood up to the authorities at the DISA riots. I really don't want this post to descend into blatant, tear-jerking status update territory, but I feel, as I'm sure do many, that during the course of this mania we're going through, it's important for us to stop and accord some respect to those that continue to fall as a result of what must surely now be classed as a national tragedy. All our debates and bills and discussions and opinions can't eliminate the damage that has been done, first of all by inaction and now by overreaction. We can never bring them back. They are gone forever. So why don't we all just stop?

Jason

How long have I been here?

I don't even know her name. This is definitely better than the last strange place I woke up in…

Ooohhh…stretching hurts, everything hurts…

'Jason, are you ok? Are you in much pain?'

That voice again…where is she?

'Jason, can you speak? Do you want some water?'

Can I speak? I don't know…

'Just blink twice if you want water.'

Blink? Ok…

'…that's good, here you are.'

Nice and cold…there she is, who is she?

'My name is Melanie, I'm a private doctor employed by Mr. Manbag to look after you. You're quite safe, here, there's nothing to worry about.'

Nothing to worry about? Doesn't feel like it…

'Can you speak?'

'I…think so…where am I?'

'You can, that's good. You're in a secure location, that's all I'm permitted to tell you. Mr. Manbag's instructions, I'm afraid. Drink some more.'

Manbag's instructions…we're still following instructions…

'Do you remember what happened to you?'

'Yes…some of it…I think…it's a bit blurred.'

'Of course, well, don't try to speak anymore. I'm giving you something else for the pain and you need to sleep.'

I need to sleep…I need…to…

Manbag

It's time to think about when the safest time to resign is. It's time to do something more worthwhile. I could travel more. I could work with kids, teaching them music or something, who knows?

There are so many things I could've done. I could've read more. I've been so...

What's going to happen to us after all this ends? Assuming it does end, at some point...

Can we remain friends? Is it possible? Will this be enough to hold us together?

Percy & Harriet

'...so that's what you think she would've wanted?'

'I don't know, dear. It's not really something one thinks about, as a father.'

'I suppose not. Unfortunately, we have to, don't we?'

'Yes, we do. I think it's a nice idea. She always loved it there, didn't she?'

'I think so. But are you sure you wouldn't prefer to have her somewhere closer to us?'

'She'll always be close to us, dear. We're her parents. You're her mother; you carry her everywhere with you, as if she were still here.'

'But she isn't, though, is she?'

'Not physically, no, but in our minds and in our hearts...'

Martha

www.onlyonebrownshoe@blogpit.com (continued)

I can't even begin to imagine how it must feel. Your only child gone: just like that. One day she decides to jump off a train platform. One day a whole country decides to jump on a bandwagon. One day he decides to resist arrest. What are we left with? What does it all mean? Is this the future for our generation? They complain about young people, they say we don't understand the value of anything, they say we don't care about real things, but look at what they are leaving us, look at what we're going to have to deal with: Skid marks from their shitegeist!

Obstructed Women

Having admitted to herself, reluctantly, that she found herself in need of help, Martha reached out to Harriet. 'But are you absolutely sure?' the young woman asked. 'I imagine it'll be very difficult to...'

'It'll be fine,' Harriet said, quietening Martha with the reassuring touch of her redundant maternal hand. She was absolutely aware of the trap posed by having another young woman in her life: in need of guidance and direction and drawn to her and her husband.

'I'm not trying to fill the void,' she said later to him after he had expressed concern. 'There can be no replacement; I know that - it's a fact of which I'm painfully aware...She just needs help, that's all, and I'm happy she came to me.'

'I wish you didn't have the experience,' he replied pensively, 'but, sadly, you do...and maybe this poor woman will find some comfort in meeting you.'

The following day, Martha and Harriet went to visit Stylus's mother. Three weeks after the riot, his body had been released: three weeks of excruciating, grief-laden, house-bound seclusion; hiding from persistent reporters whose offers to tell "his story" had fallen on proudly and resolutely deaf ears; three weeks of sitting on her son's bed as the sun had set on her semi-detached desperation, in the real world, replete with potent reminders of why she had suddenly become childless.

Finally, her boy had been returned to her after a predictably fruitless enquiry, and at that moment, the day after the funeral, his ashes were safely contained on the dining room table. It wasn't that she had wanted that to be his final resting place; in truth she had absolutely no idea how to select a spot in which to comfortably keep the urn that held her son. This difficulty had meant, that since her return the previous day, she had carried him around the house – his receptacle clutched to her bosom – as she had attempted something resembling her routine, not wanting to leave him alone in any room, while she was in another, attending to something menial enough to provide some marginally effective distraction.

Considering the cause of Stylus's death, his mother had fought hard to secure a private funeral for her son. She had worked hard to avoid the arrival of a multitude of sad and belligerent university students whose show of support would inevitably overshadow the private grief. The ceremony had been restricted to family, such as it was – a mother, no father, one grandmother, a few cousins and aunts and uncles. Harriet told Martha that she would have gone with her, had it been possible. Martha had struggled to contain her disappointment, until she had called Stylus's mother, which resulted in her being invited to visit.

For the first time in a long time, Martha had worried about her appearance. Consequently, when Harriet picked her up, the youngster appeared from her parents' front door looking, much to her mother's delight, appropriately conservative and more mature than her eighteen years.

'You look very nice, dear,' Harriet said as she noticed Martha's straight, brushed hair. She was even wearing a skirt and clean shoes.

'Don't…' she said in a self-deprecating tone. 'I feel ridiculous; Stylus wouldn't even recognise me like this.'

'That's as maybe,' Harriet said, 'but his mother will appreciate it, and that's what matters today.'

Martha smiled. Dressing up for somebody else's mother wasn't so bad, she supposed.

The car radio was tuned to Talk Time Radio:

"…some people call it positive action; others simply refer to them as fighters for swift justice. You can call it what you like; one thing we're not short of these days is names for things we don't understand."

"That's right, yes. There are, of course, several questions to be asked."

'None of which they can answer,' Martha said.

'Shall I switch it off?' said Harriet.

'No, let's wait till it gets really annoying!' Martha said.

"Is it really justice, for one thing? Is it terrorism? In these times of morally questionable acts, do we have any right to judge?"

"If you eliminate the right to be judgemental, what do we have left?"

"Questions, questions, questions: that's what we're about, today."

Martha sighed. Harriet smiled without taking her eyes off the road.

"This group has been given the name Cold Justice, although nothing has been formally recognised by any of its members."

"That's right, of course, as nothing is known about who they might be, what their manifesto is, or even if they have one or not. Any information we have has been constructed by us in an attempt to discuss the situation, and therefore not strictly attributable to the perpetrators, whoever they are."

'Let's invent information just so we can make noise,' Martha said,

'...because we can't possibly stay quiet until we know something real, can we?'

'You're very opinionated, aren't you?' Harriet said. Martha looked at her. 'There's nothing wrong with that, believe me,' she added, feeling the young woman's questioning eyes on her. Martha harrumphed.

'My mother doesn't seem to think so!' she said.

'Well, dear, she might not agree with your opinions, but I'm sure she's happy you have them,' Harriet added diplomatically.

Martha smiled.

"...so, is the cold justice of Cold Justice an acceptable symptom of today's society?"

"Caller one, you're live on Talk Time."

"Good morning. Well, first of all, I think we have to stop prefacing and tagging everything with 'today's society', as if we realise that the austerity and turbulence we are experiencing somehow move those lines which, ethically speaking, we shouldn't cross, allowing us to go one or two steps further before going too far – that somehow it's only to be expected, and we are therefore blameless."

'Finally, somebody with common sense,' Martha said.

'It's an interesting point,' Harriet added.

"...when is it ever right to kidnap and kill people? You can't justify it by saying, 'well, times are bad!'"

"Point well made, Caller one. Thank you!"

"...and another thi..."

"Caller Two, you're live on Talk Time!"

"Hello, everybody; I'd like to say, first of all, that I'm sorry for the families of those who died in the protest..."

Martha and Harriet remained silent.

313

"...I say protest because, for us, that's what it was. It was never meant to be a riot."

"It was inevitable, though, wasn't it?"

"Why, because those mysterious people turned up with their hostages?"

"Well, yes, but also because the police didn't intervene, and the protestors didn't like that."

"Do you think it was as simple as that? I was there. Where were you; there, in your comfortable studio – commenting, adding your inconclusive bullshit remarks, whilst us real folk were there, getting involved, getting our hands dirty?"

"Inconclusive bullshit remarks?!"

"Yes, that's what I said. That caller before me was making some very interesting points and you just cut her off!"

"Is that right?"

"Yes, you can't keep quiet long enough to let people talk – Talk Time my arse!"

"...and you're done, caller two, thank you for your valuable contribution..."

'I think you should call this show, some time,' Harriet said.

Martha laughed. 'It's typical that they raise some very pertinent topics,' Harriet added, 'but then never really answer any questions.'

'...and never let those whose opinions might be close to the truth speak properly!' Martha said.

Harriet turned off the radio. 'I think we've reached that point, don't you?' she said.

Martha didn't answer. The sudden silence had sent her mind back to thoughts of Stylus and their destination. Only a few quiet moments later, Harriet said, 'We're here.'

Martha looked uncomfortable, as if she would have preferred the journey not to have ended. In truth, she felt close to Harriet, despite not really knowing her that well. She would have felt more comfortable just driving around with her, listening to the radio. Strange, she thought, with a little accompanying emission of air: spending time with one grieving mother in order to avoid spending time with another. Harriet seemed to exude a sense of acceptance of her grief; it could almost manifest itself as willingness, like she had a job to do – a job that until recently, she hadn't considered possible. In the days she had wasted in bed, or with her nose between the solitary pages of a crossword book, she had tried to abnegate the idea of mourning as a process, as a path with a firm direction and a recuperative destination. She had opted instead for the wallowing inertia from which her husband was so pleased, finally, to have coaxed her. Stylus's mother, on the other hand, was different. The freshness of her grief made Martha uncomfortable – as they approached the door and rang the bell, uncomfortable – as the door opened and Stylus's mother appeared, Martha's heart pounded, she was dumbstruck. Her mouth opened but produced no sound. Harriet took charge and, stepping forward, extended her hand.

'Harriet Harrison,' she said. The soft, soothing alliteration of her name usually elicited an amiable response, but as she shook hands with the woman standing before her, she saw in her eyes the very same empty heaviness that could be found in her own reflection; the look that wasn't always as pronounced but was always there, peering out from every emotive vantage point, hiding in the corners of every necessary smile, lurking around her wrinkles; its ripple effect curtailed any awkward laugh. Drawn, dry-mouthed, dishevelled – at least by her own standards – Stylus's mother spoke.

'Caroline Farmer,' she said with more volume than seemed necessary, as if she had realised an effort needed to be made even to say her own name at such a time when all words seemed unbearable. After hearing Caroline's voice, Martha seemed to find her own from somewhere. They had met once before, when she had called round for Stylus before one of their nocturnal graffiti sessions. She had witnessed the way he and his mother got on so easily with each other. Caroline had seemed fully aware and appreciative of how different her son was and Martha had envied their relationship to such a point that, for several days after, she had found her own mother even more tedious and intolerable than usual. As she stood there on the doorstep with the two grieving mothers, she tried to imagine just what they had lost, and immediately chastised herself for assuming for one second that such a realisation was even attemptable.

Martha shook hands with Caroline, who closed her eyes briefly as she felt the force of the teenager's empathic squeeze. She invited them in, she asked them to sit down, and she offered them tea – all done with a very matter of fact detachment and a reluctance to make eye contact. Harriet offered to help with the tea. En route to the kitchen, Caroline looked reassuringly to her son's urn in the centre of the dining table as she passed. She didn't feel so bad about leaving him alone with Martha. Harriet gave Martha a reassuring look of her own.

Once Martha could hear the clinking of cups and the strained yet polite murmur of maternal small talk coming from the kitchen, she got to her feet and approached the urn. Perching on a dining chair, she reached out and placed her fingertips on the urn's lid, as if in search of some sensation whose exact nature she couldn't have defined. She sighed mournfully at the futility of her efforts. Gently she removed the lid and placed her dissatisfied fingertips into the ashes, letting their coarse dryness adhere to her moist skin. Her thoughts turned quickly to the contents of her bag which she slid gently from her shoulder. Opening it, she pulled out a spray can. It had been the last thing that Stylus had given her. Since the day of the riot, she had taken to carrying it around with her. She removed its lid carefully so as not to make too much noise. She placed the lid of the spray can into the urn and took a scoop of Stylus's ashes out of it before replacing both lids on their respective containers. She deposited the spray can in her bag, returned to the sofa and retook her position just as the two older women returned, bearing tea and a plate of biscuits which none of them would touch.

As she finally made eye contact with Caroline, Martha felt a pang of guilt at having opened the urn. It wasn't as if she had desecrated her friend and his memory; she had just stolen part of him. Part of his remains would remain with her. His mother would never know, unless Martha looked so guilty that Caroline's intuition went into overdrive. It would be likelier that the ashy residue on the teenager's hand would give the game away. She chose a discreet moment to ask if she might use the bathroom. Having left the two older women, Martha, in the spotlessly clean downstairs bathroom, let warm water flow slowly through her fingers and across her hands, watching the little particles of Stylus, her friend, disappear in a circular flow down the plughole. Eventually she turned the water off. She inspected her hands through warm eyes, a little ashamed at having washed away her indiscretion. She looked in the mirror, promised herself she wouldn't cry, and re-joined Harriet and Caroline for tea.

The two mothers were talking in a manner which suggested to Martha, as she sat back down, that Caroline knew of Harriet's situation, that information had been shared, and it was paving a tentative way on which both women had embarked – towards affiliation.

'What was your daughter's name?' Caroline asked.

'Dani,' Harriet said, 'well, Danielle, really, but she insisted on Dani.'

Martha tried to imagine what she had been like. Who had she looked like? Maybe both of them. Fleetingly, she imagined they were her parents. She assumed, based on just how nice Percy and Harriet seemed to be, that their daughter, Dani, must have been incredibly lost – how could she have left such lovely people? How could she have done that to them?

'…and you had no idea?' Caroline asked.

Harriet inhaled gently before answering.

'There had been a few signs,' she said. 'Well, they look like signs now, after the fact, of course. But before…' she paused. 'We couldn't have imagined what would happen.'

Martha looked at her with admiration. Harriet felt a little surprised at how much easier it was to talk to a stranger about it.

An hour later, Harriet and Martha left Caroline. They didn't want to outstay their welcome, despite Caroline's assuring them that they needn't leave. The three of them had spent a surprisingly comfortable hour talking, inevitably, about both unfortunate children, but also about the current state of the country, the riot, the possible outcome of the whole debacle, and Martha's studies and her future; the latter being a necessary departure from the seriousness of the other topics, but a subject on which Martha was less than keen to dwell, given that she held herself partly responsible for the swift withdrawal of Stylus's future, and consequently a little callous while discussing her own. Both Caroline and Harriet seemed content just to know that some young person still had a future, and had neither been forced by circumstance to abandon it, nor had had it cruelly snatched from them through the zeal of others. Martha tried hard to define just what she witnessed in the demeanours of the two older women. Some might have referred to it as resigned acceptance or forbearance. Whilst lying on her bed later that same day, she would ponder the women's capacity for endurance, and in light of the sheer emotional weight of what they were suffering, she would punish herself as she considered her own lack of endurance for something as comparatively innocuous as her own mother. Tolerance could be acquired, she would think, with a little effort.

As they were leaving, Caroline seemed to lose the edge she had managed to hold onto during their visit; the idea of being alone again wasn't one to be relished, despite having her son there in his urn. The fact that it was indeed only about ninety per cent of her son, due to Martha's light fingers and their dexterity in obeying her urges, would never become known to her, so the comfort provided by having him there was never diminished.

As the door closed behind them, Harriet looked at Martha who finally let go of everything, and as her tears appeared, she rushed at Harriet and hugged her with such force that Harriet was taken aback by the independent young woman's sudden need for comfort, and then by the ease with which she could imagine it was Dani she was hugging; mother and daughter's reunion by proxy was sufficient in keeping

Harriet's bigger, more mature arms wrapped around Martha until the tears began to subside and the teenager calmed down enough to apologise, saying that she had no right to be the one crying. On the other side of the door, Caroline listened in silence, considering opening it or resisting the urge to intrude on a private moment on her own door step. She really didn't want to see anymore tears; that was the conclusion that sent her back into the silence of her empty life.

Harriet was proud to have accompanied Martha, to have been there with her at Caroline's house, engaged in an act of kindness which most people her age would much rather have avoided. Harriet knew full well that she was acquiescing, she could feel it. She was allowing her attachment to Martha to gain purchase. As their hug ended in a gentle release, and she saw once again that the red-faced girl was not her daughter, the grieving mother lifted the teenager's hair from her glistening eyes, permitting her maternal need to care and to protect to take hold. She thought of Percy and how he might air his concern, but then she also thought that she wouldn't have been there with Martha if he hadn't already formed his own attachment; if he weren't already enthralled, out of necessity, out of grief, out of sheer appreciation for the remarkable young woman.

Meanwhile…

'Ow!' said Jason, as he gave Martha a look of protest.

'Oh come on,' she said. 'If I'm too rough for you, perhaps you should get that expensive doctor back. What happened to her, anyway?'

'We parted ways after ten days,' Jason replied. 'It was for the best.'

'But why, if you're still in so much pain?' Martha asked.

'I prefer not to talk about it, if it's all the same to you,' Jason said, averting his eyes from her interrogative brow.

'Shying away from questions about what is obviously a fascinating subject; is this correct behaviour for a man named Mighty?'

'It is correct behaviour for a man with a sense of decency,' he replied.

'Ok, well now you have to tell me,' Martha said. 'Come on, what did you do?'

He looked at her. He seemed endearingly pathetic, lying there on a pile of plump pillows, bruised and broken, surrounded by the accoutrements of a recovering victim. She picked up a spare pillow from the chair next to the bed and advanced upon him, jokingly, as if to suffocate him.

'Ok, ok,' he said, wincing in discomfort. 'You know your bedside manner leaves a lot to be desired.'

'I would hope so,' she replied with a smirk.

'Well,' he began with a sigh. 'It seems that I made quite a few suggestions whilst under her care.'

'Suggestions, what do you mean?'

'Let's just say that I wasn't in a very coherent state, and, well, there was just something about her white coat that…'

Martha started sniggering. He blushed.

'She had given me very strong medication,' he added by way of an explanation. 'I wasn't in control!'

Martha burst out laughing. Jason managed a smile, which alleviated some of his embarrassment.

'So Manbag gets you a private doctor, and you sexually harass her!' Martha said between giggles.

'It wasn't my fault…well, not completely,' he said. 'Anyway, it wasn't so bad. I only expressed an intention, a desire, so to speak. I barely remember it. She told me later, as she was informing me of her leaving.'

Martha shook her head in mock disgust.

'Actually,' Jason continued. 'It reminds me of a time many years ago. I was only twenty-one, and there was a young girl, just a bit older than you, that I really liked. I invited her to a party, where we spent a lot of time talking. She explained to me, with no apparent awareness of the conceit in her words, that she didn't like it when men called her attractive, because it meant that they just wanted to fuck her….'

Martha sniggered again. Jason gave her a smile of appreciation. '…anyway, she said that she preferred it when they called her beautiful, because it was more genuine. So, I replied, "Well, I think you're very, very attractive."'

Martha exploded in a fit of cackling laughter, in which Jason tried to participate, until his ribs begged him to stop. Martha's eyes glistened.

'...and that was with no medication,' he added.

The laughter continued. Ordinarily, he wouldn't have shared the story but he felt close to Martha, somehow. She certainly wasn't delicate and he knew she would find it amusing.

'Anyway,' Jason said a moment later. 'I think Manbag owed me something, considering what I've been through. It was all part of the plan, after all.'

'Part of your plan,' she said. 'I still don't understand why we all weren't allowed to know.'

'I told you, Manbag thought it would be safer if we didn't know all the finer details of each other's roles.'

'Ok, but this was different,' Martha said.

'It was very different. I've been stuck in this place for over a month, in pain, just because I took some photos.'

'It can't have been that bad if your mind was able to wander far enough that you try to get up your doctor's skirt!' Martha grinned at the invalid.

'That's very funny!' Jason said. 'It seems like a lot has happened,' he added.

'Well, some of us have been busy,' Martha said, 'while you've been lying in bed for over a month!'

…and the shoe drops

Antony Manbag opened his door and was surprised to see Workman standing before him. Manbag had never invited any of his DISA colleagues to his house. Workman's demeanour seemed even more serious and professional than Manbag had been used to. He was holding a briefcase. 'I'm sorry that it has come to this, Sir,' Workman said. Manbag looked puzzled. He had answered the door wearing his enema utensil cleaning outfit which included a fetching yet practical apron and one latex glove, the other having been removed hygienically in order to open the door. Workman, who was aware of his superior's hobbies, paid his appearance little attention. Manbag gestured for his young assistant to enter, which he promptly did. They passed through into the kitchen where Workman seated himself at the table. Beneath the mild air of cordiality, his superior espied enthusiasm which in turn produced an accompanying air of smugness as the assistant placed his briefcase on the floor next to his chair. Manbag was surprised to see it; Workman's duties had been severely reduced since his interrogation of Jason Mighty. Consequently, a briefcase hardly seemed necessary anymore, not to mention its being rather pathetic that he should resort to using one in order to cling onto some semblance of his previous stature.

Having refused Manbag's hospitality, he waited in silence for his superior to take a seat opposite him. Only then was the silence broken.

'So how might I be of assistance?' Manbag asked.

'Why should I require your assistance?' Workman responded.

'Well, it's just that...' Manbag began.

'It's just that you assume there must be something for which I lack the capacity,' Workman said. Manbag didn't even flutter.

'I assume that when people pay unannounced visits, it's because they want something,' he said. His voice still bore its amiable tone, despite his visitor's sharpness.

'...and if I have something you want?' Workman asked.

'Then, by all means, enlighten me. What've you got?' Manbag said.

'The answers.'

'The answers to what?'

'The answers to two questions.'

'Which questions might they be?' Manbag asked.

'Well,' Workman said forcefully, 'why don't we begin with exhibit A?'

'You've brought props; how exciting!' Manbag said jovially.

Leaning down to open his briefcase, Workman reached inside. Lingering somewhat, eventually he produced a woman's brown shoe and placed it in the centre of the kitchen table. It was scuffed and appeared to be blood-stained, but Manbag recognised it immediately as being the other brown shoe that would make up the pair, the other half of which he had retrieved from the platform on the day of his visit to the Contemplation Zone – the poor young woman who had made that perfect jump in brand new shoes – this one looked the worse for wear, but it was definitely it. The Disposal Team evidence tag attached to the heel confirmed it. Manbag maintained his cool as he continued to think about the other shoe, and how it had occupied that exact same spot on his kitchen table on that terrible day, the day which had been a catalyst; a companion catalyst working in conjunction with Jason's photographs to set Manbag on his current path.

He could feel Workman scrutinising his every move. He raised his eyebrows but remained silent, waiting for his visitor to explain his actions.

'This is where you tell me you've never seen this shoe before,' Workman said.

'Is it?' Manbag replied coolly.

'…and I would say it's true, you haven't.'

'So then why is it on my kitchen table?'

'I was hoping you could give me the other,' Workman said nonchalantly.

'I beg your pardon?' Manbag enquired, gauging the necessary level of disingenuousness.

'The other one,' Workman repeated. 'You took it from the platform when you went to the Contemplation Zone.'

'When I went to the Contemplation Zone?' Manbag said.

'Are you going to say you've never gone?'

'I fail to see why there's a need to say either way, and besides, why would that be so unusual, anyway? I am the Project Manager, after all.'

'That's true.'

'So then…?'

'You admit to being there?'

'Yes, once, I did go, just to get a sense of the place.'

'Which in itself is not strange, of course,' Workman said facetiously.

'But...?' Manbag added.

'Why did you feel the need to disguise yourself and then remove evidence from the scene of a successful jump?'

'What are you talking about?' Manbag asked. He allowed himself a hint of frustration.

Calmly, Workman retrieved a file from his briefcase from which he spread various photos across the kitchen table. They were still photographs from Contemplation Zone security camera footage. In sequence they showed the frames capturing the young woman's successful dash towards the oncoming train. Amongst the crowd, Manbag recognised four mysterious figures as Martha, Jason, the obstructed man and himself. The chaos which he could still remember vividly was laid out before him. Then came the final image from Workman's file.

'This one,' he said. 'Look at this one.'

Manbag looked and saw himself bending down on the platform edge to retrieve the shoe.

'Why exactly are you showing this to me?' he asked. 'You think this is me?'

'Yes, I do!' Workman replied.

'But you can't see the face; he's wearing a hood. It could be anybody.'

'You're right, he's wearing a hood. But...' he said, tapping his finger on the photo, 'if you look closely, you can also see that he's wearing odd socks – the same odd socks you were wearing on that very day!'

There was a moment of silence and then Manbag burst out laughing; a deep, satisfying guffaw which Workman hadn't expected, and found irritating.

'ODD SOCKS!' Manbag shouted, still laughing. 'That's all you've got?!'

Workman's umbrage was palpable. 'This is you, I know it is!' he said.

'How do you know?' Manbag demanded. 'Socks, fucking socks!'

Workman was surprised at his boss's language. 'I saw you wearing those socks!' he said forcefully.

'Even if the man in the photo is me, how can you possibly prove that I was wearing those socks earlier that day?' Manbag said. 'More importantly; why would I want to disguise myself, anyway?'

'Well that's a very good question, isn't it? Why would you?'

'I wouldn't, quite simply!'

'So why did you, then?' Workman pushed.

'LOOK!' Manbag shouted. He paused. Neither man spoke for a moment. Manbag calmed himself rapidly and continued. 'Let's just say, for the sake of argument, that you're right: I was there, in disguise – although it looks more like somebody with their hood up on a cold day, anyway, I digress – let's say I took the shoe.' He paused. 'What exactly are you accusing me of?'

'Tampering with evidence from a successful jump, hindering Disposal Team processing: shall I go on?'

'Please do,' Manbag said.

'How about these other hooded figures in the photo?' Workman asked.

Manbag looked at the three figures whom he knew to be Martha, Jason and the obstructed man. Martha was actually wearing a hat, but she had managed to obscure her face from view.

'…other cold people waiting for a train, presumably,' Manbag said

'Interesting,' Workman said. 'One could argue that it seems strange that the only four unidentifiable people are all standing together, almost as if they are deliberately hiding their identities.'

'Well, yes,' Manbag said. 'That would certainly be interesting, if it were true!'

'So just to clarify, then,' Workman said. 'You're saying that's not you in the photo?'

'Yes, that's what I'm saying,' Manbag replied.

'So, if I were to take a look around,' Workman said, standing up, 'I wouldn't find the other shoe, somewhere?'

He moved quickly. Before Manbag could catch him, he was already in the living room. He was surprisingly fast.

'What do you think you're doing?' Manbag shouted. 'This is my house. You've no right!'

'I've every right,' Workman said, 'for the Department!'

'Is that what you said to Jason Mighty?' Manbag shouted. 'What are you going to do now, tie me to a chair and beat it out of me?'

They were chasing each other around the dining table, where Manbag had placed the other brown shoe during his conspiratorial dinner with the mysterious three figures he'd just denied knowing.

'I could make you tell me!' Workman said. He stopped and picked up the antique enema syringe as Manbag advanced upon him. Workman turned, brandishing the intimate item. Manbag smiled and said, 'I hate to disappoint you, but it's not the first time I've had an enema syringe pointed at me!'

Workman frowned uncomfortably.

'What are you going to do,' Manbag said, 'cleanse me into submission?'

'I might!' Workman said childishly, his hand shaking.

'Now you're just being weird!' Manbag said. 'You're out of your depth!'

'The shoe's not here?'

'No, the shoe's not here. I have no idea where it is because I didn't take it!'

'Really, and I suppose the odd socks were purely coincidental, were they?'

'What happened to you?' Manbag asked. 'I had such high hopes for you; you showed such promise and you were a great Project Manager in the making.'

'And what happened to you?' Workman said, still brandishing his boss's prized enema syringe. 'You were my mentor, my leader, my hero…and now look at you!'

'Go on, then, look at me; tell me what you see.'

'I see a great man, reduced to hiding within his own creation; I see you,' he paused, 'I see…the whistle-blower!'

There was a moment's silence. Workman's accusation was out

there, but Manbag didn't want to acknowledge it with an immediate, perhaps less plausible denial.

'That's quite a leap, isn't it; odd socks to whistle-blower?'

'It all makes perfect sense,' Workman said. He put the enema syringe down on the table. They sat down. The tone changed. Manbag had to tread very carefully.

'I reported your suspicious behaviour to the Auxiliary,' Workman said dutifully.

'What suspicious behaviour? Manbag asked calmly.

'You were vacant, uncharacteristically vacant; you came to work in less than your usual pristine state of attire – unshaven – the odd socks!'

Manbag remained silent.

'You disappeared, and then, the very day you eventually reappeared, the shit hit the fan! And all of it since you met Jason Mighty…'

'So you reported me to the Auxiliary,' Manbag said. 'Reported what, exactly; that I was a little scruffy? That must have been a huge revelation.'

'She asked me to monitor you.'

Manbag's heart sank, but he was able to bear it without showing.

'Ah, so you've been spying on me, have you?' he said.

'She was worried about your usual strict regimen suddenly changing, and what that might signify.'

'Why does it have to signify anything at all?'

'Everything means something: you taught me that?'

'…and was your covert surveillance successful at all?'

'Not really; the CZ security photos are the only evidence I have.'

'All that is evidence of,' Manbag began with a smile, 'is that some people are careless with their socks in the morning!'

'You being one of them?' Workman said firmly. 'I hardly think so – most out of character.'

'Considering your position, a little caution might be advisable, don't you think?'

'My position?' Workman replied. His eyes narrowed with curiosity.

'Kidnap, torture, grievous bodily harm: you're not really in a position to throw stones, are you?'

'So you admit it, then?' Workman said, trying not to sound too triumphant.

'Admit what?' Manbag said.

'You're the whistle-blower. You leaked everything.'

'No, I didn't!'

'Then why are you threatening me, if you're innocent?'

'I'm simply warning you, advising you, as I've always done,' Manbag said calmly. 'You are in no way off the hook. You deserve to be held accountable for your actions. Gross unprofessionalism, simply put, will not be tolerated.'

'Oh, come off it, Manbag!' Workman had never addressed his boss in such a manner. 'I did what you couldn't. You knew Jason Mighty had to be treated delicately…'

'Delicately!' Manbag laughed.

'…it was a delicate situation,' Workman continued, 'and you just didn't want to get your hands dirty.'

'You got yours far dirtier than necessary!'

'I knew what needed to be done, and you can pretend that you didn't know what was going to happen; go on, pretend as much as you like, but you knew, you sanctioned it, you planted the seed and then washed your hands of it and of me, just like that!'

Workman was becoming more aggressive. Manbag kept calm. He knew that Workman was right. He'd selected him for the job based on an assumption he'd had for a long time, an assumption about Workman's character, his temper, his devotion. Manbag had known all along that it wouldn't end well. He had led his supposed new friend, Jason, into a predicament, and if he were forced to admit it, he would severely doubt his own right to solely accuse and blame Workman, and to resort to his previously all important plausible deniability in a stance against what was obviously his own unquestionable culpability. In that precise moment, he knew that he had to worry more about the Auxiliary and her interest in his uncharacteristic behaviour. Just because Workman claimed to have nothing more, that didn't mean that her higher-upness didn't either. Assume nothing.

'You exceeded your brief; you apparatchik!' Manbag said bitingly.

'Did I?' Workman responded accusingly. 'Did I really?'

Both Workman's voice and his face conveyed a smug suggestion of awareness; awareness that what he had done to Jason Mighty was exactly what Manbag had wanted, what he had implied, and what he had known to be the inevitable outcome of his delegation. Don't delegate to others what you're not willing to do yourself: another thing he'd taught him. Workman would always remember that and abide by it, whilst no longer respecting the source from which it had come.

'Did I ask you to almost kill someone? Did I ask you to immerse yourself in the task at hand to the extent that you had to be physically extracted from your position?'

'You didn't ask me, no, because you couldn't, but you knew!'

'Not only do you come to my house and blame me for your actions, throwing in the old Nazi chestnut about just following orders, but also, you accuse me of tampering, sabotage and whistleblowing. We know what you did: we have proof, we have witnesses and of course we have a victim. What do you have? Socks!'

'Odd socks! The same odd socks!'

'I think you should take your brown shoe, I think you should leave my house, I think you should forget about trying to prove to us that you have anything to offer. You've got nothing other than criminal charges hanging over your head. Remember that. Forget the socks. Go home and never come here again.'

'Oh, dear,' Workman said, 'Am I fired!?'

'I think an amicable backdown is how we'll refer to it,' Manbag replied.

Workman left eventually. He had the look of a man who wasn't finished, a man who had something to prove. He had a mentor to discredit; a whistle-blower to expose. Manbag showed him out, briefcase in hand. Neither man could ever have said that odd shoes and odd socks had ever played such significant roles in a conversation. The fact that a sartorial slip-up could be his downfall amused Manbag no end, not simply because it was entirely ridiculous, but because it reaffirmed his values of impeccable professional presentation. To be presentable was to be.

Auxiliary Nerve

'Jennifer,' Manbag said. 'Jennifer,' he repeated in a different tone. He looked at himself in the lift mirror. He considered adjusting his tie, but then chuckled at the very idea of such a thing being necessary. 'Jennifer,' he said again, tentatively. He was considering a drop in formality and a bold move towards this would be the use of her first name. She was, of course, the Auxiliary, but why? He'd pondered this before. Surely, if she is the end of the line, he thought, aren't we all her auxiliaries? He looked tired, and the skin around his eyes drooped. He thought about Workman's spying on him at the Auxiliary's behest. The lift stopped, the door pinged open and he set off down the corridor. The ultimate door beckoned and its beguiling custodian sat at the helm.

He approached in the customary silent way and then took a leap. 'Jennifer,' he said as he took the seat which her raised hand had indicated. 'Good morning,' he added. She raised her head and peered over her glasses at him inquisitively. He took her lack of response as an indication of her unwelcome receipt of his informality. Something snapped. 'What's your problem?' he asked suddenly. He'd surprised himself.

'I beg your pardon?' she responded finally. She held his gaze. She looked very serious.

'I've been nothing but courteous in all our dealings. I've shown the utmost professionalism and capability, yet I get nothing from you in return but sterile coldness!' He bit his tongue.

'Oh, I'm sorry,' she said, 'have I not given you enough attention? You: the highly-qualified, highly-capable, well-experienced, superbly-dedicated expert? Have I been remiss with the pats on the back?'

'I'm not looking for praise,' he said. 'I know I am excellent at what I do!'

'Don't tell me; you want to be my friend. Why do all you men want to be my friend?'

He looked at her and considered her question for a second.

'We don't have to be friends,' he began, 'but maybe a smile once in a while might make us seem less robotic. We're not machines!'

'That's where you're wrong,' she said directly. 'Your credentials are impeccable and your interview technique displayed an impressive sense of detachment which was precisely what was necessary to undertake a project so ground-breaking. You were hired because you were the most machine-like candidate. And now you're telling me a smile might make things run more smoothly?'

'If I'm so impressive, why did you have my assistant spy on me?' Manbag asked.

She smirked beautifully yet annoyingly.

'So now we get to the root of this petulant outburst!'

'I think an explanation is quite a reasonable request,' he replied.

'Very well. It was simply a counter-measure based on your assistant's concerns. He expressed dismay at your sudden "sartorial slump", I think was how he put it. He was worried that you may be breaking under pressure. I merely instructed him to report any further irregularities, nothing more.'

'I see,' Manbag said.

'I'm sure I don't have to remind you that your contract quite clearly states that you are subject to spontaneous monitoring to be implemented at my discretion.'

'I am well-aware of that, Auxiliary, thank you. But I think you'll find that that very clause also states that the subject is to be informed of said monitoring before its implementation.'

Manbag's tone was snippy. She knew she had lost a little part of his commitment, but she could also see that the end of the project was now an imminent inevitability.

'Let's just put this to one side, if it please you,' he said. 'We need to talk about Workman's contract and the addendum I had him sign.'

'No we don't,' she replied matter-of-factly. She sat back in her chair.

'I don't follow, Auxiliary,' Manbag said.

'We don't need to discuss Workman because he is no longer with us.'

'I'm sorry? Has he resigned?' Manbag was baffled.

'Antony,' she said, 'he is no longer with us, his contract is null and void and he will not be returning. Now I suggest you choose this point to cease any further discussion of this matter. It is over. Do you understand?'

Manbag remained quiet for a moment as he summed up the implications of what she was telling him.

'I think it's time I got back to it, then,' he said finally, getting to his feet.

'That's the spirit,' she replied. In recognition of what she knew was his complete understanding of the situation, she gave him the smile that he'd wanted.

Bringing Mighty Back

Jason's beard itched. It had become full and satisfyingly unkempt. Combined with the red baseball cap he'd just put on, he felt like he looked like someone from a little-known Americana band. He'd been hoping that his recuperation might have allowed him to put on some more weight, but as he looked in the mirror, he looked skinnier than ever. He'd been offered help by both the obstructed man and Manbag, but he'd declined politely with the firm intention of doing something for himself. It was that determination, or stubbornness according to Martha, which had propelled the young photographer out of the house to the underground station so that he could catch the train to their meeting point.

Apart from while in his darkroom, he never really enjoyed being underground. It was different to the overground train system, of course. There were no Contemplation Zones down there, although it was certainly easy to envisage the possibility. The underground had a certain quaint charm, for want of a less touristy expression, on which local councils and private owners maximised, it being something to preserve rather than modify. The tourists loved it, despite its being hugely expensive, hot, cramped, smelly and dirty. Since his interrogation nightmare, plus the subsequent isolation of his recuperation, he'd been feeling somewhat claustrophobic; an unpleasant urge to escape his immediate surroundings was becoming a familiar sensation which he hoped would be temporary. His decision to use the underground had been made in part by way of testing himself and gauging his tolerance of his newest unwelcome preoccupation.

 He was, however, enjoying being free from the house, being surrounded by people whom he could study for details, for characteristics. He'd begun writing short stories again; his preferred medium, and what he really wanted to be doing instead of the more lucrative, yet creatively less satisfying erotic stories which almost embarrassed him.

 His body still hurt a little too much to be absolutely comfortable bearing the weight of his camera bag. He clutched his Yashica, but nothing more. Of course, due to the overriding presence of retro this and vintage that in his neighbourhood – most evident in the next street where the sheer number of hipster coffee bars was reaching ridiculous heights – his carrying a vintage camera left him open to such categorisation. His beard was his saving grace, as its lack of any sort of grooming attention at least negated any suggestion of its being contrived, plus he had no piercings, no tattoos, nor did he wear glasses. He thought about this as he waited for the train, content that his camera might simply appear as nothing more than an incongruous hipster adornment on an otherwise very anti-hipster individual.

 He could hear other trains arriving and leaving on other platforms – the air, the temperature, the smell – they all changed, as did the number of people gathering in wait. Apart from the lack of sufficient workable disposal space, he assumed the logistics of mounting the Contemplation Zone project down in the underground would be mostly transferable; bringing death downstairs – subterranean suicide – now, there's a song title, he thought.

The train arrived in comparatively unceremonious fashion. Jason entered the carriage and was lucky enough to find a seat. He'd spent so much of his time in the preceding weeks trying to escape from the vividness of his memories of that terrible day. Never in his life before his encounter with the obstructed man would he ever have imagined that he would be the victim of torture; like a persecuted refugee or asylum seeker, like a political prisoner whose pamphlet propaganda contravened the dictatorial system in which he lived. In a way, when he considered it, was he really that different? His photographs had documented real events, but they were presented as a shout-out against an establishment that had cashed in on a nation's disregard for its own horrors; and look how he had suffered as a result.

A young man sitting opposite him was tentatively checking a fresh tattoo on his shin, pulling the plastic protective cover carefully away from the skin to reveal the word HARDCORE. He winced. Jason assumed he would have to grow into the responsibility of its message. At the far end of the carriage, not quite far enough for comfort, a middle-aged couple were kissing with the oblivious abandon of true passion, as exemplified by the enthusiasm of the man's wandering hands. When they eventually remembered that breathing was necessary, the man moved his head away, revealing the woman's nose to be severely deformed and, surgically speaking, seemingly in a state of reconstructive incompletion. He looked at her lovingly and kissed her again. Jason made a note of this on his telephone for future literary reference.

The train was hot. He considered removing his baseball cap but he was enjoying the shade of its brim. He would admit, at a push, to having worried about being recognised. He knew that his photos had been omnipresent whilst he had been recovering. His doctor, before she had resigned, had informed him of certain facts, as per Manbag's instruction. The Project Manager, out of thoroughness and a not inconsiderable amount of guilt, had insisted that Jason be kept abreast of some developments, once he was able to take it all in. Knowledge of just how widespread the name Jason Mighty had become had been filtered to him sensitively so as to ensure his full cooperation and therefore his understanding of the importance of lying low. It had since become obvious, in recent weeks, that people were already moving on to other scandals; other obsessions, and other household names were being created. His beard was just to indulge his appreciation of his own hirsuteness, but the baseball cap had been a humorous counter-measure, his enjoyment of which even his stubborn aches and pains couldn't mar.

   The train stopped, people got off. A one-legged man with a crutch entered and took the empty seat next to the HARDCORE youngster. As discreetly as he could, which was probably less than he gave himself credit for, Jason looked across at the monoped. He found himself wondering what happened to all the odd shoes that one-legged people don't need. Where did they all go? Did this man have a huge collection of left-foot shoes at home just discarded because he only needed the right-foot ones? Were there special shops that sold odd shoes only? He found the idea of a huge Holocaust-sized pile of discarded shoes quite depressing. He cast his eyes elsewhere lest the one-legged man should feel scrutinised. He was starting to feel overwhelmed by the extent of this exposure to the public. He'd been on his back in pain for a long time. He'd been juiced up on pain medication, the effects of which he still liked to imagine from time to time. He'd spent Christmas day being fed by Manbag, who had brought all manner of festive fare to the safe-house. He'd got through it on auto-pilot, not being fully capable of enjoying the extent of the efforts to which the Project Manager had gone in order for the young photographer to not be alone. He had missed his customary trip home and Manbag had written to his mother, pretending to be her son, and explaining that he was full of flu and would try to phone to wish them a Merry Christmas, but he couldn't promise anything. He'd started the new year feeling better, and had been attended by a small team of very sympathetic nurses who'd attentively got him back to a point where Martha had been able to visit him. He had then been taken home during the night, where he had remained. With the aid of regular visits and help, he had eventually arrived at this point, where he was able to refuse help and get himself onto a train with little fuss.

He'd thought a lot about Workman during his recuperation. Once he'd reached a certain point of communicable curiosity, Manbag had informed him of his interrogator's identity, and that he had actually met him once before when he'd been to Manbag's office with his yellow obstruction form. Jason had asked the obvious question first of all. Manbag answered in all honesty that he hadn't known the extent to which Workman would go, but he had to concede that he had expected it to be a serious interrogation. That was what they had spoken about during the first visit to the soup kitchen. Jason had been satisfied with Manbag's answer and the subsequent profuse apologies, but at certain times he'd found his mind wandering back to the persistent inkling that perhaps there had been more awareness than the Project Manager was willing to admit. In spite of that, Jason felt that Manbag had provided him with excellent care, for which he was grateful. Workman was a far more persistent presence; his voice, the solitary hanging light bulb beneath which Jason had sat, the ideas conveyed in the vitriolic, baleful pronouncements of his interrogation – these and many more images and sounds were what had populated much of Jason's time, at least in the beginning, when thinking was just about all he was physically capable of doing. He couldn't imagine Workman's presence would be leaving his imagination any time soon, but he was certainly learning how to deal with it. One thing Jason had learnt from it all, was that he was actually a strong person. He'd taken whatever they had dished out and he had remained unforthcoming, with any knowledge of the DISA leak and his alleged connection to it unrevealed and secure within his broken body. He had fought back, he had resisted their brutality, he had triumphed and he had remained Mighty.

Number 10 Commandments

The door of Number 10 opens and Terence Nimby, Prime Minister, appears to an onslaught of flash photography. He shakes hands with the policeman standing on his doorstep and gives him a contrived, familiar smile – he's in touch with the real people, he knows their children's names, he supports them. With an impressive majority, he was elected easily by a nation of voters whose ballot papers reflected the need for charisma in their representatives. Personality is what runs a country, as he, himself, had once said in an interview not long after taking office, when a belligerent interviewer had asked about his public appeal in the face of rigorous debate competition from his seemingly savvier opponents. The interviewer, being under the misapprehension that Prime Ministers should be able to answer questions and make informed decisions, was enlightened by the fresh-faced P.M. and told, in no uncertain terms, that "the people of this country are no longer interested in political discourse and long-winded explanation. They prefer a bit of charm and a reassuring smile."

"But surely, Prime Minister, that's quite insulting, is it not?"

"Not at all," Nimby replied. "This country will go further with a smile and concise language; two things you might do well to remember."

His ingratiating smile stops just short of smarmy as he lets go of the policeman's hand. He steps forward to the podium, placing his hands commandingly at its corners. There is quiet. Journalists are poised, cameras are trained on his Etonian face as the Whitehall wind provokes a modest movement of his enviably thick hair. After a cinematic pause, the Parliamentary poster boy speaks.

'Good morning, everyone. We have a busy day ahead of us, so let's keep this brief. We are presently involved in various lines of inquiry, working in conjunction with the security services and the police force. In pursuing these lines, we hope to once and for all be in a position where we can put a stop to vigilantism in this country. From this day forward, we are adopting a zero tolerance policy. Once identities have been discovered, the people in question will be subject to the full force of the law. Our laws exist for our own protection and they are to be implemented only by those with the knowledge and skill to do so, by those devoted servants who work tirelessly to keep this country safe; to keep this country great. In times such as these, we look to each other for support, we look to our past glories for inspiration, and we seek solace in the familiarity and comfort of the community. Our past is, of course, very important, but it is also imperative that we adapt and evolve together, into something new, something better. What we need is reassurance, safety for everyone, and a health service which values all its patients equally. Moving forward, we need to start afresh. This will be a serious undertaking during which we must never forget the importance of sharing information, sharing a smile and a well-chosen remark. Let your government take on the burden while you live for each other, in the now, in this moment. Now is not a time for the hand of history to be holding us back; now is a time for sound bites. Stay alert. Be safe.'

Without a moment's hesitation, journalists begin shouting

questions in an attempt to engage the Prime Minister.

'Are you going to resign, Prime Minister?'

'Do you have an apology for the people, Prime Minister?'

'When will the Contemplation Zone be closing, Prime Minister?'

'Do you regret the authorisation of water cannons, Prime Minister?'

'How do you respond to the leader of the opposition's remark that you're nothing more than a puppet who, with every month in power, seems to have more and more strings?'

'Can you admit, Prime Minister, that your government has absolutely no idea who Cold Justice are?'

From the door of Number 10, the Minister for Avoidance emerges. As Terence Nimby retreats with an unfazed expression, he is replaced at the podium by his professionally unforthcoming Minister. Nimby disappears inside, having remained for a few seconds of photographs. The most famous door in the country closes and the Minister for Avoidance holds up a placatory hand.

'Ladies and gentlemen,' he says. The hubbub subsides. 'Obviously, you have a lot of questions that require answers. However...'

Ashes to Ashes

"…Be safe! Stay alert!"

'Wanker!' said Manbag in reaction to the Prime Minister. He switched off the radio and stamped on the accelerator.

'Fuck's sake!' said Martha as she stood at the bus stop watching the news on her phone. The old woman next to her pursed her lips in shock at the expletive.

'What a joke,' said the obstructed man as he bent to put on his shoes in front of the television. He switched it off. 'Come on, love,' he shouted. 'We're going to be late.'

Temporarily, the whole country was abuzz with an ephemeral ratio of anxiety and gullible acceptance. The plethora of independently compiled opinion polls, which serviced the country's need for meaningless quotable statistics, suffered ructions as they were blasted from all angles with tripe. Social network feeds were awash with grammatically incorrect comments. Business as usual. For the remainder of their journeys, Jason, Manbag, Martha and the Harrisons, once they had set off, switched off from it all. Enough was enough. Their excursion for the day was quite different, and they were to undertake something which required absolutely no interference from the bilge that constituted news, nor did the analysis of said news need to be given any further attention. Unplug it all and forget about it: that had to be their mantra.

They gathered at the train station out of the city, free from the pressure that had built up around them, away from the Contemplation Zone, away from DISA, away from the spying eyes of Workman, and away from parents whose approval and/or interest would not extend as far as fighting for justice in a government scandal. Despite not having been all together since the inception of their plan, there wasn't much that really needed to be done in terms of formalities, apart from introducing Jason to Harriet, which occurred reservedly as they were still not sure of being absolutely free from surveillance. Nobody commented much; there was little ceremony involved in their greetings. They seemed to have reached a different level, one at which an acceptable amount of quietness had become comfortable and easy to maintain, without the need to fill it with opinions. Not even a comment was made about Manbag's costume, as they were becoming the norm.

This quietness remained as the train doors closed. Manbag had splashed out on a first class compartment for them. As they took their seats, there was a simultaneous realisation, each of them contemplating the fact that it was the first time any of them had used an overground train since their own journey had begun with two of them being involved in an "amicable backdown" stamped obstruction incident. The obstructed man's daughter had in some way provided, through her tragic death, an opportunity for her father – his appreciation of which was apparent in his smile – to meet and form such a unique bond with three other people with whom, ordinarily, he would probably not have crossed paths. They would of course never forget that her death was a successful jump from the Contemplation Zone, that what they had fought against and suffered for was the reason they were there. Martha turned from the window as the train began to move. She looked at Manbag.

'What's wrong?' asked the obstructed man, noticing her mood.

'I suppose…' she sighed, 'I suppose I'm just a little disappointed.'

'Why?' the obstructed man asked her.

'Well, we've done so much, but really it feels like so little, like we've lost in some way,' she said.

'We haven't lost,' Manbag said. 'We're still fighting; it isn't over yet.'

'He's right,' said the obstructed man. 'We can't have lost when there's still so much up in the air.'

'That's right,' Jason added.

The obstructed man continued. 'There are still two hospital executives unaccounted for. The future of the zone is unclear. After so many resignations and dismissals, the government is in tatters.'

'Not to mention the hospitals,' Manbag added.

'…and DISA?' Martha said. 'What's to become of it?'

'Well,' said Manbag with a positive inflection, 'as my learned friend here will attest: the investigation is losing its momentum with every passing week, due to the lack of discernible leads and/or evidence pointing to any individuals as being responsible for the leak.' He looked to the obstructed man, who nodded in confirmation.

'But aren't you risking, well no, basically throwing away your professional reputation by deliberately not solving this?' Jason asked the obstructed man.

'Not at all,' he replied. 'I had a very fruitful career, from which I had already retired. I have no qualms whatsoever. I can put on a suit happily every day for as long as it takes to steer the investigation in the wrong direction. I am more than willing to appear like I am past it, professionally speaking of course,' he added with a twinkle in his eye which made his wife's cheeks colour slightly, 'if it means we achieve our goal. Besides,' he said with a smile, 'I think you were under a far greater strain, really.'

They all looked at Jason, which meant they didn't see the tinge of guilt that was apparent in Manbag's demeanour.

'Ok,' Jason said. 'Yes, I've suffered, but I'm getting better, really.'

'…and of course,' Martha said with her first grin of the day, 'his injuries are very photogenic.' She pulled a magazine from her bag and slapped it down on the table. Its high quality cover displayed a close-up portrait shot of Jason looking ruggedly unshaven, the clinical colour of his facial injuries highlighted by the photographer's lighting technique. Beneath were the words, JASON MIGHTY FINALLY BREAKS HIS SILENCE.

'If "torture chic" ever becomes a thing,' Martha said, 'which is quite possible these days; we have its poster boy right here amongst us!'

Jason grabbed the magazine. 'I demanded final say on which photo they used,' he said.

'It looks good,' the obstructed man said.

They all agreed, although Manbag's positive smile was a little too forced. It was obvious to all of them that the magazine's presentation of Jason's beautifully photographed wounds poked the Project Manager's sense of guilt. The aesthetic quality of the image did convey, however slightly, an intimation of recovery, as the magazine's designer had dressed Jason in an expensive suit for the photo shoot and the image had been captured during his recuperation, from a survival standpoint. The magazine editor had put forward the idea of portraying a "look what they did to me" concept. It worked. Martha took the magazine, flipped through it to the interview, where more photos could be found, and she began reading aloud.

'*Jason Mighty Finally Speaks, by Felix Blake,*' she began. '*...about his name and much more.*'

Jason groaned.

She continued. '*Looking very much the worse for wear, the laconic thirty-year old funeral photographer seemed more interested in our equipment than in answering our questions, when we paid him a visit recently. However, we did eventually manage to get his thoughts on his recent ordeal at the hands of DISA's covert interrogators and their persuasive techniques.*

"*Not so persuasive really,*" *Mighty says in his lilting voice as we begin.*

"*...and that's because you couldn't tell them anything?*" *I ask.*

"*Yes, I had no answers for any of their questions, because there has never been any link between me and DISA,*" *he says more firmly, twisting a tuft of hair between thumb and finger.*

"*Well, that's not entirely true, is it?*" *I put to him. He bristles and looks at me squarely.*

"*Ah, you mean my obstruction incident, of course, but I'm talking about the leak specifically. I am not connected to any whistle-blowing vigilante.*"

"*But the question remains,*" *I continue to push,* "*that nobody really knows how your photos were circulated so widely and rapidly. You say it was purely coincidental. Do you stick to that?*"

"*It's interesting that you say "stick to".*"

"*Why is that?*" *I ask.*

"It implies that it's something that could change, that it's not a true answer that's fixed by virtue of it being a fact."

"That seems very sensitive for a man who's telling the truth," I say to him. At this point he pushes back.

"My understanding of the conditions of our meeting is that you wanted to talk about my interrogation and torture."

"That's true."

"Let's do that then, shall we?"

'Nicely done!' Manbag said with an approving nod. Jason smiled and then grimaced as he changed position in his seat. Martha continued reading.

' "So, why do you think they adopted such vigorous methods of interrogation?"

"I got the distinct impression that my interrogator enjoyed what he was doing, and probably knew he was going to enjoy it."

"Really?"

"Yes, absolutely," he says assuredly.

"Are you suggesting that he was experienced, that DISA had employed such methods previously?"

"No, this is one fire that doesn't need fuel adding to it. Besides, I doubt they would have had cause to use such methods before."

"But we can't know that for sure, can we?" I ask.

"You can speculate as much as you want. All I know about is what happened to me."

"Of course," I say to him. He seems almost offended by my deviating from his specific situation. He has met me today with the obvious intention of only discussing his case. "So," I said, by way of reintroducing the topic he seems determined to stick to. "Did you, at any point, wonder if you weren't going to get out of it alive?" I detect

a trace of fear lurking in the philosophical look he tries to give me.

"I was trying to tell myself all along that there was only so far they could go, but as it went on and on, it became frighteningly obvious that some Rumsfeldian rewrite was being enacted and I was the test subject."

"…and do you really feel like you were tortured?"

"What do you think? Look at my face!"

'What a ridiculous question!' the obstructed man said. Jason shrugged in recognition. Martha continued.

"'Is there some doubt relating to the authenticity of my story?" Jason Mighty asks me. There is a look in his eye which suggests he is actually concerned about my answer.

"At this point, after everything; do people still care about what journalists think? I ask him.

*"I think they wonder more about whether you **do** think. You haven't answered my question!"*

I smile at him in resignation; in recognition of his pushing me for answers. "I have no doubts about your story," I say to him. "Personally, I believe you 100%…"

"But?" he asks.

"But it's my job to question everything, especially in a case like this, where the allegations are so serious."

"That's part of the problem, isn't it?" he says. I push him for an explanation.

He continues. "In the course of this whole set of circumstances, the Contemplation Zone and everything that led to its inception: is my situation any more serious or shocking than the rest of it? Isn't the most terrible part of it the fact that the zone even opened? That it even got off the drawing board and they were able to run with it is just incredible, is it not?"

"Yes, it is, of course. You're absolutely right!" He nods seriously at my agreement. "So, tell me," I begin, trying to inject some optimism into the proceedings. "Do you see an end to all this?"

"An end to the whole thing?" he asks me.

"Yes, to everything; at least for the Contemplation Zone to close." He looks at me pensively, the nostrils of his proud nose flaring.

"The basic problem is that none of us really knows what type of resolution we're entitled to expect."

"Because there isn't one?" I push him for an answer.

"Exactly!" he says with a disarming grin. "There is no possible end to this story!"

Martha stopped reading and looked up.

'Is that true?' she asked the group. Her face contorted with the sudden disappointment of realisation. 'There isn't, is there?' she added.

The obstructed man took the magazine from her hands. 'Look,' he said, 'we have to make our own ends to the story. Do you want everyone to go to prison? Will that bring back all those successful unfortunates?' He looked at his wife who barely managed a thin smile. 'You can never fight something like this with the idea in mind that the result will be as you want it to be.'

'Then why have we bothered, then?' Martha said sulkily.

'Come on,' Manbag answered. 'You're far too clever to ask a question like that.'

She accepted his compliment without comment.

'But after everything we've done,' she began, 'in spite of it being so right, now we have people condemning us because hospitals are being forced into closure, like we shouldn't have bothered, and it would've all been better to just carry on as we were!'

'Martha,' the obstructed man said in a soothing tone, 'there are doctors and nurses treating people in car parks, in shopping centre toilets, in their spare time because, like us, they realise that something has to be done. If it is left up to those in charge, all we will have is a slew of more disastrous deaths on our hands.' She sighed, but he continued. 'There was never going to be a satisfactory end to a story like this. It might not feel like a victory, but it certainly isn't a defeat.'

'But we're responsible for hospitals closing,' she blurted out.

'No we're not,' Manbag said firmly. 'Well, you're not.' All eyes were on him. 'It's people like me: the executives, their initiatives, directives, schemes, projects; everything that has ever been put in place as a means of saving money at the expense of humans. I mean, seriously, humans – the mental health of human beings as a conveniently expendable commodity. There really isn't enough shame in the world, is there? These people just don't have the capacity to display one single iota of the amount of embarrassment, regret; they could never be sorry enough…'

In her first real attempt at magnanimity, Harriet Harrison touched Manbag's hand. 'I think you've made more than enough effort to correct that,' she said to him. It was too much for him. Tears fell from his tired eyes as he squeezed her hand tightly in his; grateful that there were people capable of such strength in his life, people in possession of such innate understanding. She passed him a tissue from her pocket as he sniffed through his tears. The obstructed man looked at his wife with an overwhelming eruption of familiarity. He was being re-introduced to those elements of her personality, every nuance of her character that had lain dormant throughout their bereavement. He could finally see HER again, instead of her grief. He had never forgotten why he loved her, nor had he imagined he ever would. Nevertheless, the evidence was there before him; and in some way, perhaps unfathomable at that exact point, he suddenly felt he had neglected her, and guilty that it had taken something of such magnitude to open his eyes again. A lesser man might attribute it solely to grief, but the obstructed man was able to convince himself all too readily that he should have tried harder. That's what he would do. He owed it to her, to them both, and to the memory of their daughter.

'Doesn't it feel a little like an ending, in some way?' Jason asked, directing his question at Martha.

'I know it's not about drawing a line under it, as these corporate types might say,' she began, nodding at Manbag and the obstructed man, '...and that little things make up the whole...'

'Sounds like she's after a job!' the obstructed man said to Manbag with a grin.

She continued. 'I find it difficult to think of hospital executives' bodies turning up in the remains collected by CZ Disposal Team workers as a victory!'

'There are still two missing,' Jason added.

Martha's face grew stern. Manbag looked at her.

'You blame us for the riot?' he asked her.

'I don't blame us, no,' she said. 'But surely we are partly accountable.' She thought of Stylus, and how some small protest might issue forth from the contents of her backpack, namely the spray can; if she could just hear his voice. How hard do I have to concentrate? That was the thought which refused to leave her: how hard to do I have to concentrate in order to remember the sound of his voice?

'We couldn't have known what was going to happen,' Jason said.

'Couldn't we?' Martha replied, looking at Manbag for confirmation. 'New vigilante groups appear every day, acting under the guise of indignation, as if their thinly-disguised brand of terrorism is somehow justified in today's circumstances!'

'She's right, Jason,' Manbag said. 'Based on the sheer number of such groups recognised to be operating in all sectors, some such incident was inevitable, I'm afraid.'

'Aren't there any police counter-measures in place?' asked Harriet.

'How do we know it isn't the police?' Martha said.

'We don't, basically,' Manbag replied, '…and, yes, there are counter-measures; there have to be. Without them, it would look as though this type of extreme action is condoned.'

'Openly condoned,' the obstructed man added. 'Let's not pretend that there aren't thousands of people whose personal opinion is one that favours such activities.'

'Without a doubt,' Martha said.

'I seriously doubt we'll ever know anything more about it,' Jason said.

'Just another fact that makes this all seem less like a victory!' Martha said.

'The victory is in knowing you've made a difference, surely…isn't it?' Harriet said.

'That depends on the difference,' Martha said. The obstructed man saw in her face what was evident also in her voice: that she was determined to see it all as a defeat, and would continue to do so without some serious coaxing from her fellow passengers.

A silence descended on the group as Martha's persistence seemed to require a pause in the proceedings. Jason shuffled in his seat, trying to limit the amount of time he spent in one position. He wanted to start yoga again as soon as possible, as soon as he could move without wincing. Martha picked up the magazine again and began thumbing through its pages cursorily, as fields and trees blurred past the train window, accented sporadically by cows and sheep and old, abandoned stations where trains no longer stopped.

In a separate article for which the magazine had commissioned urban photographers to catalogue the city's recent clean-up initiative, as implemented by a coalition of local councils, Martha saw two shots which highlighted graffiti removal. The graffiti in question had been done by Stylus, with Martha's keen assistance. The second of the two shots showed the recently cleaned surface, newly restored to its former concrete blandness; the impact of their message whitewashed, and along with it, a little trace of Stylus reduced to ordinariness, as if the art had never existed, as if their nocturnal excursions, brandishing spray cans and an appetite for defacement, had never occurred. She couldn't let that happen. She had to find some way of keeping him alive. His spirit could not be defeated with his graffiti. She wouldn't allow it. She thought about what would happen if the Contemplation Zone was finally removed; not that she could see it actually happening – her negativity was far too prevalent – but if it did, would it wipe away all trace of those who'd jumped to their deaths? If their society was such an indifferent, apathetic one, why would they remember those whom they had ignored willingly for so long, as they completed their trajectories, achieving the status of "successful unfortunate"? This really bothered her greatly. She hadn't entered into any of this for recognition, neither had her co-conspirators. They had each had their motives. But, the idea that it might all simply provoke a national, collective forgetting of why it had been necessary to act; this eventuality proved dispiritingly bankrupt, as if they lived among dispossessed citizens shepherded by corporate wolves. Manbag had been one such wolf, although he looked more like a sheep to Martha. The obstructed man had had the clearest necessity from the outset, and how much brighter he seemed now his wife had joined him in his campaign was obvious to Martha, and it warmed her soul to see it in his demeanour and hear it in his voice. Manbag had sought absolution as a result of seeing Jason's photographs. The young photographer had been the catalyst; he had made it possible for them all to fight against insouciance and attempt an exposure of a callous system of political and medical expediency. What Martha imagined was the dominant ethos of the country, or at least two of its prevailing characteristics, could be exemplified in her mind by the simple use of her parents. If their house represented the country, then her mother and father represented its lack of compassion and its apathy respectively, all of which conveniently left her as the middle ground, the under-appreciated crusader staring at the kitchen ceiling as her cereal went soggy, who didn't mind getting her hands dirty if the end justified the means. Her chief problem, however, seemed to be that she couldn't see a satisfactory end, rendering their means free from the need for justification.

    The train continued its path, away from the city and towards the coast. During momentary interludes, perhaps whilst shaving, or sitting on the toilet; perhaps with motionless hands dangling in washing up water, the obstructed man's mind had been plagued by the idea of his daughter's corporeal dwindling. From the living, breathing light of their lives, to the broken and reassembled representation of her which he had been forced to identify, to the reduction of her to her basic elements; she was dust – all they had left was dust, and it was to that final word which his mind had plummeted several times since her successful jump. However, the soup kitchen, the project, the resurrection of his professional career, and most importantly, the reawakening of his wife – all these factors combined with his new friends and his place amongst them; everything allowed him, on that day, to think of Dani, their daughter; her face, her laugh and a thousand other priceless idiosyncrasies superseded the dust, bringing her image to his mind with unwavering radiance.

On went the train to the significant location chosen by he and Harriet, where they would finally scatter the ashes at the former picnic spot of many a family holiday, where they would release her to the earth, to the air, to the sea, to continue her journey, and perhaps to release themselves from their limbo, with the vague hope of becoming fully unobstructed at last.

The spray can lid which contained the modest scoop of Stylus's ashes, currently rattling in Martha's backpack thanks to the movement of the train, would also be opened, and the percentage of his remnants would be released in a poignant, solitary moment of sun-kissed, breezy melancholia, to which her mind would return for years to come, when sunsets, road trips, music, and the earth's elements would conspire to fire neurons at that fragile part of her limbic system which had guarded the now figurative spray can which held every memory of Stylus, his persona, his graffiti, and ultimately, his death and subsequent scattering.

And so to our two progenitors: Mighty and Manbag; one bearing the scars of a battle well-fought, the other bearing the guilt of having precipitated the cause of that battle. To look at it from the bleakest point of view, the mighty scars of Mighty might as well have been inflicted by the hand of Manbag. At various low ebbs, the Project Manager would find his mind pushed into such territory by his desire to atone, at which point he would question himself strictly, demanding to know how long he should expect to have to punish himself. There was never an answer; not even an organic, fine blend one.

Sharing a train carriage with the Harrisons proved to be less excruciating than he had imagined. They were allowing him to accompany them on their final journey with their daughter; he – the Project Manager of the Contemplation Zone, the very facility which epitomised the negligence and disregard of a system that failed her, their family, and countless other wretched souls, whose leaps had left bemused, bereaved families to grieve in indifference.

Alongside the Harrisons sat Jason Mighty, whose bruises exemplified Manbag's readiness to push forward to levels where collateral damage was inevitable. Mighty had given his consent to the use of his photographs, but Manbag had facilitated this decision, allowing the photographer to go ahead without being fully aware of the risks. He could only be held partly accountable for Workman's behaviour, of course, but partly accountable was certainly effective in provoking guilt and self-recrimination. He now had to deal with Workman himself being a possible addition to the collateral damage list, as his nagging suspicion that the Auxiliary's swift resolution of that particular loose end was more sinister than a mere dismissal. What Jason had gone through was a necessary evil, and the completion of the project had been Manbag's primary concern. However, for the first time in his career, he hadn't managed to adopt his customary guilt-free objectivity, and he couldn't justify his means without acknowledging the suffering of someone he now considered a friend. He felt that Martha had been the least affected by everything, although there was the tragic loss of Stylus to take into account. In all honesty, he couldn't really tell whether she still despised him because of what he represented in her radical young mind, or if there was more to it. He didn't remember teenage girls being so complicated in his day.

The train entered a tunnel and they were plunged into darkness. They were quiet as it continued forward on its rhythmic trajectory towards the oncoming light. Their anxious minds travelled with them, but in various directions, to personal destinations.

ACKNOWLEDGEMENTS

In full acknowledgement of the inspiration for this story, I really need to cite the ridiculous condition from which we all suffer, namely, Modern Life. Without hysterical accounts of daily events both incredible and incredibly insignificant, the imagination would have to work that much harder.

THANK YOU

For proofreading, encouragement, support, understanding and patience: Concha, Debbie and Sarah.

Also

For being yourself, an inspiration: Antony.

For being Mighty: Jason.

Stephen J. Hird also self-published
CEDAR VILLAGE in 2015.

www.stephenjhird.com

Printed in Great Britain
by Amazon